MW00957837

The Explosive Nature of Friendship

Sara Alexi is the author of the Greek Village Series. She divides her time between England and a small village in Greece.

http://facebook.com/authorsaraalexi

Sara Alexi

THE EXPLOSIVE NATURE OF FRIENDSHIP

oneiro

Published by Oneiro Press 2012

ISBN-13: 978-1481875516

ISBN-10: 1481875515

For Vikki

Chapter 1

The whitewashed village basked in the summer sun, the red tiled roofs hazy in the heat. The road shimmered, the dust along its edges still. Not even a dog barked.

The kafenio, usually full of old men and farmers taking a break from work and wives, was empty. Behind the glass doors the old wooden chairs and rough tables were neatly arranged for their return. The chemist's and bakery that also flanked the town square were closed. The area in front of the church was devoid of shirtless boys playing barefoot ball. The school on the edge of the village, on the road that led into town, was finished for the day. The sun was past its highest and people were asleep during the afternoon's heavy heat. All was quiet, not even a dog barked.

The deep dull thud was felt as much as heard, tremoring the ground like an earthquake, a sickening resonance that alerted the senses. Its unnatural quality penetrated the villagers' slumbers, rousing them to an unsettled wakefulness, questioning.

Sleepy, half-dressed people emerged from doorways, looking to their neighbours for explanation. Gates had rattled, windows had shaken, a glass had fallen over. They exchanged their experiences, trying to make sense of the unfamiliar sound. They felt alarmed but could find no cause to panic. They looked across the village to the sea, glistening in the afternoon sun; they looked up the hill to the dotted houses that nestled there amongst the olives. Everything appeared as normal. Sleepy, warm, unchangeable.

Rubbing eyes, they drifted back to shady, cooler interiors, muttering and grumbling.

It was only as the day's temperature dropped, and people pulled back on their working clothes to venture outside that, clustered in unsettled groups, they heard the news, the whispers, flowing like water through crevices, until they all knew the source of the disturbance and were horrified.

Marina's life changed in that instant.

At forty-three, Mitsos' life would never be the same again and he felt he owed Marina even more. His constant remaining question: how much was he to blame for everything?

Fixed with twists of wire to the rusting metal gate at the end of the unpaved track is a homemade post box. Mitsos made it from pieces of an old wooden crate, with nails in his mouth, the construction pinned between his legs, his grey hair falling into his eyes as he worked. He was going to paint it, blue perhaps, like the sky, but then he took the time to admire the grain of the wood, rubbed his veined and age-spotted hand along its smooth surface, and left it unspolit.

Worried about the spring rains, he gave it a sloping roof using the front piece of an old drawer, still shiny and polished. The brass handle with its ornate back plate now sits uppermost to glint in the light.

A lizard is sitting on the handle, its long toes spread as it basks in the morning sun. The grasses around the gate, dotted with delicate pink and purple flowers hiding in their length, are tall after the winter rains - the rains that found their way through Mitsos' kitchen roof and dripped here and there on his kitchen floor.

At his approach the lizard disappears down the back of the gate into the undergrowth. Mitsos smiles, takes a moment to follow its progress through the undergrowth. He bends to examine the flowers tucked away amongst the grasses, but he doesn't pick them. Mitsos uses the drawer handle to lift the lid, edges the elbow of the same arm to hold it open as he slides his hand under and into the box to feel around. It is a well-practised manoeuvre. He scrapes his nails along the wooden insides to see if anything has become lodged flat, and with joy, and nervousness, he retrieves an envelope. He has been expecting this letter for days.

Mitsos looks up at the clear blue sky and mops his brow with his forearm. Even though it is hot the spring rains have not finished yet and Mitsos can feel the pressure changing. By the gate the grasses rustle as another lizard runs through them, or perhaps it is a snake.

He feels the envelope. It is thin, a single sheet perhaps. He heads up the lane towards the house.

He wonders how long the letter has been in the village. The postman, Cosmo, brings letters to the village every day. But after a ride on his moped to the central depot in town and back, he often gets as far as his home near the square and feels in need of a little time to himself and a coffee. Then he often loses his sense of urgency, and the post can remain on his kitchen table sometimes for days before it is finally delivered to its destination. Mitsos recalls that Cosmo was just as lackadaisical back in school.

Holding the corner of the envelope between thumb and forefinger, he reads the return address as he walks: Berlin. His breath catches and suspends; he stands still. The enormity hits him. He can feel his heartbeat in his chest, his pulse in his temples. If he handles it well this could put everything right … Mitsos feels an unfamiliar tremor of excitement. He puts the letter in the back pocket of his coarse serge trousers, breaths deeply to compose himself, and continues his steady pace home. There is never a reason to hurry.

The track to the house is stone and mud, much of which the rains have washed away and which Mitsos has not repaired yet this year. Some stones stand proud, the soil around them eroded. He stops, checks his balance, which is good today, and is about to kick one of the stones away when it moves. At sixty-five his vision is filmy and the edges of things appear fuzzy. He screws up his eyes and looks more closely, his slightly bulbous nose wrinkling in the effort. The baby tortoise is no bigger than his palm. Its head disappears. After a while the creature slowly extends its neck out of curiosity, its eyes blinking. As a boy, he once collected three such tiny tortoises. With wood and chicken wire he built a corral for them, the construction careful, but the next day his creep of tortoises had all gone. A mystery.

Mitsos lifts it to put it amongst the weeds by the track and continues his steady amble, the smell of rosemary drifting to him on the wisp of a breeze.

His cottage is settled in a hollow on the rise of a low hill, and from the front there is an enchanting view across the village: lichen-covered orange roofs capping single storey whitewashed houses, each crouched low, in between neat vegetable gardens. Beyond the village, regimented orange groves spread across the plain and far away to the blue hills in the distance.

Despite the uplifting panorama Mitsos no longer uses the front door, not since that day, to which fact the tangle of roses, tall grasses and overgrown succulents testifies. The featureless packed-earth rear is more private; he feels hidden here.

The kitchen is dark after the bright sunlight. Mitsos briefly closes his eyes to adjust. The small, low, dirty, thinly curtained window casts sunlight in a shaft through the kitchen, across furniture that his grandfather made. The dark polished wood bridges generations and centuries, suffocating but reassuring. The house smells ever so slightly damp since the rain.

Mitsos is fidgety and looks around for his cigarettes, which are not immediately apparent. He takes the envelope from his pocket and props it up on the painted plaster mantelpiece before commencing a more thorough search.

His kitchen, like the other three rooms in the house, is sparsely furnished: a table and chair, a day-bed, a rug by the fireplace. Everything is foggy with dust, the colours sucked out by the passage of time.

During his half-hearted search of the room he lives, and now sleeps in, he cannot avoid noticing the sink of chipped, unwashed china and blackened pans. He is also running out of, well, everything. The vegetable box is empty. The mesh umbrella keeps insects from nothing but bread crumbs and the heavy fridge no longer works, although it now acts as an admirable mouse-proof storage bin for chicken feed.

Abandoning the search for tobacco, he turns on the single tap and stares out of the window into the almond grove as he half-heartedly commences the chore with cold water and no soap. The cool running over his fingers feels delicious in the heat. He bathes his forearm and wipes his wet hand over his unshaven face.

Then he recalls that he was about to do something that was both exciting, and scary. Or was that a memory leaking into the present from another day? He casts around the room for a clue until he spots the letter, the possible answer to his one wish. He leaves the washing-up undone, dries his hand on his trousers and plucks the envelope from the mantelpiece. Wedging it in a drawer, he takes a knife from beside the sink to open it.

'Hey!' Adonis' head appears around the door, shiny-faced, shaven, clean, and then disappears.

Mitsos puts down the knife and carefully places the letter back on the mantelpiece. He steps outside into the heat, which is both beating down and rising off the compacted mud yard by the orchard.

Adonis takes a baby-seat out of his car and puts the sleeping child down in amongst the trees. He hands a large bag of bottles and nappies to Mitsos before giving him a hearty hug.

'Leni's written all the instructions on a piece of paper in the bag and sends her love ... And she asks when will you come to eat with us?' He is smiling, full of life, and smart in his suit trousers and white shirt. They have the same nose but Mitsos is aware that his is bigger, as are his ears now, with tufts of hair growing from inside them and dangling lobes. Old man's ears. His brother is smarter too. 'But,' says Adonis, 'I had opportunities that you did not, more education ...' He puts the nappy bag down by the back door.

The new car, the baby-seat, the big modern bag smelling of sweet chemicals and the noise of the engine seem incongruous outside the back of the flaking whitewashed house, flanked by patchy painted flower pots and a swept-earth yard.

'I still don't think this is a good idea. I won't manage,' Mitsos says. Baby goats are fine; he even has the patience to help a nanny to give birth. Feeding donkey foals and lambs is no problem. But a human baby – how will he know what it wants, and what if he misreads the signs? He blinks a few times and tries to calm his racing thoughts.

'You'll be fine. He's just been changed so you probably won't have to deal with that. We trust you, so you should trust yourself.' Adonis kisses the baby on the top of his head and, gently, pats his big brother on the back.

Mitsos asks, 'Have you thought what you are going to call him yet?' He does not know how to even address his little nephew, let alone feed and change him. He considers his little brother rather rash in his choice of ward for something so precious.

'Well, Leni wants to name him after our Baba but I have said no. Nor do I want to name him after her grandfather, Zorba.' He waves his fingers at his son, playing an invisible piano. 'Leni's mother wants to call him Miracle, but if we go down that route I said we should call him Science.' Adonis laughs at his own joke. Mitsos smiles to be polite but he has watched them struggle through two years on IVF programmes and the gesture does not reach his eyes.

At the time he had thought it unnatural, but then again what else could they do when they had met so late? Adonis continues. 'So we have decided on a name, but Leni is adamant that we do not call him by it until he is baptised, so he is "Baby" for now.' He smooths the baby's hair; his eyes close as if to sleep. 'Leni is very traditional in that way,' Adonis whispers to the child.

'So "Baby" it is,' Mitsos establishes. But a name does not quell his panic. He was no more than five when he found the nest of baby mice. He had picked one up and held it tight and ran to his mother to show her. His mother had been so cold. She just picked it up, from his pink palm, by its tail, and dropped the lifeless creature into the fire. 'I still don't think leaving him with me is a good idea.' Mitsos touches his nephew's hair as gently as he can, testing his control.

'It is only a couple of hours. Besides, you need to bond.' Adonis is smiling, and this time pats Mitsos heartily on his back.

'I don't think this is a laughing matter.' Mitsos is serious. He tries to console himself that the mouse was nearly sixty years ago. He had held it tightly to keep it safe from falling. What he thought would save it had killed it. Maybe he still thinks upside down like that.

Adonis slams his car door and turns his head to reverse down the track to the road. Mitsos watches him disappear as he backs into the lane, leaving the gate open. He turns to the sleeping boy. He objects to his presence. He's been alone a long time.

True, just over a year ago he had opened the shop. Adonis had galvanised him into making an effort, to become part of village life again.

They had taken on an *apothiki*, a small storage house, filled the rough wooden shelves with plastic bottles of powders, and sacks of chemicals, to be mixed with water for crop-spraying and blight-killing, lined up against mossy walls. But when the first trickle of farmers visited, mostly out of curiosity, Mitsos was abruptly aware that he still could not face the villagers. Adonis managed it for a while, but his heart was not in it either. Not one to miss an opportunity, he pays a manager to run the shop now. With relief, Mitsos returned to his solitary life, which he had been living for the past twenty years, happy to feed his chickens and potter down to the kafenio.

He finds solace in his solitude now, the gentle change of the seasons the only influence on his quiet routine. The bugs and the small beasts all around him are his most constant companions. Besides, his life is harder than people think. They don't realise how difficult it is.

He turns to the house and tries to recall what he was doing, something important ... The child makes a noise, a calm cooing as he sleeps, his eyes fluttering, his fists clenching. Mitsos looks at him again, trying to understand this noise, like he tries to understand his chickens' different clucks. Each one has a meaning if you take the time to listen. The child's soft skin beckons him to touch again, his rough fingers rasping no matter how lightly he strokes.

With the contact the boy becomes silent again and sleeps on. Mitsos envies his peace, his innocence. Truth be told, he envies his ease of living, his whole life ahead of him, unblemished.

In stages he lowers himself to a sitting position next to the child. The ground is still cool from the night, the grass slightly damp. The baby is lying down in his car seat, so Mitsos lies back, spreading himself out, picking the sharper stones from under his back. Now they can enjoy the same view – or at least they will, when the child wakes up. He can hear insects all around him, scratching and rustling. He feels at one with his land; he pats the earth, appreciating the living it has given him.

The baby's noises change. Mitsos turns on his side to look at his companion, who has opened his eyes.

‘So young,’ he says with a sigh, and leans forward to kiss the little boy, the sweet smell of infancy lingering after he pulls away. ‘I was young once. It must seem impossible to one as new as you are.’ Mitsos rolls onto his back again. Lying in the weeds and the grass, they gaze up at the almond blossom. Bright white against a deep blue sky, the orchard full of warmth and the promise of summer; the smell of the earth dominant, a hint of ozone assuring all growing things that more rain will come.

‘Yes, I was young. We all were.’ Mitsos picks a grass stem and chews on it, slowly. It is the act of a man who spends much of his time thinking, slow, ponderous.

His nephew stares at the blossoms fluttering in the slight breeze. He reaches out, wanting to touch them. Mitsos turns his head again to look at him. The infant is mesmerised by a fly. Mitsos waves his hand, driving it away, and the baby reaches for his watch, gold and shiny. Mitsos, missing the child's interest, pulls his hand back and puts it behind his head. The baby squeals as the watch is replaced by a falling leaf. Side by side, they become lost in the maze of black branches of the almond trees.

‘When I was young,’ Mitsos begins, quietly, ‘I had a friend, we were like two peas in a pod. What a pair of idiots we were …’ His voice trails off, and he exhales slowly. ‘So much life wasted.’ He looks to see if his talking is bothering the baby, but it seems to be soothing so he continues. ‘The young are so foolish, and then we grow up and get some sense, but it is too late, too late.' A tear comes to his eye, and he wipes it away. They are silent together for a long time. The leaves rustle; creatures can be heard passing through the grass. The occasional butterfly flits overhead. The world around them is alive and happy.

When he resumes his narrative his tone is serious, quieter.

'If I could turn back time, my little friend, so many things I would change. We were so wicked I can hardly bring myself to tell you.'

The baby makes a noise. 'Calm yourself,' Mitsos responds. 'I will tell you. We have a couple of hours together, for goodness' sake. If my brother is serious and he wants this baby-sitting lark to be a regular event I may even get around to telling you how I lost my arm.' He laughs sadly before adding: 'There's precious else you and I can do but talk. You being only a baby and me, well, me being the way I am now.' He looks soflty at his kin and wishes the baby an uneventful life.

Mitsos falls silent for a moment. He has been thinking about the part he has played in his own life for so long that it feels a heavy burden. He decides to share it, why not? His talking will amuse the baby and he might finally make some sense of it all, two birds with one stone. He rouses himself slightly and adopts the role of entertainer.

'So imagine us if you will, Manolis and Mitsos, young lads. Manolis always more of a man – he was a good head taller than me, with jet-black hair, blue eyes that mesmerised the women from when he was a very young age, first the mothers, then the daughters, and then the mothers again. Built like an ox and as wild as a wolf. There was no taming him.' He looks at the baby to reassure hmself that the talking will not upset the child but seeing its eyes so bright he continues, 'Next to him, your good old Uncle Mitsos was just the sidekick, an afterthought for most people. Your Uncle Mitsos smiled more, I think. Your Uncle Mitsos definitely moaned less and was too shy to have a way with the women. I think your Uncle Mitsos perhaps thought things through a bit more than Manolis did, but Manolis – well, he was the ideas man. And did he come up with some ideas, let me tell you ...'

Chapter 2

Mitsos was brushing the area at the back of the house. Years of brushing and countless feet had compacted the ground to a smooth surface, with not a weed, not a blade of grass. The flowers were in pots, geraniums, basil, bougainvillea marking the boundary. His mother had painted the pots, some white, some blue. Mitsos swept the dust into a pile and looked about him for the dustpan. He had left it inside. He swept the dust over towards one of the larger pots.

'No you don't,' his mother said, and handed him the dustpan. 'If you brush it under the pots they end up leaning. Put it over the wall.'

Mitsos brushed up the dust, watching the ants struggle to regain their balance once in the dustpan. He wondered if they would find their way back to their nest, or would they be lost forever if he put them over the wall? He had also swept up a shiny black beetle, which was lying on its back in the dust, its legs scrabbling in the air grasping for something, anything, to help right itself.

Mitsos dropped the brush and snapped a twig off one of the young almond trees. He teased the beetle, touching its feet one by one with the twig, not allowing it to grab hold. The tiny beast became quite frantic at the prospect of becoming righted, if it could just get a grip.

'Don't mess around, Mitso. I want you to go down to the kafenio and tell your father his dinner is ready. His sister is coming to eat with us this evening – we can't wait until he is good and ready today. And put on a shirt before you go.'

Mitsos let the beetle grab the twig and then put twig and beetle into one of the geranium pots. He walked with the dustpan across the hot compacted earth and then through the almond trees, the weeds cooling his bare feet, towards the back wall. But once under the trees he let the dust seep from the pan as he walked so when he was only halfway there he turned back towards the house, dustpan empty.

'Tsss!'

Mitsos looked back to the wall but could see nothing.

'Tssss, here.' Manolis' voice came from behind the boundary.

'Go away! My mum says we can't play together any more.'

'Don't be stupid! How can she stop us, we go to the same school? Besides, you laughed too.'

'Yes, but my dad says we go to school to learn, and someone who starts rumours to disrupt that needs a good ...' His voice faltered, he didn't want to finish his sentence.

'Ah! People do what they want to. They don't have to listen to any rumour I start.'

'But that's the point. No one did listen except Theo. It's not his fault he believes everything you ...' Again, Mitsos left his sentence unfinished, scared of the consequences of what he was saying.

'It was a good pirate costume he had for carnival, though! I am glad he showed up to school in it. Anyway, never mind about that. I have a great idea. Meet me in the village square in ten minutes.'

'I can't,' Mitsos said, but Manolis had gone.

'Mitso, who are you talking to?'

'No one, Mum.'

'Well, hurry up with getting your Baba.'

Mitsos dropped the dustpan by the back door and ran along the track to the gate. He could hear his mother shouting, 'Don't leave it there!' But he was gone, his bare feet burning on the mud road.

His Baba, in the kafenio, sweating in the heat, said he would come when he was good and ready, which is what Mitsos knew he would say. The knowledge of his sister's imminent arrival made no difference, in fact he ordered another ouzo, sweat dripping from his brow onto his round distended stomach. Mitsos wandered back across the square. If he hassled his Baba he would be shouted at; if he went back alone his Mama would shout. He turned just off the square, so his Baba couldn't see him through the large kafenio windows, and sank down onto his haunches by the whitewashed wall.

'There you are.' Manolis slammed his back against the wall and sank down next to him.

'Go away.'

'I have had the most amazing idea. This one is going to make you laugh and laugh!' Manolis waited for a reaction, but none came. Mitsos was drawing patterns in the dust with a stick. Hunched over his knees, his spine prominent through his chestnut-brown skin, his hair flopped over his face, he concentrated on the movement of his stick.

'Come on! This is my best idea yet. How would you like to get your own back on everyone in the village for calling us trouble makers? Get your own back on your Baba for his beatings and your Mama for her scolding?'

'I don't want to get into even more trouble.'

'You won't. This one is fool-proof. If they know that you were asleep at the time they can't blame it on you, can they? I'll call for you tonight, really late, when everyone is in bed.' Manolis straightened up, jumped and hopped a little with excitement, pulling up his dirty oversized shorts, telling Mitsos again how funny it was going to be. And then, his bare feet slapping, he ran across the square towards his home, shouting behind him for Mitsos to bring carrots.

Mitsos poked his stick around a little more before reluctantly returning home. Carrots? Why carrots?

An owl hooted. Nothing else stirred, no dog, no cat, no insect. The moon was full and big and low. It was so bright, nothing was hidden. The orange-tiled roofs had mellowed to a burnt umber, the whitewashed walls to a warm sepia. Looking across the village not a lamp was lit, no light left on.

Manolis and Mitsos climbed, giggling, over the wall at the end of the almond grove. Mitsos had been praised by his aunt at dinner for being an angel and she had chastised her brother for being so harsh. She remembered when he too had been a boy and he had … But his Baba had given her a silencing look and she did not finish her tale. Baba had patted him on the back, though, and smiled, and all seemed to be forgiven. So now he was in good spirits, an angel again, and off to have some fun with Manolis.

'Come on, we'll start at the teacher's house.'

'Start what?'

'Shh, you'll see.'

The teacher's house, a single storey like all the houses, stood in the open at the edge of the village. But the boys walked past the house, and climbed the low stone wall and disappeared round the back.

'Go and open the gate,' Manolis hissed.

The first one took some time. They stopped and started, and at one point they thought that a single night was not going to be long enough to carry out the plan on the scale Manolis insisted upon.

After the teacher's house they went to Manolis' house, which was easy, then Mitsos' house, which was also easy, and then they took it in turns to choose where next, each choice collapsing the boys into fits of giggles and new excitement.

They worked silently, and feverishly at times. The carrots proved to be very handy. Backwards and forwards they went across the village, criss-crossing their paths, working together sometimes and sometimes individually, until the coolness of the air told them it was just before dawn. A lamp came on in one house and they knew it was time to go home, to be in bed, to be woken by their mothers.

They had covered the whole village. Not one house was left devoid of their attentions.

'Mitso, you lazy head, come on!' his mother called.

Mitsos could not rouse himself from the deep sleep he had fallen into.

'Mitso, you will be late for school! The eggs will not come in by themselves. Come on, your Baba's up already.'

Dawn had just broken. Mitsos could not have been asleep for more than an hour at most. He was just about to turn over and go back to sleep when details of the night before came to him and he leapt out of bed ready to see the fun.

Without a yawn, he was dressed, downstairs, and on his way out to collect the eggs before his mother had a chance to call him a third time. He left her making her Greek coffee in the kitchen, declaring that he had never been so quick to get up and dressed before, and was there anything wrong?

Mitsos jumped over the wall at the end of the almond grove and headed higher up the hill to the chicken coop. He unlatched the hut door and the hens came out, clucking and scratching the ground, slowly at first, lazily, until the cockerel emerged, filled his chest and crowed. Then the hens all began to add energy to their steps, cooing and scratching at the ground and jostling for dominance.

Mitsos had intended to feed the chickens and collect the eggs before allowing himself to look down over the village, delaying the delicious sight of their mischief, but he couldn't resist. He took a scoop of corn and turned to survey his kingdom. All seemed as normal. He felt a little disappointed. He was not sure what he expected, but he expected something. He waited and looked harder. He could see the teacher coming out of his door. Round the back of the house he went, and there! Back round to the front, scratching his head. Mitsos held his breath.

The chickens, gathered at his feet for their breakfast, began to grow impatient so he threw the corn haphazardly over them and tossed the scoop into the bin, leaving them pecking corn off each other's backs.

He scanned the village again. The baker was pulling his donkey for all he was worth but the donkey had dug its hooves in and was not moving. Its equine teeth bared, its head up, the animal broke into a crescendo of hee-haws. Mitsos giggled. Now, close at hand through the trees, he saw his own Baba go to untie Mimi. He stopped in his tracks. He took off his cap, rubbed his hair and then walked around her as if he had never seen a donkey before.

Across the square Mitsos could see more people leaving their houses in the dawn light and standing perplexed. Mitsos was crying with laughter by this time. Manolis had been restored to a god in his eyes and he knew this was going to be a day to remember.

'Hey!' Manolis came running up the hill. 'Best place to watch from is up here!' He had an old brass telescope in his hand.

'Did you see the teacher rub his head?' Mitsos asked.

'No, I heard my neighbours swearing and then my Baba went out to see what the trouble was and then he too started to swear so I ran up here.' He turned around and flopped down to watch over the village.

'I'd better take the eggs or my Mama will wonder what is happening. I'll tell her I want to be early to school or something, for football.'

'You don't play football.'

'Yes, but she doesn't know that. See you in one minute.'

By the time he returned Manolis was rocking with laughter, the telescope still in his hand. Mitsos dropped himself down too.

'What's happening?' Manolis offered him the telescope.

'Oh, you should have seen the Papas when he came out. He was crossing himself and praying like it was a miracle.' Manolis crossed himself repeatedly to demonstrate. 'Old Kyria Roula behind the bakery just burst into tears.'

'That's not nice.' All merriment momentarily left Mitsos face, but then he put the telescope to his eye again. Grumpy old Mr Socrates, who had chased them out of his mandarin orchard by the dry river bed last year, came out of his house stretching and yawning. He finished his ritual, and to Mitsos' horror and delight he picked his nose and flicked the contents onto his doorstep. His wife, suddenly behind him, clipped him across the ear and pointed to her scrubbed entrance. What an added bonus! Mitsos could not hold the telescope still for laughing, and Manolis took over.

Grumpy old Socrates went towards his tethered donkey, his wife still in the doorway, her arms gesturing wildly. The boys could hear faint sounds coming from her, echoed off the hill, but could not make out the words. Mr Socrates walked towards his donkey and, in greeting, slapped it on its behind. Mitsos watched with his naked eyes before grabbing the telescope back from Manolis. The slap registered with the donkey and crack! It lashed out with both rear hooves, catching the grumpy old man on the thighs and sending him flying back to sprawl on his own snot-layered stone flags.

'Did you see that?' cried Manolis in wide-eyed excitement, before rolling backwards, hysterical. Mitsos hoped the Socrates was not badly hurt, and then the laugher took hold of him too. The two boys rolled about on the hillside, crying with merriment, knees bent to chests.

After a while they regained some control. Manolis complained that his sides ached, and they both tried to be serious.

They could see, all over the village, people on donkeys, each sitting on traditional side saddles, reins loose, offering their animals no guidance. The donkeys ambled here and there, eating a few weeds on the way, each taking its own sweet time. The villagers knew that if they let any donkey wander it will eventually head home.

'The only thing is,' Manolis gasped between bouts of laughter, 'when they get to where the donkeys are leading them …' He dissolved into another spasm before he could continue. 'Their own donkey won't be there either, or there won't even be a donkey because it's out doing the same thing. Mayhem!' Manolis held his sides, gasping for air. His last-minute idea to not directly swap the donkeys had been a real stroke of genius.

As time passed, more and more shouts could be heard when animals arrived and owners were not reunited. The telescope was passed faster and faster between the two boys.

Manolis developed an evil cackle when he saw the teacher, close by, arrive at a destination on his alien beast.

There began an argument, the teacher insisting on keeping the borrowed mount he was on to ride around the village in search of his own animal. The true owner would not hear of it, he needed his donkey for work. The teacher bellowed so loudly that the boys could make out some of his words from their hilltop perch. The donkey's true owner was furious, but the teacher would not dismount. The donkey's owner grabbed the teacher's legs and pulled. The teacher, riding side-saddle, leaned backwards to counteract the force.

Then, to the boys' greatest delight, the donkey's owner stopped pulling on the teacher's legs and the teacher's weight, still in counterbalance, caused him to abruptly slide backwards off the donkey, landing on his back. The yell echoed off the hillside and Manolis declared he would wet himself.

Eventually, the bell rang for school and the pair hurried down the hill, eager to see the chaos close up. The villagers with no immediate work to do were being amicable about the situation, one or two even chuckling over the prank. But the farmers who had chores to accomplish in the cool hours of dawn were furious. Those who used their mules to go to jobs in the nearby town were frantic, they would be late.

The boys did not hurry to school on the best of days, and on this day they took a longer way round, winding through the village. The donkey that had given the most trouble the night before was refusing to come out of the shed, and the surrogate owner and his wife were heaving on its bridle to no avail.

'Try a carrot,' Manolis suggested with a straight face as they passed.

They were nearly at school when they passed Theo coming towards them.

'No school. The teacher's hurt his back.'

'You're kidding!' Mitsos' eyes widened and his mouth hung open.

'Nope. Fell off his donkey,' Theo said.

Manolis started giggling, and Mitsos dug him in the ribs with his elbow.

'Is he badly hurt?' Mitsos asked. Theo shrugged.

The three of them walked together in silence until Theo ran off ahead of them to turn down his lane. As soon as he was gone, Manolis and Mitsos resumed their half whispers.

The boys had agreed not to divulge their involvement in the day's events to anyone.

'Least of all Theo – he might want to get his own back for the costume prank,' Manolis had insisted. Mitsos suggested that maybe they could share their fun with him as a sort of apology, but Manolis was steadfast.

As they neared the square they saw the first unmanned donkey. A passer-by tapped it on the rump and it trotted the faster, presumably towards home. Then they saw another and another. Someone had evidently had the bright idea of letting all the donkeys go, the villagers working together to encourage each donkey to keep going until it found its way home.

The laughter that accompanied the reunions in some quarters was matched by complaints in others. The moaners complained of time lost, interference in their personal lives, how dare they be insulted in this way! Manolis was particularly interested in the ways different people reacted. The priest complained, and Manolis told Mitsos that this made him a hypocrite. The kind little old lady, Despina, who always offered the children sweet bread at Easter complained, and that told Manolis she was a fake. Grumpy Mr Socrates, with the mandarins by the dry river bed, laughed out loud, and they both had to reassess him, and his ear-swiping wife.

Mitsos' Baba was striding towards the kafenio for his first cup of coffee of the day. He always drank it there. He drank it there before he was married and he would drink it there now. As he reached the square, so did Manolis and Mitsos.

'Oi! You two,' he shouted.

Manolis was about to run. Mitsos put a retaining hand on his arm. They walked slowly towards him.

'I don't suppose you know anything about this?'

'About what, Mr Dimitri?' Manolis put on his innocent voice and pulled up his sagging school trousers. His mother had cut them short enough for him to wear the year before, and now they no longer reached his ankles.

'Don't you give me "About what", you little rascal. Mitsos, what have you to say for yourself?'

'Baba, I have just been to school but there is no school because the teacher has hurt his back.'

'I'm talking about the donkeys.'

Mitsos was not sure how to reply to this and so stayed silent. He did his best to look innocent.

'Get home to your mother, and you, Manolis, go back to where you came from and leave my son alone.' The big man turned to mount the few steps into the kafenio and took his usual place by the window in the front corner, his look-out post.

'Catch you later,' Manolis said, with a big grin. Mitsos did not answer, but his grin was just as broad.

Chapter 3

The baby begins to make a discontented noise.

'Your old Uncle Mitsos has to agree, we have been lying here far too long for comfort, but I took it by your silence that you enjoyed that piece of village history.'

Mitsos takes his time to stand. He shakes out his legs and straightens his back. The baby begins to cry, just softly.

'Ah, you young chicken, what does that noise mean? Are you hungry?' Mitsos looks in the bag and takes out the piece of paper and reads. He checks his watch. 'Yup, food time.' He slings the bag over his shoulder and picks up the baby-seat.

He doesn't realise how warm it has become outside until he is in the comparative cool of his kitchen. He places the baby-seat on the bare wooden table and turns to the camping gas burner, by the old stained marble sink, which he uses to make Greek coffee on. He sets some water to boil.

The baby's noises are becoming more insistent. The car seat looks so unfamiliar in a room that has not changed since his first memory. He was born on the day-bed in the corner, as were his brothers.

'Now, now, little man. Let's be having none of that. This is hard enough for your uncle without a chorus from you. It seems you stay quiet for the stories, but you are an impatient little chap when you have nothing to entertain you.'

The water is taking forever to boil, or so it seems to Mitsos, and, with twisted mouth, the baby's cries are becoming full blown, his little nose wrinkles and his innocent eyes screw up. Mitsos looks around the room, but apart from the table and chairs, day-bed, pictures of his long-gone mother and father, grandfather and grandmother, and his shepherd's crook for the goats leaning by the door, there is little in the room. Certainly nothing that would entertain a baby.

'Ok, ok, I'll tell you another story, but you must agree to be quiet.' He manages to unscrew the top of the bottle, clasping it between his knees. The process of filling it and testing the temperature is nowhere near as tricky as he had imagined.

However, picking the young lad up with one arm is the struggle he thought it would be, but in the end, once sitting down, Mitsos manages to get him nestled on his lap and offers the milk, which the little boy drinks greedily. They are both content for a while. The gentle sucking noises soothe them both as the baby finds a rhythm to his sucking. Lulled, Mitsos stares around the room and his gaze lands on the envelope. He wills the contents to be to his liking. The baby pulls away from the bottle to breathe before latching back on, breaking Mitsos' concentration.

'Ah, my friend, you look so content. I remember a time when I was content …' The milk is all gone and the baby looks sleepy.

'Unfortunately, what starts with fun and laughter – and there was much fun and laughter at that age, I can tell you – can often lead to more serious places.'

Mitsos is aware that he is using the opportunity to voice all his worries but feels no shame. He has been silent so long, the same stories rattling round and round in his head. He needs to allow them to escape. This is the first person who has given him the time or the confidence to speak. Mitsos wonders what that says about him.

The baby yawns, giving a small noise that makes Mitsos smile before he continues his soothing talk.

'The donkeys were just a silly boyish prank, but what happens when you are so full of life that each step must outreach the last? That's when you need to take care. But when you are young,' he sighs, 'you do not see the path ahead clearly, you only see the next step.' He manoeuvres the baby over his shoulder and pats his soft back. 'Take Manolis' next step,' he whispers into the child's ear. 'Was it over the line? Did it foretell things to come? Would we have acted any differently if we had known where our path was leading?'

'Here, give us a hand …' Manolis said.

'What are we doing?' Mitsos' heartbeat had increased and there was a fine sweat on his brow. His spine felt cold. They were up to mischief again, and God was watching this time.

'… with this,' Manolis said, as he ran to the centre of the nave and grasped the brass font with both hands as if to lift it. 'Come on, I can't do this alone.'

Mitsos was horrified. He imagined bolts of lightning coming through the church roof at him, the voice of God bellowing through the high domed ceiling. His feet stayed glued to the spot where he stood and his jaw hung limply open. Manolis beckoned him over, but Mitsos hesitated as the icons glowered at him from the walls.

'Come on!' Manolis shouted. Mitsos was sure shouting in church was a definite sin and hurried towards him to stop him shouting out again.

'Shhhh.' Mitsos hissed. But Manolis' words were no longer a request and Mitsos found, in his fear of the shouting and of Manolis himself, that he lifted the font off its stand and the two of them, wobbling under its weight, carried it to the door. Together they tipped it up, pouring the contents over the mud and grass.

'That's holy water!' Mitsos exclaimed, as it was quickly sucked away by the cracked mud.

'Ha! He can bless more,' Manolis laughed. 'Besides, he picked on the wrong boy to preach to this time!'

The young trainee Papas was far too keen, and each Sunday he would pull aside a couple of boys.

'You boys are nearly too old for school now. How old are you – ten, eleven?'

'Nine,' Manolis answered. He pulled at his shirt collar, uncomfortable in his Sunday clothes.

'Look at the size of you! You should have been out working beside your Baba years ago. And you, boy …'

'Mitsos, sir,' he replied, standing erect.

'How old are you – seven, eight?'

'Nine and a half!' Mitsos was wide-eyed with indignation.

'Well then, you too should be out helping your Baba. "Αϱγία μήτηϱ πάσης κακίας" – Idleness, mother of all evil. How often do you read your Bible?'

On the subject of the Bible, on how infrequently the boys read it and on how far their behaviour diverged from that expected from a good Greek Orthodox Christian, there was seemingly no end. Mitsos and Manolis jiggled from foot to foot, trying to keep their attention on the priest, but it was a losing battle. The curls of smoke from the incense burner, the old lady lighting a candle, the reflective gold leaf embellishments on the icons, anything, well actually everything, was more interesting than the sonorous voice of this young trainee Papas.

Presently a distraction was provided by way of a bee landing on the Papas' kamelaukio. The bee began to crawl up the side of the tall black flat-topped hat that denoted his status, and the boys could not take their eyes off it. Manolis willed the bee, and indeed he actually prayed to God, for it to circumnavigate the black mountain and crawl down the Papas' collar. Maybe then the trainee would stop droning on.

To Mitsos' horror, he had laughed and laughed when he bragged about his prayers after they were set free.

Finally, the trainee Papas, who was too young to have grown a proper, full, official Papas' beard, told them he was posted there for a month. He added that if he could help them with anything, anything at all spiritual, then they must not hesitate; it was his calling, his duty, his pleasure to be of assistance to them in their quest for Godliness.

At last, he released them with a nod towards the door.

The air outside the church that Sunday had never smelt so fresh; running into the square, their legs had never felt so alive. Manolis unbuttoned his best shirt at the neck and pulled it off over his head and knotted the sleeves round his waist. It was hot, but more than that: to the boys, divesting themselves of their shirts spelt freedom.

'Let's go up the hill,' Manolis shouted, his bare feet already propelling him on his way.

Mitsos also unbuttoned his shirt at the collar, but he dared not take it off. What if his Mama or Baba saw him, or someone else who would tell them? He wore shoes, too. He only wore them on Sunday, once the winter had gone. They were too big and they flopped and slapped when he tried to run. As he passed the low stone wall to the almond orchard, he sank to the ground on the dusty track and pulled them off and dropped them down over the wall. They would be there when he returned.

Manolis was lying on his back in the shade of the pine trees, a dense clump of which provided a tuft of hair on the very top of the hill.

Mitsos followed suit and lay looking up at the branches, listening to the hissing of the breeze through the needles. Such a lovely, lonely sound. He presumed that Manolis was listening too, and they lay there silently, time of no relevance, lost in the noises of nature and the scent of wild thyme.

'Got it!' Manolis sat up with a start.

'Got what?' Mitsos sat up too, just to copy Manolis.

'What we are going to do to that trainee Papas. Ha! I'll show him what reading the Bible does.' And with that he leapt to his feet and did a little dance on the carpet of pine needles.

'What are we going to do to him?' Mitsos' young brow frowned in alarm, an unpractised expression, his young forehead, still too soft to form creases, creating waves.

But, as usual, Manolis would not tell. He just instructed Mitsos on the preparations he must make. He felt a fortnight would be long enough for what they had to gather.

Mitsos was a bit put out that Manolis would not share the idea with him. They had been partners in the donkey prank, when he had more than proved his worth. He held no secrets from Manolis, and it only seemed fair that it should work the other way round too. The slightest splinter of resentment crept under his skin.

Two weeks later Manolis announced that they were ready. Early morning prayers had finished and the congregation were leaving the church. The incense hung heavy in the air, and the gold leaf glowed and the brass chandeliers reflected the sea of candles offered up as prayers. The brass font, and its stand, had been moved to the centre of the nave ready for a baptism later. Manolis grabbed Mitsos' sleeve and pulled him down to crouch behind the stall of unused candles. It smelt of beeswax and mice. Manolis was giggling, but as Mitsos still had not been told what the plan was, he just felt afraid. He was going to get into trouble again, he could see it coming; he might even be committing a sin, he didn't know. But Manolis' energy was so great, his attraction so compelling, that Mitsos felt weak beside him. He stifled the whimper in his throat and by force of will turned it into a giggle.

It took time for the church to empty completely. Then all was quiet, the only movement the curling smoke of incense. The trainee Papas had gone back to the real Papas' house for his lunch. No one would return until the late afternoon for the baptism.

'Right, come on,' Manolis said. Mitsos started at the loudness of his voice in the silent sanctuary. But Manolis was unafraid and he strode to the side door. The key was in the lock, he turned it and, with both hands, pushed it opened to view the rough ground at the back of the church. A donkey with soft brown eyes grazing there ceased chewing the short stubble and lifted its head to contemplate the boys briefly.

It was then that they had lifted and emptied the font outside before replacing it on its stand.

Mitsos was hopeful that the job was complete, but Manolis grabbed his sleeve and pulled. They ran out of the side door to the bush at the corner where for the last two weeks they had made their storage in a hole in the ground, covered with sacks and leaves. Manolis pulled off the sacks and tossed one to Mitsos.

There was a stench of vinegar and goat. The odour was offensive and Mitsos tried to think of nice smells. He wondered what his Mama had cooked for lunch. His favourite dish came to mind: *pastichio* with cheese melting on top and a side plate of fresh tomatoes with that unmistakable just-picked-from-the-garden smell. He wished he was at home filling his stomach, with nothing to interrupt his afternoon but a long sleep. Instead, he was doing what? Manolis hadn't even shared with him what his plan was. Mitsos' excitement that had turned to fear was now on the edge of resentment.

Manolis nudged him, and they filled the sacks and hauled them to the church, Mitsos dragging his, creating dust that tickled his throat and made him cough. Manolis laughed all the way but still would not share the joke.

Once back inside the church, Manolis half-closed the door and put down the sacks.

He took the first bottle from his sack and poured the contents into the font. Mitsos followed suit and the font began to fill.

The smell from the brew became even more pungent as it mixed with the incense. There were also many fruit flies in attendance. The liquid stored in the goat skin smelt the worst.

'Shall we try it?' Manolis asked. But Mitsos pulled a face and wondered if he was going to be sick.

Most houses in the village had a cask or two of homemade wine. Manolis and Mitsos had been turning the tap and letting it flow into any containers they could find over the last fortnight. Mitsos had not contributed much as his Baba had remarked on how quickly the cask was emptying. Besides, he didn't like the smell. Manolis said his father hadn't noticed and he had filled bottles and jars. The old goat skin he had found in the barn, and he had filled it until it was fat with the rosy liquid. There must have been ten litres or more. It had felt terribly dangerous at the time.

But pouring the liquid into the font felt worse.

Mitsos, who was sure they had now finished, started for the door. He wanted to be at home.

'Where you going? Now we wait.' Manolis grabbed his arm, and pulled him to the back of the church. Mitsos sat stiff, frightened and just a bit bored. After a while, Manolis leaned back and put up his feet on the chairs, with the attitude of a man immune to the whole world. Mitsos copied, experimenting with how that felt. It gave him a curious sense of power, which he liked, and he began to relax and enjoy himself.

As time passed the feeling of power faded and was replaced again with boredom. Manolis drew a crumpled packet from his pocket and took out a cigarette, trying to act casual.

'You can't light that in here – this is the house of God!' Mitsos was horrified, and chastised himself for putting his feet on the chairs and letting his guard down. He sat up straight. He should have left when he said he was going to. They were piling crime upon crime, sin upon sin. God was never going to forgive them.

Manolis lit up and made a big show of drawing in a lungful of smoke.

'Here you go.' He offered the wet end to Mitsos.

Mitsos wriggled on his chair. If he took it he would be smoking in the church, and he felt that must be a sin even if smoking itself wasn't. His Baba smoked, everyone smoked. If he didn't take it, Manolis would laugh at him and call him a baby. He refused.

'For God's sake, they burn enough incense in this place. What difference will a herb of a different kind make?' He was starting to scoff, and thrust the cigarette more firmly at Mitsos. 'Don't be such a baby,' Manolis said, his face contorted with derision.

Mitsos took it and hesitated again before taking a mouthful and coughing. But, as with all new things, a little practice made perfect, and a very short time later they were both puffing like old masters. They were men. They relaxed, and after a time they lay flat across the seats, end to end, their crowns touching, passing the cigarettes back and forth.

A noise disturbed them and the boys sat upright: the sound of a door opening. Time had passed so quickly. Manolis took a last puff and stuck the glowing end into one of the sand trays for the candle offerings. The two boys then scuttled back behind the candle stall, waving their hands in the air to dissipate the smell of tobacco as they went.

'This will be good,' Manolis whispered, as the trainee Papas, with an armful of papers, came up the nave towards the templon, his black robes hanging from his thin frame. He had to pass the font which stood in the centre of the church.

As he passed, he briefly glanced at the font and then, with a slack jaw, stopped and looked again. Slowly and cautiously he took a step closer and with his free hand dipped a finger into the pungent liquid. He sucked the finger, and as his tastebuds confirmed his suspicions his eyes grew wide and he dropped his papers on the floor. He regained composure enough to cross himself several times and then ran to the church entrance. There he paused, looked back and then closed the doors behind him, and the boys could hear him locking them from the outside. His footsteps retreated at a run, and he called the real Papas' name.

Mitsos was rolling on the floor laughing but Manolis stood up and kicked him hard to get his attention.

'Come on, we aren't finished with him yet.' He beckoned Mitsos back to the font and assumed the lifting position again.

'Why?' Mitsos asked.

'Don't be thick. Right now he thinks a miracle has happened.'

'I know, it was hysterical.'

'Yes, but we owe him.' The boys lifted the font back to the side door, and as the wine seeped across the mud, turning it briefly the colour of blood, Mitsos considered what a terrible waste it was. But as soon as it was gone Manolis hurried him towards the templon with the clear intent of passing through to the sanctuary.

'We can't go in there, it's Holy.' Mitsos was beginning to think the whole episode was more than he, or his soul, could bear. Tears were threatening to fall.

'It's a room. Look, if that silly beardless Papas can go in there, how holy can it be? Besides, we won't touch anything. We just need some water. God would never deny us water.' And with a pull of the brass bowl from his side they passed through the templon. Manolis filled the font from the tap. Mitsos crossed himself, had a good look around, was disappointed by the sparseness and asked for forgiveness for trespassing. When the font was full they took it back to the nave and set it on its stand.

They let themselves out of the side door and walked as casually as they could around to the main entrance. A few of the village children were playing football in the space around the front of the church. They invited the pair to join them. Manolis said he might, but later.

The boys, one by one, stopped playing as they followed Manolis' excited, wide-eyed gaze and pointing finger down the lane to the square. Coming at a run, his black robes flying, his arms out to the side trying to retain some dignity but pumping with the effort, was the trainee priest. His face was red with excitement. Behind him, also hurrying, but in a fast-walking way, came the rotund real priest.

When the trainee was close enough, Manolis called.

'What is it, Papas?'

The trainee answered, 'There's been a miracle, a miracle I tell you.'

The boys abandoned football for the infinitely greater excitement of a real miracle, and ran round him, hindering his advance, allowing the real Papas time to catch up. A lady across the road witnessed the commotion and wandered over to find out what was going on. Armed with the facts, she quickly returned to inform her neighbour, who told her son, who went off on his motorbike to tell his friends, and the news quickly spread throughout the village. The devotees came running, the curious bringing up the rear with less enthusiastic fervour, but at a pace brisk enough that they would not miss out on the event.

The boys were all shouting questions at once, and neither of the priests could make any progress. More and more people arrived, all with their own questions, and the real Papas tried to wave them back and maintain some order, but in vain.

Finally, he took control of the situation and with raised hands quietened everyone down. Once they were silent he announced that, as senior clergy, he would go in to investigate. Once he had established the authenticity they could all see this miracle. The trainee Papas strutted with his chest puffed out in pride; his hat had been knocked to cocky angle. A sharp word from the real Papas and at least the hat was put straight.

By the time the key had been turned in the lock there was quite a crowd gathered. The real Papas opened the double doors wide and cautiously peered into the church. All was still. The papers the trainee had dropped lay scattered, white squares on the grey flag floor. But everyone's eyes were fixed on the font. The senior Papas walked gingerly up the aisle. The boys who had been playing football could not resist and followed step for step, on tiptoe. No one took a breath.

The rotund Papas exhaled loudly as he reached the font. The trainee hurried forward as he saw his mentor's shoulders drop.

'But, but …' The trainee stuck his finger in the font and then in his mouth and sucked it. 'But …'

The crowd surged forwards and one by one the disappointment spread through them. They all had to see for themselves; no one said a word.

The crowd that left the church walked with lifeless steps, apart from the real Papas, who marched swiftly to his home and closed the door with a rather loud bang.

The trainee was still by the font. No words were forming in his mouth; they had been replaced by some unintelligible sounds.

Now Manolis, who was standing outside the church doors with all the other children, was laughing. First a giggle behind his hand, which set Mitsos going. The two of them together could not hide what was bursting inside them and they gave in to uncontrollable laughter, which was contagious, and soon all the other children from the church down to the square were laughing. The one or two remaining football players were drawn out of the church by the sound of laughter, and the trainee Papas, heavy-footed, looking stunned, came after them. The laughing boys seemed to line his path, but when he got to the senior Papas' house the door was firmly closed and he had to knock and wait. With laughter ringing in his ears, he turned his face from the disapproving glances of the passing villagers.

He left the village very soon after that.

Some said he left the church.

The baby burps remarkably loudly. Mitsos manages to lift his nephew back into his car seat. Once he is settled Mitsos washes the bottle in cold water with one hand as best he can.

'You see, my little nephew, how a bit of fun can become something more. Once you have stepped over the threshold of respect for authority, if you get away with it, you know no boundaries, you begin to feel and act like gods.' Mitsos sighs deeply. 'And we did get away with it, then and later.' He gazes out into the almond grove. The corner of the window has a spider's web on the outside. The spider sits in the centre, waiting.

'I was like a moth to a flame around Manolis.' Mitsos turns around to find his charge firmly asleep.

Chapter 4

Mitsos' home is a little lonely after his nephew returns to his parents. Under the almond blossom, which provides shade from the hot sun, he can see one or two cats lying in the grass. He reaches into his front trouser pocket and finds his cigarettes. So that's where they were ... He buys the soft packets. The cellophane squeaks as he fumbles to extract one. The packet is empty.

He puts on his black flat cap and grasps his shepherd's crook, and takes one slow footstep after the other along the track and then down to the kiosk to buy a new pack. It is too warm to hurry. The crickets are singing by the gate. There is a hum of insects around the purple and pink flowers shaded in long grass. Mitsos stops to watch a moth drink nectar, its wings a blur, its proboscis extended, reaching into the centre of the petals. It darts away. He has been left with an hollow feeling after talking to his little friend. His world seems barren.

'A wasted life,' he tells the sky, and rubs his face. He hasn't shaved again, and the stubble is itching.

He stops at the edge of the village square. She is there, standing across from him. She is arguing with her daughter, who is standing at the bus stop with a large bag. The palm tree in the centre of the square speckles them in shade, hiding some of their expressions. This daughter looks like Marina; it is the younger one who also looks a little like Manolis. He remembers her when she was so tiny, opening the door to let him in, that last time he was invited to dinner. The day he made the final wrong decision.

Her voice is like Marina's.

'I am going to the island, I don't need to stay here,' she shouts.

'Come back inside a minute.' Marina's voice is hushed but Mitsos can hear an edge of panic.

Poor Marina, she looks quite distraught. He wishes he could go over and help. It hurts that she does not even talk to him. It might have looked like he was encouraging Manolis, but he didn't really want to be involved. It was for her. For her and her daughters. Even that last wrong decision was for her.

A bus pulls into the square and Marina and Eleni disappear from view. The cloud of dust, blown up by the tyres, no sooner settles than the bus is moving again. Only Marina remains when it is gone, her face in the sun, her body dappled in shade. It is hard to tell from this distance, but he thinks she is crying. He wants to hug her, to tell her he will make it better.

She could have been his reason to concentrate on his farm, to plant more orange trees, work the land more efficiently, shave in the mornings. He would have worked, dawn till dusk, just for the joy of making her life easy, for the thrill of returning home to her at the end of the day. He would have gladly earned all the money she needed to dress as finely as she could have liked, taken her to tavernas in town. Maybe they would even have gone to Athens, if she had wanted.

He hasn't seen her for some time. She doesn't look quite so beautiful any more. She seems uncared for, and stouter than he remembers. He recognises her widow's weeds from the first days after Manolis died. They have greyed with washing. This is not really surprising as it was – how many? – twenty-two years ago? How can she be wearing the same clothes? Is she that poor? She looks tired. His heart reaches out to her.

Watching her walk back into her whitewashed home, with the peeling blue shutters, behind her shop on the corner, he realises that it would take a miracle for them to be friends now. His one wish, his one dream, is to show Marina, in some way, how much she is loved by him, how worthy of love. Even if there is no return for him.

She is gone. He continues his slow tread, using his crook for balance. His steps take him to the glass-fronted kafenio which is full of farmers getting out from under their wives' feet, enjoying the chance of a nip of ouzo with their coffee without being nagged. Two or three of the farmers who are not engaged in playing backgammon or animated in lively discussion, arms flying to emphasise a point, swing their *komboloi*, worry beads, slowly between their fingers and acknowledge Mitsos with a nod as he climbs the steps. The air is hazy with cigarette smoke and the rich aroma of coffee.

His father had sat in the front corner. The floor-to-ceiling windows on two sides gave him the best vantage point. That corner is just a road's-width away from Marina's shop. Mitsos never sits there. He sits diagonally opposite, away from the window, near the counter. At the back. On his own.

He knows every man in here. They went to school together and have grown up together. But after the accident that cost him his arm he doesn't feel as social. In the back corner, by the counter, he can talk to the kafenio owner, Theo, of the pirate suit fame, as he makes coffees. Half a sentence between serving the drinks, a broken, undemanding conversation.

Mitsos makes his way to this seat now. Theo comes over, his huge mop of floppy, frizzy, unruly hair bobs as he walks, greying now but still as thick as when he was a boy. Although he was in the same class as Mitsos at school he now looks a few years younger. But then all he has ever done is to run the cafe, with no great stresses. No lost limbs, broken heart or guilty conscience.

He still walks like a boy, too, a spring in his step. His grey hair is the only real giveaway. He nods to Mitsos and goes behind the counter. He lights his single-burner camping gas stove and drops the match onto a small hill of matches that have been lit and extinguished for the same purpose. Coffee, water, patience. Theo does not rush, and always boils the coffee slowly to get the most flavour, the grounds becoming well saturated, not left as hard gritty bits that float on the surface. Nor does he burn the grounds. The froth begins to rise, and just as it is about to spill over Theo lifts the briki pan from the stove, lets the lava subside and pours the coffee into a small cup. He balances the cup on a saucer and hands it over the counter to Mitsos rather than walking all the way around and serving him as he does the other men.

Mitsos knows it is petty, but this always makes him feel a bit special. The square and the corner shop are the hub of the village for the children and half the women, and the church the hub for the other half. The kafenio is the hub of the village for the men, a sanctuary. Being treated as someone who can be handed a coffee over the counter, with no ceremony, makes Mitsos feel he does still belong even if he no longer joins in. It is a familiarity that keeps him grounded. He nods his thanks and stands the coffee on the table to settle. He always lets the grounds settle.

He reaches for a cigarette and then recalls that he has forgotten to stop at the kiosk. He turns to Theo and mimes smoking. Theo pulls his pack from his top pocket and shakes one out.

Sipping his coffee, Mitsos looks out at the world. Past the heads of his peers he can see the square. On the seat around the central palm tree sit some illegal immigrants. They look Indian. But who can tell? They could be Pakistani, Iranian, Afghan. All he sees is cheap labour. Twenty or thirty euros per day, per man, to pick the oranges. Cheaper if you hire them as a team.

Mitsos recalls an immigrant last year who had taken to wearing his socks on his hands in the winter. His shoes had been sole-less. One day Mitsos had been in the kafenio and he saw the English woman, the one who had bought the old farmhouse, take a sandwich to him. Initially he was shocked; it hadn't occurred to him that they were as human as he. He put a pair of gloves in his pocket the next day in case he saw the man again. But he never did.

Today is hot, and the illegals sit in their long-sleeved shirts, seemingly immune to the heat. One picks up a pebble and throws it at a passing dog that skitters sideways to avoid the missile. A woman crosses the square to the corner shop, a basket on her arm.

The shop used to be Manolis' store room. They had done some talking in there, smoking and drinking, going through things Manolis had accumulated.

Mitsos remembers sitting in the store room with Manolis in the first few days after he and Marina were married. Manolis had acquired some crates of whisky. Marina tapped on the door and shyly came in with a tray of coffee and some homemade biscuits. When she smiled, Mitsos felt his heart lift in his chest. But Manolis shouted at her to get out, and she withdrew in a panic. He even put his foot against the door, before she was fully out, to shut it the faster. Mitsos heard the breaking of the china cups and a sob. It was at about that time that he began to realise he quite disliked Manolis.

Mitsos sits in the kafenio for a long time nursing his one coffee. He considers an ouzo chaser but decides he is hungry instead. He leaves his money on the table and nods to the other patrons on the way out. A noisy game of backgammon is taking place in the corner by the window and most of the men have crowded round. Mitsos takes a step at a time down from the kafenio door and, not looking for traffic, crosses the road and heads to the *souvlaki* shop on the other side of the square. This fast-food outlet provides quick meals for hungry farmers and farmers' sons alike. Meat shaved off a spit with chips and tomatoes and *tzatziki* wrapped in a flat patty of grilled bread or, if you are really hungry, roast chicken and chips.

Stella greets him warmly as he walks through the shop past the take-away counter and into the 'restaurant' part. As he passes, her husband is only just visible behind the grill, where the sink and the wine barrels are. The walls in this area are lined with mirrors now misty and greasy with smeared fat.

The dining room walls are painted a pale gloss green. Two pictures, an attempt at decoration, only serve to further emphasise the starkness. One is of a ship under full sail, one of a donkey with a straw hat. The glass fronts to these are also greasy and streaked. Mitsos' usual table, at the back, is free.

The crude wooden tables have plastic cloths, hastily wiped clean with a wet rag, which are cracking with age and wear. The cloth at Mitsos' table depicts English huntsmen in red jackets on horseback following a pack of dogs with upright tails. The table next to this is patterned with intertwining brown flowers and brown leaves around the circumference. The room is not big, with only five small square tables.

Using hardboard sheets, and a wooden framework that can be seen on the inside, one corner of the room has been divided off around a toilet. You do not need to sit and eat for long before becoming aware of the lack of sound-proofing this provides. Except when it is in use, the door is always open.

Some younger farmers, only about forty years old, sit at the table by the window. The room has its own door to the street but it is not used, sealed shut with layers of paint. The patrons, instead, call a greeting as they shuffle past the counter, through the take-away. Both the window and the small square glass in the door let in blocks of sun.

Mitsos swaps his chair for one that does not wobble. He tries three before he finds a stable one. The rushes of the seat are coming loose and fluff up around the edges.

He settles onto this seat and then realises he has forgotten to go to the kiosk again. He thinks about getting up and going back, but he is here now. Later will do. He hangs his crook on the back of another chair.

Stella's husband, Stavros, can be heard grumbling in the kitchen next door. He is not from the village, he is from a town across the plain. Stella is a local, just over fifteen years younger than Mitsos.

Stavros is speaking to her in a derogatory way. It's nothing obvious, just a tone, the way he constructs his sentences and where he puts the emphasis.

Stella comes through to take Mitsos' order. She looks tired, but she puts on a smile and adds a bounce to her step. Too skinny, Mitsos thinks, she should eat more. She sits and puts her notebook on the table, pencil paused, the sun pouring light into her dark hair.

'What can I get you, Mitso? The usual, or something different today?' Despite her obvious fatigue, her eyes shine with life. She is wasted on her husband.

'Hello, Stella. How are you today?'

'Etsi ketsi, so so, as they say. We have one chicken ready, but the sausages need another five minutes.'

'I'll have lobster and champagne.' Mitsos grins. He has been coming in here since Stella and Stavros opened the shop, seven, eight years ago, and the food is always the same, simple but tasty.

'Yeah, right, lobster and champagne. I'll just sit my husband in a boat to go get the lobsters. I'll fly to France for the champagne. With a little luck he will drown and I won't come back.'

Mitsos' levity drops. 'Is it worse than normal?'

Her voice falls to a whisper and she glances in the direction of the kitchen before replying. 'I don't suppose so, but some days are harder than others. Oh!' She suddenly smiles as she remembers. 'How did your baby-sitting go with your nephew?'

Mitos laughs at the recent memory. 'It was not as bad as I thought it would be. I managed, shall we say.'

'Any difficulties?' She nods at the flat shirt sleeve tucked into the waist of his trousers.

'Well, I sat him on my knee.' Mitsos lowers his tone; he is not one to speak about his disability but Stella has always been understanding. 'It was difficult, but I did not make him cry,' says Mitsos, and recalls how he'd leaned right in to the boy, and scooped him up close against his chest and then sat down, left ankle on right thigh, and let him sort of slither down into the crook of his knee to feed him. Mitsos sits tall, proud of his achievement.

'Good for you. So will Adonis bring him again?' Her smile is a ray of sunshine.

'He wants it to be fairly regular, so Leni can continue with this part-time job she has got. I don't think they are short of money, I think she just likes the stimulus.'

'Stella!' Stavros calls from next door.

Stella gets up suddenly. 'Chicken and chips,' Mitsos says quickly, and Stella leaves the room.

She soon returns with his lunch.

'Your lobster, sir, and your champagne.' She puts his plate of chicken and chips in front of him with a bottle of beer. As he didn't order the beer, he knows it is a present from her. She chops his chicken for him. He smiles at her, this act of kindness no longer embarrassing as it was in the early days. She briefly smiles back, wistfully, before returning to the take-away.

Chapter 5

Mitsos looks at his chicken and thinks of lobster. That was another of Manolis' pranks. Although it is much more than a prank when you are a teenager and you are making money from it.

At that time the sea was their second home. They sailed it, swam it, walked alongside it, pulled things out of it, threw things in it. They felt they owned it.

Mitsos chews his chicken and looks at the picture of the sailing ship on the wall.

He remembers the first time they went out for lobsters: the calm of the water, the smell of the salt. The sun, just rising, orange-gold on the horizon, reflected off the sea so they had to shield their eyes as they looked out towards their destination. Mitsos sat at the oars feeling as free as any boy could wish to feel. Manolis was at the bow, directing and pointing. He was the captain.

The motion of the boat soothed any remaining trepidation that Mitsos felt. A seagull flew low overhead. He kicked the nets at his feet to make more room for his ever-lengthening limbs. He leaned back with each stroke and gazed up at the enormous expanse of blue sky, settling into a lazy, soporific state.

Mitsos no longer enjoys the sea. The lobsters had made them rich, briefly, even by today's standards. Rich for teenage boys from a village. He dips his chicken into the lemon sauce.

That evening they went into town and spent money like it was water. They were at an age when they passed from boyhood to adulthood and back again on the whim of a fleeting emotion. That night they were men and everyone knew it. The girls flocked around blue-eyed Manolis, and they were treated like kings. They danced in the bars and drank like fish. And that was only the first day.

But at what price, Mitsos reflects. He squishes a large chip into two with the edge of his fork. They may have just been teenagers, but it was the fishermen's living they had played with. Taking lobsters from their pots was no different than taking food from their tables. Manolis had told him nothing of the plot, as usual, to get him to row out to sea. He had talked cleverly about all lobsters still in the sea being free but – and he could own up to it now – it had been fear, on the first day, that made him continue to row the boat as Manolis hauled up other people's pots to take their catch. After that it had been the money, not his clever arguments or his threatening manner. The lobsters fetched a good price at the local tavernas.

He had heard his Mama and Baba talking when he was in bed one evening. It was when he had been too hung-over to go with Manolis. He heard the words 'lobsters', 'theft' and something about the fishermen issuing a clear warning. He had felt such relief that he had not gone out that day.

Ignoring the chips he is eating, Mitsos' stomach knots at the memory of his Mama saying how relieved she was that Mitsos was not involved for once. His Baba had cleared his throat.

Mitsos rests his fork on the edge of his plate and swallows some beer to wash the food down.

The word 'theft' had lingered in his mind back then, and still does now. He had not thought of Manolis as a thief, but lying in bed that night he saw how he had taken food from the mouths of the fishermen's families. When he heard his Baba clear his throat l it occurred to Mitsos that his father did not believe he was not involved, which would mean that he too was a thief. Is that why he cleared his throat? As he lay awake listening to his parents and struggling with his conscience, he still had several thousand drachmas under his mattress. He thought long and hard. But he didn't give it back.

Mitsos wishes he had given the money back, given it to someone. It would have been one less burden to carry.

He mops the juices of his chicken lunch off his plate with a hunk of bread. His chest feels knotted with the recall of the lobster incident, even after all this time. He knew what they were doing was wrong, but at the time he felt he had no choice. Without Manolis he would be left with his older brother who was a bully, his younger brother Adonis who was spoilt, and his parents. His Mama nagged and his Baba was a drunk and needed little incentive to take his belt off.

Manolis was his escape. Maybe he should have gone further. There was a village lad who lied about his age and joined the navy. Maybe he could have found other company – Theo with his fluffy hair and his pirate suit, perhaps. Mitsos chuckles.

He pushes the memories away with his plate and leans back to digest his food, picking contentedly at his teeth with a toothpick.

Chapter 6

Mitsos watches the farmers goading each other on. Chairs are scraped, table tops banged with hammer fists, arms over shoulders mark affiliations over points of view. Genially swearing at each other, they sound crosser than they actually are. After ten minutes or so Stella puts her head round the door to ask if there is anything else Mitsos wants. The young farmers call her over for their bill. One of them has had too much ouzo with his lunch and is a bit cheeky. The other two try to act sober to chastise their friend. They apologise on his behalf, level all manner of obscenities at him, overcompensate with politeness towards Stella and leave a big tip. Stella is unmoved, she has seen it all before, and she knows they will be in again tomorrow, laughing as if nothing has happened They file out quietly, smiling but subdued. Their conversation is now on the afternoon's work. Stella pockets the tip.

She turns to Mitsos. 'Ouzo?' He shakes his head and declares the food was very good. Stella smiles briefly, but fatigue wipes the smile away. Mitsos looks towards the door as she sits down at his table. The plastic table cloth crackles as her knees push against it. She arranges the salt, pepper, oil and napkins, in an abstracted way.

'He's gone out.' She moves her feet and Manolis can hear them unsticking from the old vinyl floor covering.

'In that case, can I get you anything?' He injects a cheerful note into his intonation.

She lets out a half laugh and then brightens. 'Yes, behind the radio by the sink there is an open bottle of ouzo, the better stuff. Let's have a nip.'

Mitsos is quick to get up, but slow to cross the room. He hurries as best he can. The grill has been set up behind the counter with just enough room for one person to cook and serve. Behind the grill there is a narrow mirror-tiled space with shelves for glasses, misty from the grease of cooking. The old marble sink is full of pots, and a line of dirt where the sink meets the wall contrasts with the white of the marble. The floor is darker round the edge than where people have walked it smooth over the years. There is just enough space for one person to wash up. A radio is perched on the sink's edge, and this too has grime in all its recesses; the handle has kitchen paper wrapped around it that looks as if it has been there for weeks, compressed, tattered and no longer white. Next to the ouzo is a bottle of gin with no cap. Mitsos returns with the ouzo bottle under his arm and two glasses pinched between finger and thumb. He pours them each a generous measure.

'How are the English lessons going?' Mitsos asks, sitting down. Stella has confided in him that she is taking lessons from the English lady, Juliet, who bought an old farmhouse in the village.

She takes her frizzy hair from its elastic band, smooths and rebinds it, leaving a fluffy end. Mitsos thinks of rabbit tails and smiles.

'Good. Thank you,' she says in English before reverting to her mother tongue. 'I quite enjoy it really. It is all part of Stavros' plan. More business. Being able to talk to tourists. Tourists! Round here?' Stella's laugh is cold. 'But it's something new. I do it at her house so it gets me out.'

They sit silently for a while. Mitsos stares at the decoration for maybe the hundredth time. The room has a bare feel, like the kafenio, but with feminine touches such as the prints on the walls and the ceramic horses and swans along the shelf that runs around the walls above head height. He recalls that it was a barber's before Stella and Stavros opened the *souvlaki* shop. He hadn't been a very popular barber. Not a villager. No one knew him, and he didn't last long. Before that, it had been a place to buy sacks and barrels. An old couple had lived in the part with the toilet, and the sacks and barrels were in the other half. He had gone in with his Mama as a child to buy mouse traps that the old man made. The shop smelt of wood and dust. Mitsos remembers that the traps didn't work, and this pleased him.

'He wants to get help in.' Stella breaks the silence.

'Stavros? In here? What does he mean, "help"?'

Stella sighs. 'He says if we get a foreign girl in to work she will bring her tourist friends, that or we will attract a lot more local farmers.' Stella smiles, but there is no sparkle and the smile does not reach her eyes.

Mitsos can hear the sadness in her voice. She used to be so in love with Stavros, but his muscles have become fat and his belly is so big he could be pregnant with twins, all in the seven years Mitsos has known him. When they first opened the shop he was like Manolis, with his bright blue eyes hypnotising the girls. Mitsos imagines the type of foreign girl Stavros would employ and feels a wave of sadness too. He cannot look at Stella.

'I am sorry,' he says.

'Take my mind off it, Mitsos. Tell me of your glory days.'

'The more I think about them, the less glorious and the more stupid they seem.'

'We are all stupid when we are young. Have you ever met anyone who hasn't got things in the past that they would change?' She sounds far away.

They fall silent.

'Which do you think hurts more, the things we do, the things done to us or the things we don't do but wish we had?' she asks.

Mitsos considers before answering, rolling the clear liquid around in his glass.

'I am beginning to think that all the things we have done might be ok if they came from a good heart. It is trying to work out if you have a good heart or not that is the tricky thing.'

'But even if we do something from a good heart, if it is misread by others and it hurts people, what good is the good heart?' Stella asks.

There is a clonk of a goat bell, followed by another. A clicking of hooves and more bells follow. The clicking becomes a gentle drumming, the bells a cacophony of clanks and dongs and knocks. The tops of brown and white heads can be seen passing the window. Curling horns, inquisitive noses, flicking ears. The procession continues until a man with a stick brings up the rear. The sound of the bells diminishes until it can be heard no more.

'If we could see into each other's hearts and understand each other's true motivation no one would be hurt … and no one would be accused,' Mitsos replies.

'But no one takes the time,' Stella muses.

'Except lovers.' Mitsos surprises himself. He feels his cheeks warm and fumbles in his pocket for change. He mutters an excuse and leaves.

Light fills his senses out on the street; it even smells warm. Vasso, who is writing numbers in a book in her kiosk cocoon, apologises that she has run out of his usual brand of cigarettes. He could go to Marina's shop, she suggests, but he decides he will just do without. He turns up the lane to his house. Whitewashed walls on either side, a familiar incline.

He halts. A beetle hurries across his path and disappears into the wall, between the stones. Mitsos wonders if he has a world inside the wall, if the gaps between the stones where the soft mortar has washed away are his roads, the spaces between the rocks his houses, places to rest or store food. If he shares his world with other insects. A village within a village for the creepy-crawlies.

He leaves the beetle to its secret world and continues his slow climb

It is getting hot, too hot to do much, maybe time to have a nap. He is glad to reach his yard. The hinges on the back door creak since the last rains. The kitchen colours give the illusion of cool, whites and pale green. The faded cotton curtains keep out most of the sun but it is still very warm in the house. He hasn't taken up all the winter carpets yet. His steps kick up dust, from the rag-rugs; it swirls in the sunbeams, settling to a hover, before being caught in unfelt currents. He must roll the dust traps up and put them away until next year.

The envelope catches his eye. He had forgotten all about the letter; maybe he meant to forget. This could fulfil his dream for Marina. It might also make things worse. He could insult her, embarrass her. He could inadvertently ridicule her.

Interaction with other people is confusing. His good intentions seem to have a habit of turning out bad.

He picks up the envelope, which feels thinner than he remembers. Perhaps it is bad news. He looks again at the post mark. His German is non-existent and his English was never as good as Manolis', but he can read the word 'Berlin'. He feels a shiver of excitement through his chest; his stomach turns over and flutters. He swallows hard, and blinks rapidly for a moment, stifling his feelings. Nothing is certain until it is certain.

He takes a knife from the drawer and slips the envelope half into the drawer to trap it. He eases the knife point under the edge of the letter's flap. The cut along the edge is neat. Mitsos puts the knife on the draining board. He looks out of the window over the sink, aware that the next time he sees this view his whole position might have changed – or might not. He can see only one cat in the shade of the almonds. The compacted earth yard is unswept and there are weeds growing here and there. The remaining plants in the pots look as if they have died, and the pots need repainting.

There is a single sheet of paper in the envelope. He draws it out carefully, using his teeth to hold the envelope. He smooths the letter open on the table. It is all in English.

Mitsos sits heavily. He chastises himself. Of course it is not in Greek ... Why would it be in Greek? English – the universal language. His energy fizzles away. He recalls his teacher chastising him for looking out at the herding goats during English lessons back in school. Then he could not imagine a reason in the world why he needed to listen. His shoulders slump and he feels for his cigarettes, and then remembers he has none.

Who can he ask to read the letter to him? Stella knows some English – she is getting lessons from the foreign woman. But he is not sure he wants Stella, or more accurately Stavros, to know his business.

He sits and thinks. He wonders whether Stella will continue her English lessons if Stavros gets foreign 'help' in. Probably, if it gets her out of the house and the take-away. But meanwhile, who can read the letter?

The English woman herself – of course.

He can't remember her name. Stella had said. Everyone had said her name when she first moved into the village. Juliet, that was it!

He will go to see Juliet. She is an outsider, she has no one to gossip with. Although he has heard she is friendly with Marina. Well, he will swear her to secrecy.

He puts the piece of paper back in the envelope. He carefully replaces it on the mantelpiece, in the centre, and lies down on the day-bed in the kitchen.

Chapter 7

Mitsos taps tentatively on the metal gate at the top end of the lane. It has taken him the best part of a week to gain the courage to make the visit. Today he feels able to walk without his crook.

The gate has a metal arch over it, covered with bougainvillea, which creates a frame for the view of the front of the house. A strip of land down the side of the house leads to a back garden. There are flowers in all the borders and the place looks very cared for.

He has been to the house before, but that was forty years ago. It belonged to a friend of his parents then, a nice old lady. She died and her grandson inherited it. His parents said he let it go to rack and ruin, renting it out to Albanians back when they were illegal immigrants.

Now they live side by side with Greeks. Now Albanians run businesses.

Well, this Juliet is making a nice job of restoring the garden.

An Asian immigrant appears from the back of the house. Mitsos takes a step back and wonders if he can just walk away. He takes out his hanky and wipes his face as he turns to retrace his steps. It is hot and the lane offers no shade. A lizard darts across his path.

'Do you want Juliet?' the immigrant asks in Greek, his eyes scanning Mitsos' empty sleeve as he turns again to face the house. Mitsos raises his brow; he didn't expect such fluent Greek, and the man's accent is not that bad.

The immigrant misinterprets his hesitation and asks again, 'Do you want Juliet?' in English. Mitsos' feels his eyes widen. He tries to cover his surprise by quickly asking, 'Where is she?' in Greek. He would rather speak directly to her anyway. That is how things should be done, face to face, person to person. These days it's all middle-men, telephones and computers. How can you judge a person, build a relationship, if you never meet them? The world has become so complex, impersonal.

'She has just gone to the nursery for some plants for the garden. Would you like to come in and wait? I could get you some water.'

Mitsos ignores the Indian, Pakistani, whatever he is, and turns to walk away. He wants to keep this simple, get the translation from Juliet and leave. It is not a social visit. He does not want to talk to immigrants. A car approaches up the narrow lane.

'Sir, this is her now,' the immigrant calls. Mitsos wishes he could carry on walking away. This was a bad idea; he cannot let people he doesn't know into his personal business. In a small village that is a recipe for disaster. If people find you are doing well they get jealous and put obstacles in your way. Only if they hear you are doing worse than them do they leave you alone. Everyone in the village talks of nothing more than how badly they are doing, to appease their neighbours. But he is trapped between the car and the gate in the narrow lane; there is no escape.

The woman driving the car smiles. She has striking golden hair. Mitsos cannot help but smile back.

The immigrant opens the gates wider and Mitsos steps aside to let the car pass.

She is light on her feet as she jumps out of the car, and she puts out a hand towards Mitsos.

'Hello, I am Juliet, welcome. How may I help you?' Her Greek is fluent.

Mitsos closes his mouth, which he can feel has just opened a fraction at the enthusiastic welcome. He struggles to form his reply.

'Hello, I am …' He glances at the immigrant and does not finish his sentence.

'Oh, excuse me, this is Aaman.'

Aaman puts out his hand to shake but Mitsos is very slow to respond and in the delay Aaman retracts his. Juliet turns to him and talks quietly of the plants she has bought and where to put them. Aaman takes the plants round the side of the house, out of sight.

'So, Mr …'

'Mitsos.'

'So, Mr Mitsos how can I help you?'

'I have some very private business I wish you to help me with.' Mitsos looks towards the house. He is not comfortable talking about this in the open; you never know who is listening over the wall. He is keenly aware of this fact because once upon a time it had been him hiding behind walls … and Manolis too.

Juliet takes the hint. She leads the way and offers him a seat on the sofa. The room is entirely white, with a white floor, white walls, white sofa. There is a bookcase full of books, neatly arranged. It is alien to him but the place has a very calm feeling. He looks at Juliet, feeling he knows her a bit better for seeing inside her home.

'I have a very personal, private document I wish to have translated. It must remain private.' He chooses a hard-backed chair.

'I see.' Juliet reclines on the sofa.

'Will you do it?' Mitsos is not sure how such a conversation should be conducted.

'Is it long or short? For one copy I have a minimum fee for anything under two thousand words, and if it is longer there is an additional cost per word.'

Mitsos looks blank. It had not occurred to him that she would charge a fee. He has no money on him and precious little elsewhere. 'Er …' He does not know how to phrase it. 'It is just a letter.'

'Oh!' Juliet lets out a gentle peal of laughter and her spine curves softly as it relaxes. 'You mean you just want me to read a letter to you?'

'Yes.' Mitsos reaches into his breast pocket and takes out the envelope. He removes the single sheet which he carefully straightens, pressing it against his thigh. He passes the sheet to Juliet, who has to lean towards him to reach it. He is slightly reluctant to let it go.

'It is from …' Juliet begins.

'I know who it is from. All I want to know is are they going ahead or not? Is it a yes or a no?'

Juliet scans the page, folds the sheet carefully, reaches over and takes the envelope from Mitsos' knee, returns the missive to its place and hands it back. He takes it in a daze, eyes wide, replaces it in his breast pocket, clenches his fist, his shoulders drawn back. He looks ready to pounce.

'They are going ahead,' Juliet replies without ceremony.

Mitsos begins to smile, and then he opens his mouth wide and shouts 'Opa!' and tenses his fist and shakes it by his ear; his whole upper body judders. Juliet is now grinning at him. He stands up and offers her his hand, which she takes, and he pulls her to her feet, and spontaneously draws her towards him and kisses her on both cheeks. He regains control and feels his cheeks colour, and bows his head.

'Thank you, Mrs Juliet, thank you.' He studies his sandals. His spontaneous reaction battles for attention with the news just imparted.

'All I did was read a letter,' Juliet says.

'Ah, but you did it so beautifully.' He looks up at her and grins widely before taking his leave. When he is by the gate he turns back to see Juliet leaning against the doorframe looking after him, smiling. He purses his lips and presses a tall finger against them. Juliet nods, zipping her lips with her hand. They both smile and wave farewell.

Mitsos hops and skips, as well as he can, all the way down the lane to the square. Such a weight has been lifted. He feels years younger. His balance returns, or at least it's better.

He briskly mounts the steps to the kafenio and takes a seat in the window. He wants to see the world.

He orders an ouzo from Theo, who makes no comment on the change to his decades-long seating ritual. Theo just smiles and nods, his hair flopping, a frizzy crown. He serves an ouzo and pats Mitso on the back as he walks away, a gesture of support for whatever has happened, unconditional.

The square contains its usual assortment of children playing, women talking, immigrants waiting and dogs. The colours seem bright, the sunlight brighter. The children, wearing primary shades and dazzling whites, seem happy. The women's housecoats, shouting tropical flowers and swirling designs, make promises of faraway places. Mitsos has always hated such bold designs but right now they seem to add to the pure joy of life. A dog runs around the immigrants; one of them pats him, no one throws a stone. Vasso, in her wooden box, is looking out, smiling. The sun saturates the colours and creates strong contrast with the patches of shade. Mitsos puts his hand to his breast pocket where the letter is safely stowed.

A stout but striking woman comes out of the pharmacy, dressed in blue, a blue like the sky. Mitsos studies her. She seems familiar, and he realises it is Marina. She is not wearing black. Mitsos cannot think what this might mean. Generally women who lose their husbands do not come out of mourning. Whatever her reason for wearing blue, she wears it well, and she looks like she has lost some weight, although she remains a lovely curvy lady. Mitsos shuffles on his seat, pulls the crotch of his trousers into a more comfortable position and straightens his shirt.

He is acutely conscious of his new-found power. He checks that the envelope is still there. Marina stops to chat to other women. She smiles, she looks happy, and Mitsos is glad to see this. She laughs, and Mitsos can see the girl he first loved. What a life he would have given her. The sons they would have had.

But now, what does he do now? He can now show Marina his love for her but in what way? He must not be clumsy or crude, or the whole thing could backfire. He must be careful, considerate, see it from her point of view. But what is her view? It is more than twenty-two years since they last spoke. She was a girl of just twenty-eight then. It occurs to Mitsos that a lot can happen in that time, that he doesn't really know her anymore. But he is not convinced people really change. And he is sure he loves her anyway.

Marina looks directly at him. He swallows hard; he can feel a pulse at his temples and a bead of sweat breaks out on his forehead. She looks away again. But Mitsos, empowered by his letter, leaves his table and trots, as best he can, down the kafenio steps and across to Marina.

'Hello,' he begins. She stops walking abruptly and looks at him, searching his eyes, and then at his empty shirt sleeve. They have not been this close to each other since that day. She closes her mouth, which had opened in the surprise of the encounter, and turns to walk on. 'How are you, Marina?' He wants to tell her that, however she is, he can make it better.

'What do you want?' Her tone is neutral.

Mitsos feels his stomach drop. There is a sudden pain in his chest. 'Please, Marina, I want to know how you are.'

'I am fine.' She looks in the direction of her corner shop, where she is heading. She looks at the ground, her eyes flitting backwards and forwards, and then she makes the slightest turn in her shoulders to face him.

'I am fine. How are you?' Her voice is still neutral but her eyes make contact. His stomach flutters and his knees give a little and he swallows as his mouth has gone dry.

Mitsos does not want to have a conversation on this superficial level, but he is lost for words. He looks in her face. She is so much older now. 'I am fine. Is the shop doing well?'

'Yes, thank you.' Her shoulders make the slightest turn from him; she is going to walk away. She is holding a newspaper, which she now raises above her head to shade her face from the sun.

'Marina ...' He decides to take the goat by the horns. 'Marina,' he repeats, 'I am so deeply sorry.' Her gaze is level, and she looks him straight in the eyes. Mitsos wonders how many people at the kafenio are watching him. He is now part of the daily play. He also wonders if she is going to slap his face. There is a glint in her eye. Has he made the situation worse? 'Really ... deeply ... sorry.' He tries, but can only think of the same words again. The words he has wanted to say for twenty-two years. He can feel tears pricking at his eyes. The words seem empty, not the balm he thought they would be.

Marina takes a breath. Her stout chest lifts, the blue material pulls tight. Mitsos shifts his weight to ease any strain there may be on his trousers. 'I am not,' she says quietly, her sentence dropping at the end into a definite full stop.

'What?' Mitsos' forehead lifts.

'I am not sorry for what happened. Well, I mean, I am on one level, of course, but for what you are sorry, I am not.' She doesn't smile, but she does walk away.

Mitsos can make no sense of the exchange. All these years he has presumed she was angry, sad, lonely, hating him. His envelope does not seem so powerful now; it cannot bring clarity.

He can feel the eyes of his peer group at the kafenio on his back. He cannot stand there on his own much longer. But he is so confused by Marina's words that after two steps towards his home he changes his mind and walks as briskly as he can to Stella's.

There is music and laughter at Stella's take-away. The same young farmers are there, and some older ones that must be at least fifty, their trousers held up with twine, their skin like leather sheets drawn tight over their bones, shirt sleeves rolled up, missing teeth framed by happy smiles. Stella has turned the radio on and they are singing along to popular Greek songs. Mitsos thinks that on this particular recording the singer has a voice like rusty nails in a metal bucket. But the passion is strong. He sings of what he would like to eat, but with such an intensity that he could be singing about love. Mostly he wants fish, particularly red mullet, *barbounia*.

Fish be damned, Mitsos would like one day of love, one evening, one hour, when he can release all the care he has to offer and be cared for in return. People do not recognise how lucky they are.

The farmers sing with the same passion. In the corner sits a foreign girl. Her bag is on the floor beside her, and she clearly does not know what to make of the situation. Stavros is sitting at her table, pouring ouzo. The farmers stand to perform; they interlace arms, hands on shoulders, and dance in the tiny space. Stella moves chairs and tables out of the way, her sad eyes on Stavros who is grinning and flirting with the outsider. The girl looks slightly afraid.

One of the farmers is full of life; the lunchtime impromptu singing has brought energy to his limbs. He is feeling good, he has *kefi*, an appetite for life, joy. His hair is greying at the temples and his hands speak of years of toil, the skin thick and hard. But at this moment he is alive, his heart is full, he wants to dance, dance like there is no tomorrow, no fields to dig, no olives to tend. To dance as if his life depends on it. He climbs on a chair and then jumps onto the table. It wobbles and threatens to collapse, and the other farmers and Stavros cheer. But it holds his weight and he dances with his head brushing the ceiling, his friends on one knee clapping to encourage him. Outwardly, he is blind; there is only the music and the movement.

The girl claps self-consciously. Stavros shouts 'Opa!' The girl giggles.

The man on the table pauses on its edge. He is a youth again, he crouches low and then springs from the table, completing a somersault to the floor with an unsteady landing, but he does not fall, and everyone cheers. No one looks more surprised than he does that he is successful.

Stella spots Mitsos, but he is backing out of the shop. He does not want noise now, he needs to think. Stella nips across the room to him.

'What is it?' she asks.

Mitsos tries to rearrange his face, take off whatever expression has prompted Stella to ask such a question, to leave his countenance blank.

There is always a chair outside the shop, for when business is slack and Stella just wants to sit and watch the world go by. She brings another chair from inside. The dancing and singing continue but the distance dilutes the intensity. The air is fragrant with goats. Somewhere on the hill a cockerel tells the time, incorrectly. Mitsos thinks it might be his bird. The damned thing crows all day long. He sits.

'So?' Stella plops down and leans back in her chair, stretches her legs out in front of her and crosses them. She crosses her arms across her floral dress. It is the short dress with no sleeves. She is so petite she can wear such things and still look pretty, even though she must be in her late forties. Not, Mitsos thinks, promiscuous as some might look in such a skimpy tunic.

He wants to ask about the blonde foreign girl inside but he has the impression Stella would rather be distracted than questioned. He pushes Stavros' behaviour from his mind.

'I just talked to Marina.' Mitsos quietly relates the conversation. Stella is the only person who knows of Mitsos' secret love. The many lunches and dinners he has taken here have, slowly, over the years, unintentionally, cultured a friendship. She knows his story from the moment he and Marina first met.

He considers telling her about his visit to Juliet, about the letter. He could do with her wisdom on the best way to deal with it, but he does not trust Stavros, and after all they are married, maybe they have times when they are close. He decides not to. He tries a different angle.

'What do you think Marina needs most in the world?'

'In all honesty, she needs what no one can give her.' Stella does not hesitate in her reply.

'What's that?' Mitsos answers, with hope in his voice.

'She needs a memory of a husband who was good to her, who thought about her and who provided for her. With a memory like that she would feel like a different person. She would feel valued and loved and lovable. As it is, she sees herself as unlovable, worthy of neglect and unworthy of being put first. You can see it with her children. She sees them as having so much value and herself as having none. She does everything for them she can, breaks her back for them and just considers it the "right" thing to do. Over the years she has neglected herself more and more, and that has all come from him.' Stella pauses and Mitsos stays quiet, taken aback by her passion. 'Sorry. Did you want such a full answer?' She smiles, but she is turning her head to look inside her shop. Stavros is still at the girl's table but the dancing has stopped. He is giving her an apron and pointing to the grill.

Mitsos leans over and pats her hand kindly.

'And you would know, Stella.'

Stella lets a tear fall.

At home that night Mitsos sits on a chair in his kitchen. It creaks every time he moves. The sky outside is dark and the white almond blossom glows in the moonlight. He recollects Stella's words. 'What she needs most is a memory of a husband who was good to her, she would feel valued and loved and loveable.'

These words have an unsettling effect on him. It is almost as if he can think of a way to make everything right again but it just won't form into something concrete. But as he cannot – and would not want to – raise Manolis from the dead, her memory of him will remain the same. He dismisses these niggles as a deep desire for something that cannot be fulfilled.

An owl hoots outside the window. He opens the door to let in any breeze there is; it is still very warm. The owl is on one of the nearest almond trees. It blinks at him through the opening. He kicks off his sandals and pulls off his shirt and trousers. He stands naked in the moonlight, slightly sagging, slightly wrinkled, and yet he has the surest of feelings that his life is only just beginning. Something is around the corner.

He slaps his chest and then laughs at himself. He yawns and lies down on the day-bed. The air is now pleasantly warm; he will need no sheet, no pyjamas tonight. He stretches his legs out and rubs the stump of his arm. It still itches all these years later. He smiles again and stretches some more. Something is definitely coming.

Chapter 8

Adonis sounds his horn as he pulls in through the gates. Mitsos is wandering around the orchard. He has just been up the hill to collect the eggs and he still has the bucket with him. One hen has been broody for a week and now there are no eggs in her box; she is hiding them to sit on. But he knows this hen, she will not sit for long, they will go cold and then she will start again with new eggs. Each time the eggs will be lost and will go bad somewhere, waiting to be stepped on.

He raises the bucket in greeting. Adonis leaves the car door open and walks across to Mitsos.

'Broody hen, eh?'

How's the little man?'

'Have you tried in amongst the pine trees up at the top? He's fine, sleeping.'

'First place I looked. Do you want to take some back with you?' He lifts the bucket.

'Leni will be pleased. What do you do with them all?' Adonis peers in the bucket at the speckled brown eggs. Mitsos is content that Adonis managed to escape the farm way of life. His schooling lasted until he was sixteen and then he immediately got a job in town. He completed his national service as soon as he turned eighteen. A better job and a flat in the nearby town followed swiftly. He continues to manage the shop in the village that sells fertilisers and pesticides. He is a natural businessman.

Anyway, he has rarely collected an egg or tilled the soil, or sat with the goats. Mitsos feels coarse next to him. Clumsy. Unshaven. But he is happy for Adonis. He looks down at the bucket of eggs.

'I'll eat some, sell some to Stavros at the *souvlaki* shop, give them to you.' His attention wanders and he grins through the car window at his nephew, who has woken up. He puts the bucket of eggs down to wave.

'Ok, here's his stuff. Leni says "hi" and "thanks".' Adonis lifts the baby from the car and handing him over he climbs into the driver's seat. Mitsos puts his nephew down by the bucket of eggs and shuts the door on Adonis. The window is open and the air coming out is cool. Mitsos wonders at the modern world.

'Going to tell me his name yet?'

'At the baptism.' Adonis' head is already turned to back down the track.

Mitsos picks up his nephew in the car seat and wanders in the almond orchard swinging the baby as if he is the bucket of eggs. He would still like to find where she is laying them. 'So, my fine young man, how are you?' The baby gurgles, his hands outstretched for a passing dragonfly. Mitsos wanders a bit more, looking for the broody hen's nest until, lazily, he sits on a stone that has fallen from the top of the wall at the far end of the orchard. He puts the baby-seat on the ground in front of him and takes a good look at his kin.

'I have had some good news since I saw you last, and between me and you I think things are going to change, somehow, in some way.' The baby claps his hands and Mitsos slaps his leg to imitate the sounds. And they smile at each other for a while. Mitsos pulls a face, but soon returns to his serious topic. 'My little friend, it gets tricky now. What is the best way to go about things?' He looks through the trees. 'Women are sensitive creatures.' He sits, watching nothing in particular, his gaze altering distances in practised unawareness. He can hear a tractor in the lane and, behind him, goat bells on the hill, a hollow, flat sound.

He pauses, aware of flying insects, birds singing, branches rubbing one another and the broody hen strutting across the orchard towards the front garden, and then continues.

'Women. You won't know about women for some time yet, and believe you me, the longer that time is the better because once women are in your life you have never known pain like it. Pain in the head, pain in the ears, but the worst, pain in the heart …' The baby makes a laughing sound and Mitsos laughs too. 'So you think it's funny, do you? Well, let me tell you it didn't feel so funny back then.'

His heart had tightened. His stomach felt as if it had turned around in his body and he forgot how to breathe. She was lovely, with dark brown hair loose around her shoulders, slim ankles, her head held at a confident angle. The way she moved mesmerised him. He watched her choosing tomatoes, her slim fingers feeling the firmness of each one, caressing the smooth surface, turning them over to inspect all sides. She handed her bag to the vendor to be weighed with a smile that sent shivers down his spine. She was young, almost too young, and her innocence surrounded her like an aura. So pure, so unspoilt. Had he made a terrible mistake by refusing the match? Mitsos vaguely recognised the girl. Her family was from the village, but since he had last seen her she had turned from a child to a woman.

He was twenty-nine at the time.

Other girls he had met through the years up until that point were of no consequence. Either he and Manolis had met them in the bars in nearby towns on a Saturday, which was an introduction demanding no respect, or they were pious village girls in church on Sunday. None had touched Mitsos' heart.

At that age Mitsos and Manolis were not as close as they had once been. In their late teens they had finally been reined in by their families when Mitsos' family boat received an unwanted lining of oil-based paint.

Manolis had found the tins on a beach and persuaded Mitsos to take the booty back to the village in his family rowing boat. As they pulled on the oars in the heat of the midday sun, the lids had popped off several of them and a layer of paint flowed into the bottom of the boat.

That alone would have been enough to arouse Mitsos' father to a fury but on top of that, some days later, there was a rumour of paint having been stolen from a hardware store, and Mitsos' Baba decided enough was enough.

He organised a meeting with Manolis' Baba and they agreed the boys should no longer see each other. To this end, they were finally enlisted to do their military service, which sent them to different regions in Greece, and they didn't see each other for two years.

When they came out, Mitsos with honour and Manolis in shame, they were doomed to finally share some of the strain of the family labours if they intended to carry on living at home. When Mitsos' Baba said he must 'work beside him on the land', he really did mean right beside him. It had been a shocking wake-up call even after the regimented life in the army. And when the long day had finished and his elder brother and father went home to relax, he was consigned to cleaning every last bit of the now very encrusted paint from the rowing boat with sandpaper and wire wool. It had taken weeks.

That was the beginning of a long period of sensible living, at least for Mitsos.

At this time his older brother was already engaged and most evenings were spent taking his wife-to-be out. His younger brother, not even nine years old, was always in bed and fast asleep before him.

One evening Mitsos was lying in the room he shared with his brother, not able to sleep for the heat, when he overheard his mother and father talking about arranging a marriage. As he listened, his name was mentioned. Enraged that his life should be planned for him, he jumped from his bed and burst into the kitchen ready to challenge them.

'I do not want an arranged marriage,' Mitsos stated as firmly as he could, the rage causing his limbs to shake. His father took a long draw on his cigarette and shook his head; his mother tried to calm him.

'You need to settle down. They are offering a reasonable dowry and her parents would come and work on the land beside you. It's not a bad deal. See it as free labour for the price of a meal.'

Mitsos was lost for words. He valued his freedom, his independence. He felt shy around women; it would be hell having to spend every evening with one. What would he say, what would he do? He would have to wear a shirt all the time, know what time he would be home and, worst of all, be responsible for her happiness. He had seen bad husbands and what happened to their wives. He had vowed he would never be the same. He would not take a wife unless he was sure he could make her happy. As he didn't have a clue how to make a woman happy, he reasoned that marriage was clearly not for him.

His mother, over the next few days, had gently tried to plant lots of ideas in his head as to why it would be a good idea. But he was adamant, and finally, after months of fruitless discussions, the subject was dropped.

Mitsos was relieved, and he unburdened himself to Manolis. Manolis teased him relentlessly about marriage, but Mitsos did not really mind. He was happy to have escaped his fate, and soon Manolis dropped the subject too. Greek men, he had said, do not marry until they are forty, and even that was too soon. 'This gives us over ten years, my friend,' he had laughed.

It was nearly a year later, when Mitsos was in the nearby town with his Mama, helping her with some heavy shopping, that she spotted and pointed out the girl to whom his marriage had nearly been arranged. That was when his heart had tightened, his stomach felt as if it had turned around in his body and he forgot how to breathe. If he was ever going to marry then it had to be to a girl like this.

'Is she still single?' Mitsos asked his Mama.

'No, she is engaged to someone else in the village.' The surge of emotion induced by this statement cut through his chest and wrapped a cord around his throat. He did everything he could to dispel the feelings. He refused to look at her any more and did his best to focus on the tomatoes, the heat, the sun, the bad points of all women. A little old lady in black pushed past with her basket of shopping. He consoled himself with the thought that the girl would one day be old and fat. He was best off free. He breathed again and looked away.

Days later he was sitting with his father in the kafenio, in their usual spot, with windows on all sides, when he saw her again. She was on the back of a cart being pulled by a donkey, coming straight towards them. The cart stopped in the square and she climbed down with the help of, presumably, her father. Her mother was there also.

'Ah, so they have come to live. This is going to put a stop to his ways.'

'What, Baba?'

'Them.' He jerked his coffee in the direction of the girl and her family. 'They have a small house here, more of a storage barn really, and a little land. That is why they are marrying off their daughter. They need more land to be able to live, merge their land with someone else's. Dowry and daughter for land. Simple as that. But you, of all people, know all this.'

But that was not the question he wanted answered. 'Put a stop to whose ways?'

His Baba opened his mouth to reply but instead a laugh came out. It began as a short throaty scoffing noise but grew and grew until he was laughing so much his belly wobbled. He wiped a tear from his eye and tried to compose himself to speak again but the laughter returned. All the men in the kafenio turned to see what the merriment was, but only Dimitri knew and he was unable to put a sentence together. He slapped his thigh and looked again at the girl and her family until his laughter subsided.

'Well, my boy,' he finally managed, 'you wouldn't marry her, but they were determined to find someone who would.' He wiped his eyes and took a sip of coffee. 'The deal was not so tempting, as the dowry was not so large and the parents will be a burden all too soon. It is not a good start for a couple.' Mitsos thought he had finished speaking, as his Baba had taken another sip of coffee and put his cup down. After a minute he continued: 'But there is always someone fool enough to take any offer.' He turned his attention from Mitsos and nodded his head towards the girl who had sat down on the seat by the square's central palm tree. 'Who you see there, my son, is the future Mrs Manolis.'

Mitsos swallowed hard, but a lump caught in his throat. He could hear his heart beating in his ears and the hairs on his arm stood on end.

'That is not funny, Baba.' Mitsos heard himself but the voice did not sound like his own.

'Ha! You will miss your friend, eh?'

Mitsos had no thought of his friend. He stared at the girl sitting quite still as her Mama and Baba took their things from the cart. If he had never seen her again he might have forgotten her, but if she were to marry Manolis he would see her often, if not every day. His heart leapt at the thought of seeing her every day and, in a mad moment, it seemed like the perfect solution. He could see her but not be burdened by her. Enjoy her company but leave when he wished. But no sooner had the thought flashed though his head than he felt a sickness in his stomach. It was not all right for the girl. It was not right for someone like Manolis to marry someone so pure. He could guess what someone like that needed, and if he couldn't guess he could learn. Manolis would neither know nor care. She would not be happy with him. In fact, he could see nothing but misery for her.

'It's impossible!' he blurted.

'Yup. They put the deal together after your refusal about a year ago. I think you made the right decision – the deal was not a good one,' his Baba replied.

'She cannot!' Mitsos' voice sounded as if it hadn't broken.

His Baba turned to look at him. Mitsos stared down at his coffee, picked it up, took a sip, trying to control his responses. His hand was shaking so he stood up declaring he needed the toilet and left the table.

The toilet stank and, as usual, there was no paper. He wiped his face on his shirt. Mitsos could not understand his reactions. He tried to think logically but all he got were images of the girl in his head, and a fury ran through him when he thought of Manolis. It could not be; every fibre of his being rejected the truth of his Baba's words. The whole idea was ludicrous. Manolis himself would not allow it. His family would not split off a portion of their land and give it to him. No, the concept was beyond reason. It just would not be. It could not be. His Baba had been misinformed. He took several deep breaths and calmed himself before returning to his coffee.

'You ok?' his Baba asked.

'Yes, fine.' He looked out of the window but the seat by the tree was empty. The donkey, still shackled to the cart, was sleeping where it stood. The girl was gone.

Chapter 9

The baby sleeps away the morning. Mitsos sits on a chair by the back door, the bright sun on his face, gazing and dreaming. Adonis brings a letter from the post box when he comes to collect his son. It is from Mitsos' lawyer. Mitsos recognises the writing and puts it on the mantelpiece to read when his brother has gone. Adonis makes a speedy departure, as usual, accepting neither coffee nor a seat, eager to return to his modern air-conditioned car, leave the old life behind. After he's gone Mitsos remains sitting in the kitchen.

He stares at the new envelope, but his eyes are drawn to the pattern created by the black smoke stains up the front of the fireplace where the smoke escapes in the winter when the wind blows from the south.

It is a wide fireplace with iron hooks in the back wall on which to hang cooking pots. The mantelshelf bears cut marks where his father, and probably his father before him, used it as a narrow table. He can remember his father resting there to saw through rope on a worn leather goat collar to take off a bell. His mother had shouted at him for gouging lines in the plaster but his Baba had argued that it was cut all over anyway so what did it matter.

His elder brother's initials are carved into the plaster on one side. Mitsos can remember the day. His brother had felt the belt as a consequence of this action, and had been made to paint the whole fireplace too.

Pale green. Mitsos has always disliked the colour, but has never done anything about it. Not when his Baba died and not when his Mama died.

He stands and picks up the letter and puts it in his breast pocket and smooths it flat. It is beginning to feel real.

He is hungry and has no food in the house. He will go to Stella's again.

Stella is sitting outside in the warmth. It is too early for most people's lunch. She has the same short flowery dress on. She sits with her legs extended, slumped in the attitude of a sulking child, sucking her frappé through a straw. She pushes herself up in the chair a little and shields her eyes from the sun with her arm as he approaches.

'Early for you, Mitso.' Her hair is frizzy from the daily heat of her job. She usually has it tied back but today it rests on her shoulders. Mitsos can imagine her in a more serious dress with ribbons in her mane. She is a woman who is easy to look at, petite, lithe, strong and a little bit wild.

'You alone?' Mitsos speaks quietly.

'He's gone into town. Something to do with a deep fat fryer, he says, but he has taken the English girl with him. Abby. She works here now.' Stella sniffs in adamant defiance. 'You hungry? I have made a new batch of lemon sauce for the chickens but they won't be done for another hour or so. Chips will take over twenty minutes as the oil's not hot. So I can only offer you beer, ouzo or good company.'

Mitsos looks at the paper cup of frappé.

'Or you can go across the road and get a frappé and a cheese pie from the new sandwich shop and come and join me here.'

Mitsos pulls a chair from inside and sits next to Stella on the roadside.

'How was the baby-sitting?' she asks.

'Fine.'

'You seem distracted. What is it?'

'Did I ever tell you of Manolis' and my first big disaster before he got married?'

Stella laughs at the thought, drains her coffee with much gurgling and sucking, puts the empty paper cup down on the ground and settles back. She does not answer but is clearly ready to be entertained. She watches the woman who lives across the road, next to the sandwich shop, come out in her housecoat and sweep the road in front of her house. Mitsos follows her gaze. He has seen this a hundred times before, all over the village since he was a boy: women brush and even wash the pavement and roads in front of their houses. Normal life. A young village girl walks past in a T-shirt declaring she loves New York even though, Mitsos is sure, she will never have been there, never have been further than the nearest town probably. He wonders if the next generation will feel they belong so much to the village that even the road is theirs to sweep.

'Go on then,' Stella demands impatiently.

Mitsos is pulled back from his daydreams to recall the past.

Mitsos' father dying, when Mitsos had just turned thirty, surprised everyone. Cancer, they said. There was talk that it came from the chemicals that the farmers sprayed on the oranges. Ever since he could remember he had seen his Baba spray the oranges each year. First with a hand pump, pumping away, surrounded by the poisonous mist making rainbows in the sun. Then later on his tractor, in a cloud of high-pressure venom, each tree well covered, along with his Baba and no doubt his Baba's lungs.

It is only recently that some farmers, or workers, have begun to use masks when they spray, but most still do not.

Just before he died, his Baba said he felt unwell and wanted to see the doctor. That alone told Mitsos it was serious. Doctors were characters from the cinema, to be avoided in real life.

He had gone into the town one day for the purpose and had not come home that night. Mitsos' mother went into town next day and found him in hospital. Then he was dead.

His elder brother was making ready to leave to go and live in Corinth, his new wife's home town, where she had land more fertile than any in the village. His younger brother had been reading in his room, a skill Mitsos never really mastered. Mitsos had just returned from taking the goats to pasture, the odour of the beasts still on him, when a taxi pulled up at the end of the track and the driver said he had been sent for them all by their mother.

A little confused and with some trepidation they all, including his brother's fiancée, piled into the taxi and were driven to the hospital to find her distraught. She sobbed and wailed, her hanky flying, as she expressed her loss, her anger, her abandonment. Her emotions were terrifying. The boys stood in a line, dumbfounded. It was Mitsos' elder brother's fiancée who took a step towards her and put a consoling arm around her shoulders, his brothers following her lead. Mitsos had found her despair too alarming and remained motionless.

No one missed Dimitri, except his widow, perhaps, but the boys weren't even convinced that she did all the time. They felt only relief. Mitsos' elder brother tried to make his escape all the sooner, but his mother needed him now. Then the lawyer came.

There was a Will, it all went to the boys. The choice pieces of land went to the youngest, as he had the most distance to travel to independence. The eldest, on the presumption that he was the wisest, was left the worst piece of land, in this case a piece of saline-soaked sandy soil fit for only growing beets. It had been the family joke. Dimitri, the eldest boy in his family, had inherited it and now it would be passed on.

The two younger boys had laughed when they heard that the eldest would get the beet plot. It felt like a reprisal for his bullying. It was a flat piece of scrub land, stony, sandy and pretty useless as it was down away from the village by the sea. The salt water soaked into the soil, making it all but incapable of growing anything but beets. Mitsos' and Adonis' sides had ached laughing at their brother's lot whilst their mother sat in her room and cried.

It was the same evening, with no Baba to govern his movements, that Mitsos went into town and chose a bar in which to get drunk.

The bouzouki player was good and the wailing clarinet player was loud; another man sat nursing an accordion to very little effect. The usual types of suited men sat in groups and pairs, ties pulled loose. The smoke hung like an eiderdown over the tables and chairs, giving a metaphoric atmosphere if not a breathable one.

Who should be there but Manolis. He seemed to be on the same mission as Mitsos judging by the number of empty shot glasses before him. He had grown lean with the army and farm work, and his eyes were darker blue than Mitsos remembered. His dark mass of curls seemed bleached, presumably by the daily sun, to give it golden flecks. There were two women sitting with him, one on either side. When he saw Mitsos he hailed him loudly, jumped from his stool and greeted him with a bear hug. Mitsos was flattered by his enthusiasm, as well as the admiring looks that Manolis' interest generated from the women he was with.

'What's new?' Manolis asked.

'Not much,' replied Mitsos. 'Baba died.' Manolis congratulated him on his new-found freedom and asked what land was his now. The women were dismissed; this was man's talk.

Mitsos downed a whisky and told the tale of Adonis' and his hysterics over the beet land. Manolis congratulated him again and refilled his glass.

Manolis told of his gambling prowess, which added to his income, as he took his father's workers for their day's pay night after night.

'What do they live on,' Mitsos asked, 'if you keep winning their earnings, and where do they sleep with no wage to pay for a room?' Manolis said they could always eat oranges. His Baba, whom he was now calling by his first name, Costas, (in fact he was calling him Old Costas), had put wide shelves up in the old barn and rented the berths out nightly to illegal immigrants. It was cheaper for them than a hotel, safer than under the trees, offered some protection from police raids and, if they had no money to pay after gambling, they were offered half-price berths whilst they worked for free to pay off their debt.

Manolis laughed his evil laugh as he told of one man who owed him so much that he had to work for a month for nothing to pay him off.

Mitsos had had enough whisky by this point to find it funny, and the two of them became increasingly loud. In the end they stopped buying single refills and bought the bottle so they could fill their glasses at will. Two unsavoury-looking girls came in and attached themselves when they saw the bottle, and the four of them drank until Mitsos thought he would fall off his seat.

'We best go where the landing is soft then,' Manolis said, and took the bottle, his glass and one of the girls out into the night.

The other girl took Mitsos' arm but he wriggled free and told her to wait, he needed the toilet. The door to the facilities also led to the alley behind. Mitsos made his escape, fell over some soggy cardboard boxes of kitchen waste, used the wall to support himself, flicked pieces of unidentifiable food from his shirt, and staggered his way round to the front of the bar, to see Manolis and the girl disappearing towards the beach.

He could not hurry, his legs would not allow it. Manolis was getting further and further away. The girl's white shirt glowed in the moonlight and the bottle swinging from Manolis' hand glinted. They disappeared from sight behind some eucalyptus trees at the beaches edge, but Mitsos knew Manolis' haunts.

He needed another drink, and he hoped he would catch them up before the whisky ran out. The town seemed quiet now, and he wondered why he had ditched the other girl.

He had reached the eucalyptus tree when the girl in the white shirt ran back past him towards the town.

Mitsos swayed onwards to the sea's edge to find his friend.

'Silly whore!' Manolis was shouting and turning circles, his arms outstretched. His head thrown back, the moon on his face, he made the noise of a goat and threw himself down on the sand.

Mitsos collapsed beside him and snatched the bottle.

'Whatswaswrongwithsherthen?' Mitsos' words came out as a stream and there were too many 'esses'.

'Ach!' Manolis made a swift full arc with his arm and dismissed the crying girl from his mind.

The bay was so still, the water without a ripple, a path of light to the low-hung moon; the coast on the opposite side of the bay dotted with lights, the land black against the dark blues of sea and sky. Mitsos appreciated the beauty, although it puzzled him that there were two moons. He could hear the faraway putt-putt of a night fishing boat, a dog calling another dog, and goat bells once in a while. It was the music of his country, the sound of his home. He was revelling in it and presumed Manolis was doing the same.

'Got it!' Manolis slurred and stood up. He ran to the sea and in up to his knees, and dipped his head in the cool water, flicking his hair back as he came up. He returned, soaked, with only the odd patch of dry on his shirt.

Manolis stopped looking at the two moons and turned his attention to the two Manolises standing before him. He shivered at the vision. He put his head on one side. 'Got what?'

'I have our future. I have our wealth laid out before me. I have all the girls you could wish for and I have the most fun way to make a living. Are you in?'

At that point, for Mitsos, sleep was a far more attractive proposition than any amount of wealth or girls, and he lay down in the sand using his arm as a pillow. But Manolis was dancing from foot to foot as if he were a boy again, not a grown man, the moon turning his blue shirt silver. Mitsos had seen it all before and closed his eyes. Manolis tried to rouse him but sleep was all but upon him. He felt Manolis grab him by the arms, and before he could get his bearings Manolis was dragging him backwards through the sand. Mitsos felt disorientated. Bright moon, midnight blue, pale blue shirt. He closed his eyes and wondered if he had wet himself, but as the level of wetness rose, he opened his eyes and saw he was in the sea. Manolis continued to drag him.

Mitsos tried to find his feet but the sand shifted under his weight and there was no getting up. The water rose to his shoulders and splashed in his nose, in his mouth. He coughed and choked but still his arms were being pulled. His head went under, panic rose in his chest, he twisted and squirmed and the grip on his arms relaxed at last. But still Mitsos could not stand, the sand was shifting, he could not tell which way was up. He kicked and floundered with his arms. His fight for survival cleared his head quickly. He turned onto his hands and knees and rose to a squatting position. He gulped some air and lost his balance, but he had seen he was facing the shore. On all fours he pushed himself forward as fast as he could until the water shallowed. He gasped some more air and the panic subsided. He crawled further, his head out of the water, crouching, then standing. A hand came to steady him. He slapped it off and stamped up the beach and sat on the rocks, catching his breath.

'You nearly bloody drowned me!' Mitsos shouted.

'I needed you sober.'

'Go to hell!' Mitsos stood up to walk away. His toe touched the bottle of whisky. He picked it up. Manolis put his hand out to claim it but Mitsos flung it with all his strength into the sea.

'Hey!'

'Go to hell.' Mitsos was up by the eucalyptus trees. Manolis ran after him.

'Listen, this is it, all our problems solved.'

'You being dead would solve all my problems!' Mitsos never forgot these words. He even wanted to take them back as he said them, but part of him meant them. He was horrified by his own feelings. He was not the man he thought he was. But nor was Manolis, who had nearly drowned him.

Manolis had stopped walking as he spoke and stood, a dark shape under the trees, the moon on the sea visible under the branches behind him.

Mitsos had turned to say, 'That was too much.' But he did not make it clear whether the near-drowning was too much, or his own harsh words. Manolis would interpret it as he chose. He did not move.

'Come on, we are friends, no?' Mitsos felt an increasing need to erase the effect of his words so he could forget he said them.

'Are you with me then?'

'I don't know until you tell me the plan.'

'Do you want me dead or are you with me: which is the truth?'

Mitsos was in a corner. It felt familiar – but wishing someone dead, that was not the man he wanted to be.

'I am with you, Manolis.' His words came out as a sigh.

'Right, here's what we are going to do.'

Manolis put forward his dream, painted in shining colours. With his arm around Mitsos' shoulders, his silver words proved, without an inkling of a doubt, that it would be successful and they would not only be rich but also happy. The work itself, he said grinning at Mitsos, his eyes on fire with intensity, would be nothing but fun. All Mitsos had to do was swap his prime land with his brother's beet field.

His brother, when told of the wish to make the swap, had felt it was a harsh joke but Mitsos (urged by Manolis), to prove he was serious, took steps to do it legally, and soon the field was his, his brother laughing.

Manolis had bought double whiskys all round when he heard the transaction was complete. The next day he arranged to meet Mitsos at the beet field and told him to bring any spare boards, wooden props, chipboard, old doors and discarded windows with him. Mitsos' Baba had rebuilt the chicken shed before he died, and pieces of the old shed were stacked against the new. Mitsos loaded the lot onto a cart and towed it to the beet field with the tractor.

They resurrected the chicken coop, down by the sea's edge in the beet field, extending it and raising the roof. To the front they built decking onto the sand and lined up some roughly made tall stools against their improvised counter. When it was finished they painted the whole thing with bright orange paint that Manolis had acquired from somewhere. Mitsos stood back to admire their handiwork, but Manolis took a hatchet and cut palm leaves from the trees along the lane to the beach and they nailed them all over the hut.

'Hawaiian style,' Manolis said, but he did not laugh in the work as he had done when they played the donkey trick, or even the paint scam before the lids came off. There was a seriousness that made Mitsos feel uncomfortable. Manolis' emotions seemed to be all over the place; one minute he was angry, the next hysterically jolly. Mitsos found it difficult to keep up. The carefree boyish attitude that characterised him for so long had been rarely in evidence during their work.

When the job was finished Manolis took a board and wrote 'Beach Bar' in big letters across it and nailed it to the chicken coop's roof.

The bar was open for exactly three days. On the first two no one came, even with the first drink free for the ladies.

On the third day they put up balloons and signposts, hung hammocks from the eucalyptus trees that bordered the beet field along the sea side, and had drunk a fair amount before the first guests arrived.

The man from the hardware shop brought his son and his son brought five of his friends. They pooled their money behind the bar and the drinks kept flowing. Three tourist girls came next and ordered cocktails Mitsos had never heard of, and as they drank they joined the boys.

Manolis invented all manner of drinks, blues, greens, reds. The clients seemed as perplexed as Mitsos as to their provenance but Manolis declared they were 'Greek style' whenever the question arose, and the mood was such that no one really cared as long as the alcohol kept flowing.

More people arrived, mostly tourists.

Manolis turned the radio on in his car, the volume on full and all the doors open. The party really started kicking.

The music must have drifted over the water, as more and more people came. Twice Mitsos had to go for more bottles whilst Manolis held the fort and flirted with his blue eyes at the western girls.

The second time Mitsos returned with more alcohol Manolis took him to one side and thrust him a handful of notes. 'Here, keep it safe. You will have all the money you need to buy your land back if we carry on like this tonight.' Mitsos looked at the amount in his hand and felt slightly sick at the responsibility of having so much money. He looked around the back of the bar for a place to put it but everywhere seemed too open, or too obvious. He stepped into the night and stuffed it down his trousers and returned smiling.

People kept coming and Manolis stuffed more money into Mitsos' hand. Mitsos was half drunk and felt, once again, that Manolis was truly a god.

Until two sober-looking men in black shirts arrived.

'Hey, have a drink boys,' Manolis offered. When he held out his hand for payment that was their signal and they identified themselves.

'You must close the bar immediately.'

'You have no licence,' the taller man added.

The second man stepped forward. 'Greek law says you cannot build on the beach. Also, you had no planning. It must be pulled down immediately or you will receive a heavy fine.' Along with his briskness he was clearly enjoying his power. Particularly when he said they would face a hefty fine.

Manolis protested and waved his arms about, and opened the till to show how empty it was.

'How much money you have taken,' the taller man explained patiently, 'is not the question. The law has its penalties.'

'You will be informed of the consequences. Meanwhile, we strongly suggest you dismantle the bar.' The shorter man smiled as he spoke.

'Which, incidentally,' the first man added sniggering, 'looks more like a chicken coop.'

Then they left.

A balloon popped. Mitsos jumped.

Manolis began kicking chairs, bottles and glasses in the sand. He was beside himself and he could not vent his anger enough for it to subside. Mitsos tried to talk to him, to work out the problem, but Manolis was speechless. His eyes shone with anger and something that, to Mitsos, looked a little like madness.

Manolis jumped into his truck, started it up and revved the engine hard. Mitsos felt afraid. He saw two people sitting on the far side of the bar, kissing. He ran to them and grabbed the boy by the arm. The two rose, protesting. Mitsos did not release his grip but swung the boy nearer the trees, out of the way, the girl following.

The revving truck's doors slammed shut as it jolted forward and crashed through the chicken coop, splintering the dry wood into kindling. Mitsos put his hands in the air, and his mouth fell open. He had guessed Manolis was going to take this action, he had seen it coming, but the reality of the event seemed too dramatic.

'Panayia, mother of God, stop!'

Manolis backed off the pile of firewood and climbed out of the truck, grinding broken glass on plywood pieces.

'Every time you try to do something in this town some jealous bastard gets in your way. Who told them, eh? Who tipped them off? Some jealous bar owner, that's who.'

'But Manolis, we have spent the day telling everyone we met there was a bar here. No one needed to tip them off, we advertised ourselves.'

'No. Someone tipped them off for sure …' He jumped back into his truck and shouted through the open window, 'I'll find a way to get even,' and he laughed that strange chilling laugh as he drove away.

Stella is watching his face as he tells his story. As Mitsos turns to her she closes her mouth. There is a sudden crescendo of noise. A boy of no more than eight years old rides past on a moped, revving the engine and trying to do a wheelie. He rounds the corner at the square and the sound dwindles.

'What happened next?' Stella asks.

'Well, the licence people got in touch very soon after that. It is amazing how some wheels turn so slowly in Greece and others are like lightning. They contacted me as I was the land owner. We got a fine, and when I went to Manolis with the official paper he said, "I gave you the money." I thought the money he had given me was my half. It seemed very unlikely that Manolis would give it all to me, even if it was only for safe keeping. But he said it was, so I paid the fine and was left with nothing.

'Except a beet field.' Stella laughs dryly, sliding down in her chair and crossing her legs out in front of her as she looks up towards the square.

Chapter 10

Mitsos takes the envelope from his pocket. The rustle of the paper attracts Stella's attention.

'What's that?' Stella asks, shielding her eyes to see better. Mitsos wouldn't mind sharing it with her. It would feel like a weight had been lifted to share it with at least one person. She is probably the only person he would feel happy telling. He doesn't intend telling his own brothers. The older one is a bully, has been all his life like his Baba, and the younger is happy as a town dweller now, so his opinions would be biased towards the modern world. No, this is his business, and if he is going to tell anyone then it will be Stella. She won't judge or condemn, and she wouldn't want anything for herself or cause trouble. She will probably offer some sound advice, if she says anything at all.

He opens his mouth to speak. But then there is Stavros. He is not a kind man. Mitsos doesn't want Stavros to know his business. If it wasn't for Stavros he would probably eat chicken and chips more often. In fact, if it wasn't for Stavros he would take Stella out and have someone else cook for her, in a taverna in town, God knows she deserves it. But taking her out would mean taking Stavros too, and he has no desire to spend any time with him at all. He closes his mouth again and puts the envelope back in his pocket.

His foot begins to jiggle, shaking side to side rapidly. He nearly spoke without thinking. She is just too easy to talk to. He doesn't feel he has control of himself.

'I have to go.' He stands.

'But you haven't eaten. The chicken will be ready any minute now.' Stella sounds almost alarmed. Mitsos feels tempted; he is hungry, but he needs to think. Recalling the beach bar has changed his perspective. Manolis owed him. He needs to talk things through, even if it is just with himself.

'I'll get a cheese pie from across the road.'

'Oh, ok.' She sounds disappointed but Mitsos cannot make out of it is due to the loss of business or the loss of his company. It sounds like she will miss the company but that is surely just his own misplaced ego wishing, his desire to talk to someone twisting his perspective. He is a one-armed sixty-five-year-old farmer; she is just a girl in her late forties. He is not so lonely as to be delusional to the point of thinking she holds anything more than a casual friendship for him. He is just another customer. Besides, she is married. To Stavros.

He puts his hand in his pocket to pay and then realises he has not bought anything.

'See you tomorrow?' Stella crosses her arms across her chest.

Mitsos nods, but it is more an acknowledgement that she has spoken than a consent. Guarded.

He concentrates on his balance as he crosses the road. He has not brought his shepherd's crook with him today. He buys a spinach and feta pie, with a thick crumbly pastry made with olive oil, and makes his way to the kiosk.

Vasso apologises profusely, blames the striking lorries, blames the ordering process, blames the entire Greek system for Mitsos' cigarettes still not having arrived. Mitsos looks at the other brands. They do not appeal. He cannot be bothered to get used to another flavour. He will wait. Vasso gives him a packet of chewing gum as compensation.

He turns up the lane towards his house. The whitewashed wall where he had squatted all those years ago, drawing in the ground with a stick when Manolis had been jumping around trying not to tell him the details of donkey-swapping idea – it seems so long ago.

He wonders, if he had declined that one piece of mischief, would all the rest have followed? Would he have ended up with the beet patch rather than the prime agricultural land left him by his Baba? If he had avoided Manolis from the beginning and not been there when he got into trouble the first time, over Theo's carnival suit, maybe he would not have been cast as a trouble maker and people would have treated him differently.

If he had been treated differently, more kindly, softly, maybe he would not have been so busy fighting to be himself, so headstrong; he might not have felt the need to take the stance that resulted in him turning Marina down. Maybe he would have grown up working on the farm by his Baba, making his Mama proud, and accepted the offer of an arranged marriage and been happy?

What a bloody hypocrite Manolis turned out to be. All that teasing he had done over the potential arranged marriage, and then he accepted the very same girl.

Mitsos turns into the track towards his home and kicks the gate open. It reverberates. He kicks it closed and fastens it, shutting out the world, the people who treated him like a trouble maker, the wrong decisions he made, all on the other side of the chipped painted metal gate.

He heads up the track, looking at his feet. The leather on his left shoe is coming away at the toe and the sole scrapes as he walks, but he doesn't care. He wants to rip it more. Tear it apart and throw it to the wind. Rend his life apart and let the pieces be taken away on a gust. He lifts his chin to the sky, and through clenched teeth and closed lips he suppresses a wail, moisture running from the corners of his eyes back across his temples and into his grey hair.

He stops walking and waits for the feelings to subside but the anger is bubbling. When it turns inward he wants to explode, howl, shout; when it turns outward he wants to do harm.

How could Manolis have not played fair over the beach bar when he, Mitsos, had put up his land, his inheritance, as a sacrifice? What sort of a friend would do that? No, a friend would not do that. A self-centred, hypocritical, ignorant villain would do that.

He howls again, from the pain of the one-sided friendship, for the lack of care, the absence of love. His lips bitten between closed teeth, the sounds rumble in his chest until he gives in and opens his mouth and hisses, 'What's wrong with me?'

A bird squawks from the nearest tree and flies off over the hill.

Mitsos' feelings dwindle and rationality begins to return. He wipes from his temple to his hair line with the back of his hand and draws in a deep breath. His sadness feels heavy in his chest, a rock on his lungs, his mouth pulling down at the corners.

How far back had Manolis not been a friend? It was obvious when he returned from his national service that he had changed. He was much more self-obsessed. The boy was gone. He still had the charm and command but not in the same capacity. The girls didn't flock around him in the same way. Even he, Mitsos, had only gone along with him because he had nearly been drowned. No, not because he had nearly been drowned, but because he had wished Manolis dead and felt guilty.

Mitsos blinks and dismisses the uncomfortable memory. He has reached the brushed-earth yard and changes his focus to look out at the world. He hangs his bag with the spinach pie in it on a hook by the back door.

The almond blossom is so thick now that hardly any black branches are visible. Right at the top a few twigs appear as black lines etched in the deep blue sky. Blossom clings in clusters to their length. Years of hard pruning have brought good crops but left nubs and angles where branches have been hacked off. These stumps offend Mitsos, the suppression of life, organisms forced to grow in a particular way because of damage inflicted on them when they were young.

Mitsos looks up to the sky. Not a cloud, deep blue, another scorcher.

He has wandered the length of the grove to the wall that Manolis once hid behind before the donkey swap. Mitsos puts a leg over the low wall; it had seemed so much higher then. He puts his hand on the top to maintain his balance as he lifts his other leg over. The land climbs sharply up to the hen-house.

It had been his old hen-house, too, that the villain had driven over; there had been no mention of that. He could have used it elsewhere.

He probably wouldn't have, but that is not the point. It was not Manolis' to drive over with his truck.

Mitsos expels air noisily through his nose and looks around him.

Whilst he is up by the chicken coop he has another look for the eggs hidden by the broody hen. The chickens cluck as he approaches, expecting corn. It is a soft, homely sound. When he was very small, he had tamed one until she could be held. In the end she would only eat corn if she was sitting on his knee plucking grains from his hand.

Then there had been the engagement and the marriage. He picks up a stone and throws it with all his strength out across the roofs of the village.

The engagement party demonstrated how cruel life could be. Everyone was at Manolis' family's house, the three brothers, their parents, neighbours, Mitsos, his brothers and their parents. And in she had walked with her mother. She looked terrified. She daren't even look up. Mitsos wanted to grab her by the hand and run from the room, take her somewhere she could grow and blossom unconstrained, without deformity. But he hadn't; instead, he had drunk too much ouzo and watched silently.

She lifted her eyes on occasion, just for a second, to scan the room. Her head stayed at the same angle, chin to the ground. She repeated this gesture a few times and Mitsos realised she was looking for something. Manolis was between his two brothers and they were all getting heartily drunk, not one of them paying any mind to the girl he was to marry. When the three brothers gave an almighty cheer and raised their glasses together she looked up and gave each one of them a hard stare. Realisation came to Mitsos that she didn't even know to which one of these buffoons she was engaged. His heart reached out to her. Manolis had not even bothered to introduce himself, let alone put her at her ease. It was in that moment, on top of the recent beach bar rip-off, that Mitsos began to hate him. For a second time, he wished him dead. He had been shocked at the strength of his own feelings.

His mother came and stood beside him.

'How old is she, Ma?' Mitsos asked.

'Just turned fourteen.' Mitsos tried to swallow. The wedding was scheduled for the next week. He gulped a mouthful of ouzo to loosen the lump in his throat.

The festivities had gone on all night. Manolis and his brothers became more and more drunk until they went outside to celebrate with a gun in the garden, shooting the stars. Mitsos watched Marina, who jumped at the sound of every shot. He could stand it no longer. He walked over to her as she stood by the wall unnoticed, an unsipped glass in one hand and a plate of untouched food in the other. He took the plate of food from her and put it on a side table.

'Marina ...' But no words would come. He waited, but his thoughts were scrambled. He urged his brain into action but for some reason he began to internally question whether he had fed the chickens or not. He raised his hand to touch the fingers that held her glass.

Marina's mother bustled over to chaperone the exchange.

'Congratulations,' whispered Mitsos, and Marina's mother led her away.

That was the moment he made his pledge. He had let Marina down by not consenting to his marriage to her, and now she had a lifetime of that villain Manolis to endure. If she became unhappy it would be his fault. He could not undo the situation and so he pledged that he would look after her from afar. He would look after her by trying to get Manolis on the right track. He would guide Manolis and plant seeds in his mind to make him the best husband it was likely he could be. He would stick by Manolis so the money would not all be spent, so that he would not stray from her and so that he would get home every night. He would play bodyguard, chaperone, financial advisor and spiritual guide to her husband-to-be. He would be Manolis' friend in order to be her friend. He owed her that much at least. Beautiful Marina.

He went home.

Manolis asked him to be best man. Mitsos, despite his newly kindled hatred, agreed to this, his first conscious action to fulfil his silent pledge to Marina. Manolis, who seemed just as fed up about his wedding as Mitsos was, decided to go out the night before his wedding. Mitsos accompanied him.

He was laughing loudly and turning his blue eyes on every girl that came into the bar. Mitsos had known him long enough to understand that he was looking for an opportunity, a single girl he could take down to the beach in the moonlight. Mitsos wanted to cry out 'Have you no respect for your marriage to Marina tomorrow?' but he knew Manolis would laugh in his face and so he stayed quiet.

The bar was filling with young tourists in their late teens and early twenties. There were some Greek boys of the same age lining the walls. Mitsos smiled. He and Manolis were now thirty. They might feel like boys but they no longer looked liked boys. To these young girls they would look like old men compared to the youths leaning casually around the bar.

'What are you smiling about? I have to get married tomorrow,' Manolis barked above the music.

'Why?'

'What do you mean, why?' He drank down his whisky and caught the barman's eye, nodding for a refill.

'Why did you agree to this? Why are you still agreeing to this? Call it off, Manolis. You are not a man for marriage.'

'Don't I know it! But I have no choice.' Mitsos waited, nodding for Manolis to tell more. 'I had a little bit of fun.' He took a swig of his whisky. 'You weren't around. It was whilst I was in the army. Well, this fun …' He drew it out, looking into his glass. 'It wasn't …' a long drag on his cigarette '… strictly legal.'

'Did you get caught?' Mitsos shouted in his ear above the music.

'They tried to expose me, talked about a very long spell in prison, but they had no evidence. They told my family. When I came home my Mama went through everything, seeing what needed washing, mending, you know. Well, she found the evidence.'

Mitsos didn't know what he was talking about but nor did he want to know. 'So?' he asked.

'So time passed and nothing. Then they were approached with this marriage deal. They gave me an ultimatum: marry the girl and settle down, or else. So I said or else what, thinking the worst they could do was to throw me out of the house, which they wouldn't do, as it would look bad to the neighbours.' He scoffed at this, mumbling to himself about his mother's pretensions until he continued loud enough for Mitsos to hear. 'But no, they dragged up ten years ago when I was in the army. I said that was done with, there was no evidence, and that's when they dropped the grenade. All this time they hadn't said a word, just sat on the evidence, knowing that one day they could, and would, use it against me.' Manolis drained his glass and caught the barman's eye again. 'And these are my parents, unconditional love and all that.' The barman poured.

'Maybe a wife will be a good thing, keep you focused, a reason to work hard in the olive groves?' Mitsos said emphatically.

'Tshh, absolute goat droppings. I will marry the girl because I have no choice. That will take a day, but then life as normal as far as I am concerned. Sure, we will move into her house just on the corner and she will cook and clean instead of Mama, but that's it. They can't bully me into being a dutiful husband.'

'What about the girl?' Mitsos lit a cigarette but did not offer one to Manolis.

'What about the girl? She means nothing to me!'

'Yes, but her happiness will depend on the sort of husband you are ...' Manolis interrupted gruffly, before Mitsos could finish his sentence.

'Then her parents should have chosen more carefully.' He slammed his empty glass on the counter and slipped off his bar stool. He homed in on the nearest pretty girl and walked straight up to her. Mitsos watched. Manolis put his hand on the wall behind her and leaned right in to say something in her ear. She laughed. He leaned in again and said something more. She laughed again. He went towards her and whispered again. The girl looked shocked, dodged under his arm and ran to sit back with her friends, a group of tall blonde tourists. They all dipped their heads towards her and Mitsos could see her mouth moving, and then the table of girls broke into laughter like a pack of geese sounding an alarm.

Mitsos smiled. Manolis stomped out of the bar.

The wedding was unremarkable. Mitsos performed his duties and they were duly married. The rings were blessed. The *stefania* – crowns – were crossed above their heads three times. When the Papas said Manolis could kiss the bride Mitsos' stomach flipped over. He had to put his hands in his pockets to stop himself from launching a punch at Manolis. But Manolis allowed Marina to give him a peck on the cheek; he offered nothing back, not even eye contact. Marina was crying.

When Marina became pregnant so fast Mitsos had the fantasy that they were becoming a happily family. It was better than imagining the alternative. The baby was born; it looked like Manolis, but the man himself was not interested. 'It'll keep her busy,' was all the comment he made about it. But Marina was still a girl, and she spent more time outside playing hopscotch, her mother calling her in when it was time to nurse the weak little thing.

The poor baby died within months of its birth. Mitsos wanted to comfort Marina, and he pressed to spend more time at Manolis' house. It didn't take long to find out that Manolis no longer occupied the marital bedroom. Mitsos felt such relief; the thought of Manolis forcing himself upon her was more than he could bear. But Marina looked tired and unhappy either way. She had aged quickly and lost her girlish bounce. There were arguments about money, fuelled by accusations by Marina's mother. Marina herself never offered a word. It seemed that under Manolis' care his portion of the farm was not doing well and there was not enough to support them all. In the arguments, Manolis would spit that they, Marina's parents, should move out if they were not satisfied, and this would bring tears and fear to Marina's eyes.

Mitsos knew of no one whose life was enhanced by Manolis. Like a mosquito, there was no point to him, just irritation. He wondered if Marina wished him gone. Or worse.

Mitsos leaves these thoughts behind as he walks past the chicken coop up into the pine trees to the stone. It is a rock he has sat on many times over the years since his parents died. The pine tops hiss in the wind, a lonely but comforting sound. Under the trees it is silent, the fallen needles muffling all sounds, bringing a stillness that Mitsos has only ever experienced up there; no insects, no small animals rustling. As a boy he would come and lie in the pine needles to get away from his Baba when he was too drunk. They were soft and warm and smelt sweet, and so thick he could scrape out a trench with his bare hands where he could hide from anyone coming seeking him who could not be bothered to climb the whole of the hill but instead just called from past the chicken coop.

As he lay face down in his foxhole, his face buried, his fear would subside as the softness of the needles and the familiar scent of decay soothed his senses. He would breathe again, and by then his Baba would have given up trying to find him.

His elder brother left soon after his father's death; they never see each other now. There had been phone calls a couple of times, when a new child was born to him. His inherited village land sits uncared for; he will not pay out for a manager to work it. Mitsos harvests the olives for him and takes a cut of the profits, but the longer the trees are neglected the less oil they yield. It is almost not worth the effort now.

His younger brother has had the sense to give over his portion of the land to a paid manager and is making a small profit whilst working in the town. He also pays someone to run the shop that provides fertilisers for the farmers, and gives a token cut of the profits to Mitsos because they had set it up together and Mitsos provided the initial capital.

Apart from that there is nothing really left of the family except this new thread of him baby-sitting for his young brother's first-born. But he has nothing in common with his brother. There is twelve years between them, and his wife is fifteen years younger than that. There is nothing to say. Mitsos is of the old world. His life might as well be over. He rubs his shoulder stump, and a darkness engulfs him.

The village lies before him. He can see all the way over the plain to the town. The land between it and the village is dotted here and there with new houses, the gaps slowly closing as the town seeps across the fertile land, orange groves disappearing.

The village itself is also expanding. Areas between farms have maisonettes built on them for grown-up children who do not want to live in the old ways. The old stone farmhouses themselves are being skimmed over with concrete so the undulations of the stones are lost and crisp corners replace soft curves. The sagging, lichen-covered handmade deep red roof tiles are swapped for factory-made bright orange, interlocking, straight-lined, watertight versions.

It seems that the modern ways want to squeeze all the soft, curvy, beauty out of the world.

The cockerel crows, waking Mitsos from his mental meanderings.

He chastises himself. Thoughts of Manolis often take him to gloomy places in his mind. He had become so resistant to any of Manolis' scamming ideas towards the end that it carried over into the rest of his life. He had wanted no idea manifested anywhere; he had wanted everything to stay the same. Unchanged. It felt safer that way.

'Mitsos, you old fool, you are forgetting where you are now. Life does move on, and the proof is in your pocket.'

He takes out the envelope and taps it against his knee.

'You no longer have to think like a tired old man with no power. See the new houses as progress, accept that the younger generation want things to be different. You did when you were young! It is for the best. But now you have the chance to be part of all this newness too. Live a little and forget Manolis.'

He looks again across the valley; it is quivering in the heat. There is life! There is progress! When he was not much more than a boy he had rejoiced as they laid the tarmac road to the nearby town. The old folk said it was unnecessary, a waste of money; it would encourage gypsies into the village and townspeople to come for days out, leaving their rubbish and looking down their noses. What was the use of that, they asked. But as a boy he could see it would benefit everyone. The produce they grew in the village was taken to the town more quickly as tractors and cars replaced donkeys after the road was built. The village developed an income and people prospered.

And so it is now with the new houses and sharp edges.

He must make an appointment to see his lawyer.

Chapter 11

Mitsos has been sitting so long it is an effort to stand, partly because his legs have gone to sleep but partly just because he is surprisingly comfortable. Thoughts of being part of the modern changing world, not just a powerless bystander, have released a feeling of contentment. Positively contemplating is a pleasant novelty: firstly thinking he has a future, and secondly being happy about it. He still hasn't thought of the best way to deal with Marina, but at least they spoke the other day, which is progress. He runs his hand through the pine needles before he stands. On straightening, he picks a needle from under his nails with his teeth and spits it back to the ground, the smell of soil and tree sap on his fingers. He waits for the pins and needles to leave his legs.

When Marina and Manolis were first married, Mitsos, in his early thirties, had, slowly, learned to talk to Marina. Mitsos even believed that through their brief and awkward conversations she had picked up that he was trying to guide Manolis towards doing the things that were best for her. But whether she knew or not, he gradually became her support, until he was someone to whom she could tell her woes. The first time she confided in him he hadn't even seen it coming, and when it all came out he instantly wished it had not. It causes him pain to even think of it now. It was when Manolis was in jail after the bike scam.

Mitsos smiles wanly and shakes his legs. He can hear goat bells from behind the hill, and a woman shouting, muffled behind closed shutters, down in the village; a hint of rosemary is in the air. A solitary, small, puffy white cloud hangs in the blue expanse. At least he had held his ground and firmly refused to get involved in the bikes himself.

'No.' Mitsos was emphatic.

'What? Do you want to be a dirt-poor farmer all your life? Come on, come in with me.'

But Mitsos would not risk his money (or his land) in any more of Manolis' schemes after the beach bar incident, and he could see how his money would almost certainly be needed this time and that there was good chance it would be lost. Besides, with Manolis, he was sure somewhere along the line it would be illegal.

Marina came in with two Greek coffees. She smiled at Mitsos.

'What are you two planning?' Her tone sounded cheerful but her eyes darted, wary, nervous.

'None of your business, woman.' Manolis' chair fell back as he stood. He didn't pick it up but glared at Mitsos on his way out.

'What's happening, Mitso?' He loved the sound of his name on her lips.

'He's had another idea.' He took the cup of Greek coffee she offered; the other she put down on the table. She began to leave the room, then she paused. So gently, hardly noticeably, she touched the back of his shoulder with the ends of her fingers.

He was staring down at his coffee, but with the contact he twisted his neck to look up at her. Her eyes were moist, fearful. 'Ok, I'll stay close to him,' he said before he took a quick sip of the coffee, thanked her for it, smiled and hurried after Manolis. Marina was in the last days of her eighteenth year. She looked thirty.

Manolis rented a dilapidated shop front in town. Not much more than a store room, it had a window on one side of the door and it smelt damp. Inside was dim even with the lights on. There was a collection of flower pots in one corner and a pile of fishing nets in the other. It stood on a fairly main road next to a fast-food shop on a corner which was frequented by tourists simply because its name was written in English, 'Mary's Corner'.

Well, he didn't exactly rent it; rather, he convinced the owners to take a share of his profits each month in lieu of rent.

'This way, when I have a good month, you will make even more than your proposed rent,' he smiled, his blue eyes on the old woman of the landlord couple, his hand on hers, like a devoted son.

The building that was to be the shop had originally been built by this couple, when they were young and had time, energy and enthusiasm, as an *apothiki*, a storage room for nets and fish boxes. Now, too old to fish every day, they depended on this rent for their income. They had little education and Manolis seemed an exciting, modern businessman client to them. They were easily charmed. Mitsos' heart went out to the owners. He warned them that the rent might be very small or even nothing in the winter when there was little trade. Manolis had scowled at him. Mitsos held his tongue and in his silence reasoned that he did not want to see a monthly debt on the doorstep of Marina's house, so he said no more.

The second part of the scheme was also easier than Mitsos had expected. He accompanied Manolis round the nearby villages in his truck. It was spring and the flowers on the roadside were abundant. Cascades of orange over walls, tall purple flowers growing from the rich soil. Yellow blooms clustering in groups. They drove with the windows down, the promise of summer flowing through the cab. Mitsos held his hand out of the window, catching the warm air. The scent of the flowers came in waves, changing with the colours. Behind the flowers, row upon row of orange trees, the fruit hard and green, no bigger than Mitsos' thumb-nail.

'There's one.' Manolis said.

A motorbike, abandoned. Farmers with fields and fields of oranges, hills of olives, bought mopeds and rode them around their land, or around the village, without tax or insurance. But when they broke down there was a problem. The law stated that motorcycles and mopeds must be officially declared scrap before they could be physically disposed of or there was a hefty fine. But to declare them scrap they must be legal, taxed. If the tax had lapsed it must be brought up to date, making years of back tax due in one payment. So a broken machine would just lie around the farmer's land, creating an eyesore, slowly rusting into the grass.

Sometimes the mechanical problem would be minor, but it would be just another job that the farmer had to do and so it would be left; he would just walk for a while, like he had done in the old days. Then, after a winter, the engine would seize and the problem was bigger. Sometimes there was no problem, the farmer was prospering and wanted a new bike, a lighter model, something more reliable; but, again, the old one could not be sold or exchanged without paying the back tax.

Manolis had learned a great deal about mechanics in the army, or so he said, but, as with anything to do with Manolis, Mitsos was never sure. He gave the bike a cursory look. If the problem was too serious they would move on. If not, they would find the owner. This time they went to find the owner.

'So you'll tax it and insure it and I get a cut of any rent you make from it?'

'Exactly,' and the farmer shook Manolis' hand and helped lift the rotting bike onto the truck.

'Well, "go to the good",' the farmer said, using the traditional parting phrase.

It only took a few days to collect a dozen such mopeds.

'Manolis, I don't want to put you off, but if each of these needs from two to ten years' back tax to make them legal then you're going to have to be very wealthy before you even start,' Mitsos said, as they stood looking at the collection of rusty and decaying bikes lined up against the damp brick wall inside the shop-to-be, a misty light filtering through the dirty wired-mesh windows.

'Well, I asked you to come in with me, but if you are not going to help I will have to find another way. You've pushed me into finding creative solutions.'

'Such as?'

'Pass me the electrical screwdriver.'

And the topic was closed. Mitsos left, without passing the screwdriver, and made a mental note to restrict his presence to short visits every couple of days. It was clear he was not welcome.

Within two weeks eight of the mopeds were working, after a fashion. The others, beyond repair, were consigned to the back of the shop, in various states of disassembly. 'For parts,' Manolis said.

The working bikes were lined up outside on the pavement, their back ends up against the shop. In front of them Manolis had lined up plant pots, one in front of each bike, into which he had planted some very nice geraniums. Mitsos wondered where the flowers had come from. Out on the pavement he had crudely painted a sign in English which announced:

Rent Mopeds
Small Moneys
Big fun

'Are they legal?' Mitsos asked.

Manolis took a step into the shop and picked up some papers. He returned outside and pulled the plant pot from in front of the nearest bike. The number plate was now clearly visible, 'ANO 150'. He handed the papers to Mitsos who checked them against the number. This one had only needed one year's back tax, which had all been paid. The bike was also insured. Mitsos wondered if he had made the right decision not to go in with Manolis in this venture. It looked like he was finally trying to make an honest living like everybody else.

'How did you afford the back tax?' Mitsos asked.

'The man at the tax office could see the potential of the business.' He gave Mitsos a hard stare. 'He also liked to play cards.' Manolis put the papers away. 'And drink ouzo.' He chuckled to himself.

'For one year's back tax, yes, I can see how you could get that to work, but for all eight bikes?' Mitsos walked to the end of the line. 'This one, for example, needed six years' back tax. That is a large wager for a government worker, and more than his job is worth to forge the papers for you.'

'You are talking to me like a business partner.' Manolis took out a cigarette but did not offer one to Mitsos. He lit it and looked down the road, leaning against his door post.

Mitsos left.

Mitsos reported all these happenings to Marina. She remained unimpressed.

Each time Mitsos passed by the shop there were tourists there talking to Manolis. Sometimes there were no bikes, all of them rented out. The geraniums looked well cared for. Mitsos wished him well.

Summer was approaching fast. More and more tourists could be seen every day, in yellow shorts with pink T-shirts, hats that were too small, and socks with sandals; back-packs worn round the front, a Kodak in one hand, a guide book in the other. They came in twos and they came in packs. The Americans were scrubbed so clean their faces shone; the English always looked crumpled, as if they themselves had arrived scrunched up in a suitcase. The Asians were pristine, aloof behind expensive cameras.

Mitsos ordered a meat, chips and tzatziki wrap, a *gyro souvlaki,* from Mary's Corner. Mary looked well for her age, and served him quickly with a smile and a kind word. Mary's Corner had been the treat promised to him if he went to market with his Mama when he was small. Mary had seemed ancient even back then. He took his *gyro* outside and sat on one of the plastic chairs at a red plastic table with a cola logo painted on top. He was right next to Manolis' moped shop.

A motorbike pulled up, and the uniformed rider kicked the stand down and marched up the street with his helmet still on. Mitsos nodded at the policeman as he went past and into Mary's.

He came out again with a tray. He looked at the two tables; the other was taken by two people in Hawaiian shirts wearing ankle-socks and walking boots. He looked at Mitsos and nodded at the chair at his table. Mitsos kicked it out for him.

They briefly summed each other up. Mitsos, at thirty-three, his hair a little too long, wearing rough, practical, worn clothes, looked every bit what he was, an orange farmer. The policeman put his tray down and took his helmet off, revealing a neat crew cut. He smoothed his hair back. On his tray were a *gyro*, coffee and his wallet, which was open, a picture of two children staring up at the world.

'Nice looking children.' Mitsos made conversation. The policeman smiled; he seemed warm, genuine. Mitsos had seen him before somewhere.

'Yup, Mary's very proud of her grandchildren.'

Mitsos recalled seeing his face serving in Mary's Corner. He was her son. Mitsos smiled at him warmly now he had placed him.

They sat watching the traffic go by.

A bike pulled in next door. 'ANO 150'.

Manolis lined the bike up in front of the shop and placed a plant in front of it.

The policeman stirred his coffee.

The couple with Hawaiian shirts left and went next door. They disappeared into Manolis' shop.

Mitsos watched a lady across the road walking her dog, which stopped to relieve itself in the middle of the pavement. The Hawaiian shirts flashed past and their moped came to a halt at the junction. 'ANO 150'. A busy bike. Business was booming for Manolis.

A woman came out of a shop opposite and began to argue with the lady about her dog, pointing at the dirt. The dog's owner tried to dismiss her and get past but the woman insisted. She pointed to the shop whose door was in direct line with the dirt but still the dog owner did not want to know. She walked on. The complaining woman went into the shop. She came out again in less than a minute, smoking, and leaned against the door post, looking bored. The dog dirt remained on the pavement.

Another bike pulled in next door. Two girls got off. 'ANO 150'. Mitsos frowned. He nearly spoke without thinking but then pulled himself up. How could it be? Did the guys with the Hawaiian shirts let the girls have the bike, and if so why were they back so soon?

'What was the registration of the bike that the guys with colourful shirts took?' the policeman asked him.

'No idea, not the sort of thing I would notice.' Mitsos looked across the road.

Mary's son finished his coffee and took out a pack of cigarettes, and offered one to Mitsos. Mitsos pulled out his lighter and cupped the flame as he sparked it to life. The policeman bent over the light, his cigarette glowed, he looked above Mitsos' hand and beyond. He focused. His expression hardened. Mitsos followed his gaze, still lighting his own cigarette. A young man and his girlfriend were pulling in next door. The man had stopped the bike for his girlfriend to get off, before bumping it onto the pavement. The bike's registration plate read 'ANO 150'.

Manolis came out of the shop, and steered the bike up against the window and placed a plant pot in front of it. Beautiful orange-red geraniums.

The policeman drew on his cigarette. Another bike was coming along the road. This one was being pushed. Manolis waited for the bike to come to him. The bike-pusher was furious, shouting that this was the second bike he had been given that had broken down; his morning has been taken up with pushing the darn things back. The number plate was not visible as it was obscured by parked cars and the 'Rent a Moped' sign. The customer pushed it around to face the shop front. Now the bike rider himself was obscuring the view.

'One thousand drachma says that registration number is ANO 150,' the policemen said, and slapped a note on the table. But before Mitsos could reply the tourist had moved, and they could both see that the policeman was correct. 'Right!' The policeman stubbed out his cigarette, gathered up his things, and turned to wave through the window to his mum. 'Work to do,' he announced and strapped on his helmet.

Mitsos watched, not sure if he should – or could – do anything.

The policeman beckoned to Manolis to come out of his shop, leaving the arguing client first shocked and then smirking. With a leather-gloved hand, the policeman pointed at one of the bikes and asked to see the documents. Manolis got the papers and proudly handed them to the policeman, and pulled the plant pot away to display the number plate of the chosen moped, 'ANO 150'.

The policemen read through the documents and nodded, everything was correct. Manolis grinned. His head was held high. The policeman folded the papers and handed them back. Mitsos did not want to know what Manolis was saying but he could hear the clichéd snippets all too clearly. 'The good work that you do … thank goodness we have the police force …' Mitsos cringed. The policeman waited for Manolis to stop talking and then casually walked along the row of bikes.

'Are your plants not too exposed here in front of your bikes?' The policeman asked. Manolis looked at him with a frown, blinking. 'Or maybe the exposure isn't enough?' Manolis opened his mouth but no words were formed in reply. 'Perhaps if they were in the shade of the bikes …' The policeman moved one pot to the side of a bike. Manolis sprang into action.

'Oh no, thank you, but no, they are really fine where they are.' He tried to move the pot back but the policeman put an arm across Manolis' chest to stop him.

'I think it will stay there.' He stared at Manolis, unblinking, before turning his attention to the next pot. In a last-ditch attempt to divert his attention Manolis slapped the policeman on the back and suggested they go for a coffee. But the policeman was not to be deterred. He pulled each pot to one side and stepped back to admire his handiwork. He invited Manolis to join him. The policeman took out his cigarettes and offered one to Manolis, who accepted, but Mitsos could see Manolis' hands were shaking as his head bent over his lighter.

'What do you think?' the policeman asked. 'Much better exposure now!'

Mitsos stood up and walked into the road so he could see the bikes from the same angle as Manolis and the policeman. The lined-up bikes' number plates read:

'ANO 150', 'ANO 150', 'ANO 150' …

'Manolis, I am arresting you for,' he counted the bikes in front of him, 'six counts of avoidance of tax, renting motor vehicles without insurance …' Another moped pulled up, and a laughing couple jumped off. 'Make that seven. And no doubt there will be many other laws that you have broken with regard to renting them out in this condition.'

'Six,' Manolis barked.

'Sorry?' the policeman said.

'Six, that's the legal one,' Manolis replied, and pointed to one of the bikes.

'Seven, no eight,' the policeman replied as two more bikes came round the corner.

Mitsos watched Manolis being taken away by the policeman. He wondered if he should have done something. Manolis' shop door hung open and the bikes were still lined up on the street. He checked that the policeman was out of sight then walked over to the shop and wheeled the bikes inside. Tools lay scattered about the interior of the shop, and there was a wooden box on a shelf. Mitsos checked the box. It was full of money. He tucked it under his arm.

Chapter 12

The kitchen table, scrubbed smooth by dutiful wives over the years, rocking on the uneven stone-flagged floor, sat between them, the box of money open in the middle. The room was cool, the shutters closed to keep out the heat. A broken lath allowed a streak of sun in, hitting the back of a chair, a picture of Marina's mother on the wall, freshly picked tomatoes in a bag on the floor; the same shaft of light made dust dance over the drachmas in the box on the table.

Mitsos had thought about taking what he felt he was owed. Half of the fine for the beach bar, for example, the price of a new chicken shed. But all he felt he was owed seemed trivial compared to what he felt they both owed Marina. She would have been safe from this life she was leading had he married her, if he had taken the time to meet her, even once.

'But I cannot have it. He will ask where it has come from. He will shout. He will …' Marina wiped away a tear that hadn't fallen and leant back in her chair away from the table, leaving the sentence hanging.

'Does he …' Mitsos could not finish his sentence either. The thought of Marina being harmed by Manolis choked him.

Marina put her hand to her mouth and turned her head away. Mitsos leaned forward over the table.

'Look, I know there is never money in the house. Well, here is your chance to have something to draw on. His shop was left open. He will not be expecting to see this money again. He will presume gypsies have taken it.' Marina looked up from the two black butterflies embroidered onto her handkerchief that she had been stroking. It was her nineteenth birthday. The box of money was a poor birthday gift.

'Take it and hide it away. Then you do not always need to be waiting for him to come home to ask him for money. You can buy food when you need it, not when he demands it. Come on, Marina, you need to look after yourself a little bit too.'

'Too late,' Marina said.

Mitsos looked up from the table sharply. New tears were running down her face. She stroked the embroidered butterflies more frantically, using the hanky to dry her face in between the pacifying action.

Marina did not volunteer to explain her comment.

'Marina?' Mitsos touched her hand holding the hanky. The touch was all it took. Marina's chest swelled, her face contorted and from her throat came a wail. She wrapped her arms around her face and sank onto the table.

Mitsos was at a loss as to what he should do. He stood up, wondering if he should run to fetch her mother, but he did not want to leave Marina alone, so he sat down again. He put a hand out to stroke her hair but pulled it away before making contact; he was afraid of his own emotions that this action might unleash. He decided a hand on her back was enough. He patted her and then stroked her. The noise subsided. Part of him wished he wasn't there to have to deal with all this emotion, but another part relished the role.

She lifted her head. She looked hard and the tears had stopped.

And that was when it came, the unwanted confession that lingered in his head, gave him nightmares at night and made him wish, again, that Manolis was dead.

'The day you two went to find bikes. He came home late smelling of oil. He was full of himself. He said he was going to be rich and that I should be grateful to him. Then he took the ouzo from the cupboard and sat at this table and poured two drinks. I was standing by the door and I said I didn't want any. He stood up quickly and in one stride he was beside me, a hand in my hair, pushing me to the table.

'"Drink," he said, so I drank. He refilled the glasses and said "drink" again. Where he had pulled my hair was throbbing and I felt afraid so I drank.'

'I will kill him.' Mitsos stood up. Marina tugged on his sleeve to make him sit down again; she had more to say. Mitsos tried to control himself. He did not want to hear more, but Marina's need was greater than his own. He looked into her sad face and sat down again, the wooden chair interrupting the momentary heavy silence as it grated against the floor.

'A bottle of ouzo between us, and I do not drink. I couldn't stand. He was talking and talking, about how successful he was going to be, and then he lurched towards me. I had no idea what he was doing and then I realised he was trying to kiss me.' Her eyes flicked to the ceiling and back to her hanky, her mind looking for an escape from the memory. 'He had not tried to make any physical contact since the baby died.' She thought for a moment, shook her head and corrected herself. 'Since I first knew I was pregnant. We are not familiar with each other, we have our own rooms,' her voice trailing off.

'I know.' Mitsos did not want to hear any more. He stared at a patch of flaky green paint on the wall that revealed a brown colour underneath. They sat silently for a while and he began to think he had been spared further detail.

Marina stared blankly at her hands, folded in her lap, crumpling the hanky, stroking the embroidered butterflies. When Manolis tried to kiss her she had turned her head away and that made him angry. He stood and held her head in his one hand, twisting her hair tightly against her skull, and he pulled her face to his. Marina tried to pivot away again but his grip was too tight; she felt the individual stands of hair being uprooted one by one. She was afraid. An image came to mind of the goats, wide eyed, the sickly smells of fear before they are slaughtered.

Manolis held her face still with the hand that was not holding her hair. He kissed her and then looked to see how much he had upset her.

He had let go of her face, but still keeping a grip on her hair with his other hand he reached over to the table, took and swallowed a whole glass of ouzo in one mouthful. He looked back at Marina but his focus was gone. He kissed her again and she tried to force him away but his grip on her hair tightened. He pushed her back and the chair she was sitting on went over backwards.

The knuckles of the hand that was holding the back of her head cracked hard against the floor, with her skull bouncing on top of them. He swore. She was on her back and he was all but on top of her. He kneeled up and looked at his knuckles. There was blood.

The back of his hand smacked her across the face before she saw it coming and then he started pushing up her skirts. He shouted in a deep evil-sounding voice that she was an animal and therefore he would treat her like a goat. Marina did not know him.

The room swam from the ouzo and from his fist. Her skirts lifted despite her frantic attempts to pull them down. One hand was on her throat as he rummaged with his trousers. She tied to claw his face but the elbow of the hand holding her throat came up and cracked her across the chin. He finished his fumbling with his own clothes.

With a sudden jarring she felt her back arched involuntarily; the pain was deep. Her head knocked into the door post, she put her hands up to brace against it. He grabbed her wrist, bound them together in a single graps and twisted them behind her head, affording her skull no protection as it knocked again and again. She could feel it growing wet and sticky.

Mitsos twitched. His gaze was jolted from the paintwork as through barely opened lips Marina began to share details of what she suffered. He could hardly hear her, but despite not wanting to know found himself straining to listen.

'I tried to leave my body, shut down my mind. The ceiling, stained brown with cigarette smoke has drip marks where condensation has pooled the colour.' She did not look up to confirm this. 'His breath, sweet with ouzo and sour with his mind, was in my face.' She took some little breaths and recollected how the smell of his sweat grew until his face contorted, his hand came up from her throat over her face, his fingers feeling her face, in her mouth and she bit. She bit so hard she tasted blood almost immediately. He let out a wail, but halfway through the sound confused and his body tensed, his face muscles relaxed and she knew he had had his way.

Mitsos sat stunned. Marina was drained white and looked numb, powerless.

As if to order, the church bells began to toll. A funeral.

A dog barked, declaring its loneliness.

A child shouted, 'Mama.'

The heat of the day settled in the room.

The house was still.

Mitsos put his hand on Marina's back, gently, sensitively, patting, stroking, small movements.

They sat silently for many minutes.

'I am pregnant,' she said. Mitsos removed his hand and looked away.

Marina's rage exploded.

'What are you thinking? That I choose this?' Her voice was loud and harsh. 'You think I would choose to become pregnant in this life of mine, to him?' Marina looked him full in the face. Mitsos could not look back. She was angry, but not at him. She stood up, kicking her chair back, and with aggressive movements took two glasses from the cupboard and a bottle of water. There was no denying the heat.

Mitsos recovered himself and jumped to his feet. 'Sit down, let me.' He poured her a glass and she swallowed it all and he poured another.

'Forgive me, God, but I wish him dead.' Marina crossed herself. Mitsos did not answer. He could feel his muscles shivering with rage. If Manolis came through the door now he would not take many breaths. That would be a better birthday present for Marina. But the thought was too bitter, and he too crossed himself and whispered a prayer asking for forgiveness, and commanded his rage to settle as he sat down again.

They sat for a long time. They heard the sound of goat bells, the animals being brought in from pasture before the afternoon's meal.

'Should I go and see what is happening to him?'

'Who cares?' Marina slowly gathered up the money from the box. Mitsos wished it was more.

'So that you know when, or if, he is coming home.'

'Yes, I suppose.' Now she had the money in her fist she looked at it as if she were not sure what to do with it.

Mitsos picked up the empty box. 'I'll get rid of this on the way.' He tried to smile at Marina, but he felt he had brought all this upon her. He had no right to smile. Now he must pledge to look after her child as well.

Mitsos took his *regina*, a three-wheeled half truck, half scooter, into town, and parked in front of the police station. It was an old building, originally a housing block, now grey and crumbling with age. There was a wooden kiosk, with a window, erected outside the main doors. A policeman sat inside reading a comic.

'An acquaintance of mine has been arrested. Can I find out what is happening?' Mitsos asked. The policeman put his comic aside and looked Mitsos up and down. He stood and opened the side door to his hut, and stepped out and stretched.

'It's a hot one,' he said, and taking keys attached to a long chain from his pocket he opened the door to the station. 'Third door on your right.' Mitsos stepped through the door and the policeman locked it after him. He wondered if all the police had keys.

Smells vied for dominance, stale cigarette smoke and burnt coffee, wet dust and sweat. A big woman, in a cross-over housecoat, broom in hand, a dirty rag wrapped around the bristles, was mopping her way down the corridor, dark wet patches under her arms, a cigarette dangling from her lips. The light reflected off the wet areas of floor; she had missed many patches. She looked up. Mitsos said hello but she did not reply, returning to her work.

The third door on the right, a greying white, was unmarked. He knocked but there was no answer. He pushed the door open and called 'Hello' through the crack. Again, no answer. He opened the door. Two large policemen sat at grey metal desks; both ignored him. One was eating a sandwich whilst reading through some papers.

Mitsos stood in front of his desk and the policeman, without looking up, indicated using the papers in his hand that he should approach the other policeman, the other desk. The second policeman was writing on a form. He continued to write for another line before he, also without looking up, indicated a chair against the wall. Mitsos stood by the chair; he did not want to sit. There was a fan on full blast moving the warm air but not cooling it.

Behind the policeman was a narrow sliding internal window which, presumably, gave air to the next room. It was open and Mitsos' attention was drawn to it as he heard the murmuring of many voices. The next room was large and had a cage inside it, and there must have been some sort of skylight as the sun's rays fell in the cage, cutting men and bars diagonally.

Mitsos wondered why there was a free-standing cage inside a room: why not just lock them in a room, then the room is the cage? It reminded him of a poster for the circus, showing a circle of bars with a captured lion roaring. But it didn't thrill him or amuse him, it saddened him; the people inside an exhibit, dehumanised.

The men who prowled in the cage had taken their shirts off. They stalked back and forth with restless energy. There was nowhere to sit; none of them was still. He recognised cultures. The Filipinos stood out with their diminutive height and straight dark hair; they seemed to outnumber everyone else. Egyptians were noticeable by their curly hair, some frizzy; they were dark with straight noses, and they also looked thin. Gypsy characters with shoulder-length hair felt the most threatening to Mitsos. In amongst them, Manolis. He too had taken his shirt off and walked back and forth. He looked angry; he looked like he did when he was plotting. Mitsos thought of Marina, and an animal power ran through him demanding violence, harm, blood.

'Yes, what is it?' The policeman looked up from his writing. His eyes were different colours, one brown, one green.

Mitsos, flummoxed by the unexpected, fumbled his words. 'You brought a man in today for not having papers for the mopeds he was renting?'

The policeman didn't even smile; he didn't even seem to notice. 'Yes, you can bail him out. He is to appear the day after tomorrow before a judge.'

'How much is the bail?' The policeman looked through his ledger and pushed the book towards

Mitsos, who read the sum. He and Marina had that much between them easily; it was not a high bail.

'You want to pay it, or do you want to leave him here?' The policeman asked in a monosyllabic voice, looking back at his forms.

Mitsos did not reply. The policeman became engrossed in his form again. Mitsos waited a while and then slipped out.

The church bells' ringing brings Manolis back to the present. The sky is getting dark. It is even darker where he is standing under the trees. The lights in the village come on one by one, spreading their way towards the town, merging, uniting. He cannot see the crisp lines in this twilight, only the progress of the village towards the town – and vice versa. Mitsos slowly moves. Time to sit inside with a glass of ouzo and a cigarette before bed.

By the time he is stepping over the wall in the almond grove he notices he is tired all over. The owl hoots. Mitsos looks for it. It is sitting on the same branch outside his house. It swivels its head and looks back at him, blinking.

'I thought I had done right leaving him in jail, Mr Owl,' Mitsos calls up to him. 'To give Marina a break …' But that Sunday Marina could hardly hold her head up in church for the looks and the whispers, and Mitsos knew he had made the wrong choice.

'But, in truth, Mr Owl, I did not do it for that reason.' Mitsos turns to the house, his head hanging low, and says to himself, 'I held the power. I, personally, wanted to punish him.' He is muttering now. 'My wish for revenge brought misery on Marina.'

The back door is standing open and, in the dark, there is a cat prowling for scraps in the kitchen. It panics when it sees Mitsos and runs into a chair leg, then goes in the wrong direction. Mitsos turns on the light and stands still. The cat freezes for a second and takes its bearings before shooting outside past Mitsos' legs. It has scratched a hole in the rubbish bag and bits of tissue and some very old potato peel have been pulled out onto the kitchen floor. Mitsos sighs. He kicks the mess out of the door. He will deal with it, if the wind has not taken it away, in the morning.

He pours himself an ouzo and reaches for a cigarette and then, with a tut, he remembers he still hasn't any. He thinks for a moment and vaguely recalls an image of a different brand of cigarettes he had bought once when his own was not available, but which he had found unpleasant and had thrown in a drawer somewhere. It was not a kitchen drawer, he is certain, as he uses these regularly; and the drawers in the bedrooms are all full of clothes. He ambles through to the room at the front of the house. His mother had arranged it as a room in which to receive guests. For a while after her death he would sit in there and smoke and look down over the village. But it does not enjoy the last rays of the evening sun and there is no cheer in the room, just grey padded seats with faded pointless cushions. She kept it immaculate but no one ever came to visit. He pulls the whole drawer out from the dresser and takes it into the kitchen where there is still light.

There is a pair of scissors he has been looking for; he puts them to one side. A pack of cards. A small ball of twine. Some Sellotape that looks like it has melted to itself. Mitsos throws this towards the bin, but it misses and rolls away under the kitchen sink. The mice can have it. His mother's prayer book. Some papers. He takes the papers out. They are newspaper clippings. He turns them over and there is a picture of the pink boat. Mitsos gasps. There are more clippings, and Mitsos reads again about the scam which made him finally give up on Manolis.

Chapter 13

'They are your own brothers.' The air smelt salty.

'If they didn't want to lose they shouldn't gamble.'

'What difference does it make if you own your family's boat outright? Use it all day and give them a fish and they would be happy. But you're not planning to fish all day, are you?' The image of Manolis as a full-time fisherman would not settle in Mitsos' mind. He looked her over; she was a tidy little boat.

'I am not going to be out in it at all.'

'Then what?'

'Will you join me this time?'

'If it is legal.' Marina was heavy with child. Mitsos wanted to help, if he could.

'Yes, it's legal. That's what gave me the idea. We would be outside the law; they couldn't touch us.'

Mitsos looked down at the boards on the pier beneath his feet and shook his head. For himself he wanted no part in it. But for Marina … 'If it is legal and it stays legal I will help.'

'Right, let's take my boat to town then.' Manolis emphasised the 'my' as he jumped on board and started the engine, the diesel growl drowning the cries of the gulls, as he waited for Mitsos to release the mooring lines. Mitsos watched the swells, and when the boat rose to meet the level of the pier he hopped on board, shaking his head, still not convinced.

The sea was so clear that Mitsos could see the bottom in the harbour, ropes and anchors half buried in the sand, small fishing nibbling around them, quivering seaweed hanging like ribbons. He coiled the ropes flat on deck and stood at the prow. The wind generated by the boat's motion blew his thin shirt and rough working trousers against him, flapping behind. The sea and the sky merged into one, just a thin white line indicating the edge of the earth. Mitsos looked seaward so there was no land in his sights. Across the water was Crete, further still Egypt and Libya, places he had never seen, and probably never would, but he could dream.

They motored out into the bay.

Movement in the water. Mitsos looked down into the sea. Dolphins accompanied them, turning on their sides, looking up at him, making eye contact, before darting in the bow-wave, streaks of grey in strips of blue, edged in a froth of white. There were moments when life was perfect, usually when he least expected them.

They reached the town harbour too soon; the dolphins veered off and went their way. He felt curiously sad to see them go.

Manolis cruised round the harbour and then pulled in alongside a long ugly boat twice their length.

'She doesn't look very seaworthy,' Mitsos remarked by way of conversation. He wondered why they hadn't docked against the harbour wall itself, where there was plenty of space. He raised his hand to point to a better spot, but Manolis replied, 'She looks perfect.'

Mitsos, realising by this curious answer that the boat had something to do with why they were here, looked her over more critically. One glance was enough to convince himself that he wasn't going to sail her and risk his life, whatever the plan!

'Manolis, she will sink!' he exclaimed.

But Manolis was laughing with his own secrets and sounded the boat's loud, rude air horn.

A rough-looking man came up on deck on the big ugly boat, and Manolis climbed on board and shook hands with him. They walked up to the bows and talked quietly. Mitsos walked to the stern, his instincts telling him to not get involved. He whiled away the minutes looking at the reflections on the water, thinking of Egypt and the Middle East, Paris and London, mystical places. He became lost in his thoughts, the sun warming him, his muscles relaxing.

'Done!' Mitsos felt a slap on the back, and he tensed and turned. The rough-looking man was now on board Manolis' boat, starting the engine. Manolis unhitched the rope tethering him and the man took off laughing, the sea churning in curls behind his newly acquired vessel.

'What have you done?' Mitsos felt ever so slightly sick. He already knew the answer to this question, but it seemed so improbable, so ludicrous.

'I am now the proud owner of this money-making machine.' Manolis spread out his arms to encompass the big ugly vessel. 'I swapped it for the family boat and he gave me a little bit of cash on top as I played hard to get.'

'You played hard to get? More like you've been had.' Mitsos was appalled and felt a sweat break out down his back.

'Which is why you will always be just a farmer.' Manolis turned his back on Mitsos and went to start the engine.

'You're going to sail her?' Mitsos felt he was in a state of shock and tried to calm himself.

'Just to the village.' Manolis grinned.

'I'll walk.'

At that Manolis tutted his annoyance and Mitsos began the journey back to the village on foot. He had not gone more than a few hundred metres when an old man with a straw-laden donkey joined him from a field and walked with him. They chatted about this and that; the old man shared his flask of water with Mitsos and the time passed quickly. He was back in the village in time to see Manolis round the harbour wall, the big boat chugging like an old man.

'So you're alive, then?' Mitsos said as Manolis shut the engine down to idle.

'Damn thing wouldn't start.'

Mitsos said nothing.

'Hop on now. We are not going to moor her here. I want a bit of privacy for what we need to do – I don't need the villagers scoffing and mocking. We'll just go down there and put her by the old pier.' Mitsos felt a misgiving which must have shown on his face as

Manolis added, 'If we sink on the way you can swim that far!'

Mitsos jumped on board with reluctant limbs and the two of them took her to a more private mooring.

'Right, let's gut her.' Manolis was childlike in his eagerness.

'Are you not going to take her out of the water and seal her properly and make her watertight?' Mitsos had done this many a year on his family's small rowing boat, the first job to be done when overhauling a boat.

'Yeah. I'll borrow the tractor tonight but I want to get started. Come on.' And with that Manolis dipped his head below deck and began to throw everything that was moveable out onto the pier.

'Hang on, that's a perfectly good net …'

'Who needs nets?'

'And that's a sound bit of board …'

'We do not want boards.'

And so it went on, Mitsos trying to salvage useful items, Manolis intent on gutting the boat completely. The pier began to be overloaded and bits and pieces fell off, some into the water, others sliding over the far side into the bamboo which was growing in abundance.

By dusk Mitsos had had enough and said he was going for something to eat, and why didn't Manolis accompany him on the walk to the village as Marina would surely have his supper ready. He mopped his brow with a large hanky and eased his back straight. The sun shone relentlessly during the day; it was not the weather for all this activity. Manolis said he would go back into town to eat.

'I'll let Marina know, then, shall I?'

'Do as you like,' Manolis replied, not looking at him but wiping his hands on an old towel he had found inside.

Mitsos intended to go into Marina's and tell her what had happened but he simply could not bear to bring her such news. She would find out soon enough. As he approached her door along the dusty street he slowed his pace and then walked with a soft step, but as he passed her door it opened.

'I saw you coming. I was looking through the back window.' Marina was not smiling, but there was an air of hope about her. Mitsos shrank from being the one to extinguish it.

'Hi, Marina. Manolis wanted to let you know that he will be going into town to eat – business, I guess.'

'Oh.' But the hope was still there. It was not Manolis she hoped for so much as good news, perhaps, as to what was happening that would affect her life. She seemed to be unsure of what to say next. 'I have cooked *pastichio* for him.'

'Well, it is a dish he can eat cold.'

Marina looked up the street; the sun's heat was keeping people indoors. 'You want some, seeing as it's cooked?'

'Well, I ...' But he could not finish his sentence; too many emotions strove for dominance. In his mind this offer showed her kindness, which in turned kindled his love. The thought of eating alongside her without Manolis present put him in Manolis' shoes, the man at the head of the table, and this somehow kindled his passion. The passion brought feelings of guilt and the guilt glued his mouth shut. Marina turned into the kitchen leaving the door open and, with hands wrapped in towels, took the dish out of the oven. Mitsos could smell the hot butter and his stomach rumbled. Marina was putting a portion onto a plate, one of those acts done without much thought.

'You can either eat it here, or standing on the step.' Now she smiled as she turned her head and saw he was still in the doorway.

Mitsos went in.

Over the course of dinner Mitsos revealed, in bite-sized pieces, the events of the day. Marina put her fork down every now and again and slowly went white, eating less and less. Mitsos, to make the whole affair sound better than he thought it was, tried to put a positive light on it. He said the vessel had potential, that he thought Manolis had got a good deal, if you wanted to make such a deal, and that he felt this idea, whatever it was, might be different from the others and that she must remain hopeful. In short, he tried to sound enthusiastic.

Marina listened silently until he had finished eating. As he took the last mouthful, and put down his folk, she said slowly, as if with much thought:

'It sounds like you encouraged him.'

'No, oh no.' Mitsos realised he must have overdone his enthusiasm and now tried to put the right level of reticence in his voice without belying that he thought the whole situation a disaster.

'You think being there when he swapped the boats and agreeing to help him is not encouraging him?' Mitsos could not return her penetrating stare and he dropped his head. He knew he was in an inexcusable position, but also knew there was nothing he could have done.

'Did you not think of me and this child I am carrying?' Her tone of voice was rising, and Mitsos found that as the emotion in her voice increased the pressure in his head pushed out thoughts and words would not come. He scrabbled in his mind to describe to her what happened. How to explain the positive slant, and the foreboding, but in a way that would not make her worry the more. He wanted to explain why he was so involved with this project. But how, without divulging his guilty, love-ignited, secret pledge to her? The *pastichio* sat heavily in his stomach. His hand covered his mouth as he suppressed a burp.

'Marina, I did think of you and the child. He is going to do his mad schemes anyway, with or without me. You know he will.'

'So you chose it would be with you, which just encourages him. I thought you had changed when you refused to go in with him over the mopeds. I thought maybe you even cared.' Mitsos could see tears forming on the lower rims of her eyes but he backed away as the volume of her voice rose.

'I am not encouraging him, I am just being there to make sure he doesn't get into trouble.' Mitsos could hear the tone of his own voice, defensive, pleading, but loud. He could hear how shallow his words might sound, but he could not begin to tell her how much he cared.

'You did not stop him.' She was all but shouting. Mitsos could see she was so emotional, so angry she didn't know how to contain it or where to release it. She was on the point of losing control or breaking down into floods of tears. She lashed out, 'You two have been playing these games, these stupid schemes all your life, before I was ever around. What a fool I was to believe it would change now just because I am pregnant. I am an idiot to think you might help me. I talked to you, I trusted you.' She stood up suddenly. 'Get out. You and him, you are the same.' She paused, thinking for a second. He waited wide-eyed, mesmerised, until she added, 'At least Manolis is honest in his contempt for me, but you, you pretend to be nice and friendly but all the time you are no different.'

Mitsos stood. He felt cornered, he felt a switch had been played on him. 'I was not there when he tricked his brothers out of the boat. Were you?' Mitsos' voice sounded harsh; he swallowed several times and there was a pause, a silence.

Marina's breathing slowed. 'Yes,' she said. The tears still had not fallen but she relented, and her voice dropped. She put a hand on Mitsos' forearm, inviting him to stay, and then turned, hand on belly, and sat down again, her new load making the unpractised descent awkward.

'He invited his brothers round for dinner.' She pointed to the chair Mitsos had been sitting on, as an invitation to sit back down. 'I did my best to cook well, served them in the courtyard. After dinner, out came the whisky so I took myself off to the kitchen to wash up and generally stay out of the way.' Mitsos hadn't sat down; he still felt hurt. Marina continued anyway, recalling how Manolis played the generous host and invented toast after toast, until out slipped his cards, and before the brothers knew where they were they were involved in a riotous game, first betting for cigarettes, then this and that old bit of family furniture that they each had inherited, then on to betting for olive trees one by one until whole orchards had changed hands. Finally, everything was put into a pot and the deal was the sole ownership of the family fishing boat which, at that time, they took turns to use. If you have a fishing boat you always eat, you are never hungry: it was a heavy bet.

'But I could see from where I was standing, drying up the dishes, that Manolis was cheating. I was appalled to see him use sleight of hand, as well as a lot of whisky, against his own family.' Her face was like stone, tears gone, a hardness around her eyes.

Her hardness scared Mitsos. He was still standing by the door she had suggested he leave by. He was not really listening to her account, but was hanging on to the accusation she had flung at him that still pierced his heart. He still felt he needed to protect himself, to let her know how much she had hurt him.

He had tried so hard for her, and she attacked him for it. It was not fair.

'So you saw he was cheating and you did not stop him. You did not tell his brothers and yet you accuse me of encouraging him because I am there when he makes a deal he has already set up?' Mitsos' voice is quiet. Part of him feels the need to say these words but another part of him does not want to hurt her.

Marina's mouth falls open. 'I just told you of this terrible thing Manolis has done to his own brothers and you use it as ammunition against me to make yourself look better?' Her mouth dropped open, her eyes wide, and colour flushed her cheeks. 'That is the last time I confide in you, Kirie Mitso.' She used the formal address and stood, crossing the room to open the door for him to leave.

No sooner had he left than Mitsos was wishing away the things he had said. He had always been terrible with words when emotions became heightened. He walked, his stomach heavy with food, his heart heavy with remorse. His logic disappeared, the thread of the argument became tangled in his mind, words would evade him and a feeling of injustice would escape him in sentences he would later regret. He had defended himself, and the cost was his delicate relationship with Marina.

Mitsos had flattered himself that she needed him, that she needed an outlet, someone to confide in. Whether she did or not, that privilege was now gone.

Cross with himself, he decided to make amends by putting even more energy into helping Manolis do whatever he was doing to make it a success for Marina and her child. If this scheme succeeded, she would surely forgive him his hasty words. Consequently Manolis and Mitsos spent weeks of concentrated energy working on the old boat. Occasionally they laughed and it was like old times, but mostly Manolis was silent, intense. After gutting the boat the two of them spent a week fitting knee-high boxes to line the inside. They used pallets and orange crates that they mostly found washed up on the shore, and a few Manolis produced from other dubious sources which met with disapproving glances from Mitsos, but no words.

The sun beat down on them as they laboured, the heat causing them to sweat more than the effort of flexing muscles. They drank gallons of water, and several times a day Manolis sent Mitsos to refill their bottles.

Towards the end of the week a rather nervous, plump girl came with huge padded cushions that she shyly told Mitsos she had made. Manolis told her she was a good girl and slapped her on her behind. She blushed, and then she smiled and began to arrange them for him on top of the wooden boxes, with more of an eye for Manolis than for what she was doing.

The radio from Manolis' truck was taken out and installed in the boat along with two huge speakers from his house which he said he had won from a young bar owner in town.

The trial of the system brought the first curious children from the village. By the time it worked properly they had a good-sized crowd of youngsters hanging round the pier. Still Manolis divulged the details of his plan to no one. Slowly the villagers came in ones and twos. They declared Manolis and Mitsos had gone mad and began to come on a regular basis to see the work in progress, and to poke fun.

'Are you planning on wooing the fish into the boat with music from the speakers?' the butcher asked.

'Or do you expect the fish to die laughing?' the taxi driver called.

'Do you think the padded seats will be comfortable enough to gut fish whilst you're sitting up, or will you be lying down to do that?' asked Yorgos, who owned a little land behind Mitsos' house and struggled to feed his seven children.

'Or are they only after catching mermaids?' his eldest son retorted, which set all the assembled crowd laughing.

At one point Manolis pulled the hull out of the water and made a half-hearted job of caulking her, which was the only work he did that made any sense to the locals. They had plenty of advice and observations to share at that point and there seemed to be someone from the village present to give an opinion at all times, which did not please either of them.

Once the hull was sealed to Manolis' standards he set off for a nearby town where he had heard the hardware shop owner was very fond of poker. He did not invite Mitsos, and returned a day later with gallons and gallons of paint in a colour Mitsos would not have chosen.

On the second day of painting Manolis paused, and between bouts of laughter he said, 'When I got home last night I had paint all over me. Marina took one look and asked if it was the colour we were painting the boat. When I told her it was she said she felt she might never leave the house again, lest she die of shame.' He crumpled into laughter and dipped his brush back in the pot of bright pink paint. Mitsos understood her point of view; he too found it difficult to look people in the eye any more. He could not share Manolis' mirth.

Finally, Manolis declared the boat was finished. Mitsos thought the inside looked more like a bedroom you would see in the films. Manolis took this as a compliment. However, there were no words to describe what he thought of the pink exterior. Manolis replied that he should get with the times, this was the swinging seventies, and added that he should let his hair grow a bit more and that his side parting looked stiff. Mitsos had not received such a comment on his appearance since his mother died and was quite taken aback by the observation. He had presumed Manolis just couldn't be bothered to go to the barber's, and it surprised him to learn that his shoulder-length hair was a conscious choice.

When the two of them manhandled the barge into the water – Manolis pulling with a complaining donkey at the front, and Mitsos pushing, using poles for leverage, at the back – the whole village turned out to watch it sink. In the bright sun there was much calling and cheering as they rolled up their sleeves and helped to launch it, but it stayed afloat, its colour against the blue ocean like a profanity in church.

They slowly towed it through a calm sea behind a rowing boat, the pink monster's engine being the last thing on the list that Manolis intended to spend his time on. The village children ran along the shore shouting and jeering, accompanied by barking, frisking dogs excited by all the commotion. The village elders leaned wisely on shepherd's crooks, removed their caps and scratched their heads, declaring they had never seen such a thing, and the women, in housecoats, giggled behind their hands before returning to their cooking, the name 'Marina' caught on the wind of gossip before they returned indoors.

Once they had reached the town, it was not long before a new crowd had gathered around them. Taverna and bar owners came down to see the spectacle, shop owners took a break from smoking in their doorways to get a closer look, tourists took pictures and the priest asked if they would like it blessed. Mitsos stood sentry whilst Manolis disappeared. He returned with a truck full of boxes. Manolis and Mitsos unpacked the boxes, stocked the shelves inside with glasses and bottles. Mitsos did not ask where they had come from, Manolis did not say; the writing on the boxes looked perhaps Egyptian.

Finally, Manolis put up a board on the harbour's edge, leaning against a bollard. With a brush loaded with the same lurid pink paint they had used on the hull he wrote, in big letters:

'The Love Boat Bar'

Mitsos, and everyone else, finally understood.

Chapter 14

The villagers stopped laughing when, on the first night, young tourists and curious locals filled the padded, music-drenched interior until the bar reached capacity and people spilled out onto the harbour side. It was an oasis of colour and light and joy in the night dome of stars.

Mitsos was diligently on the look-out to keep Marina's husband out of trouble, and he worried enough for all three of them. He knew that nothing was successful in Greece without some illegalities, the law being so complex that if you fulfilled your obligation in one area you broke it in another. He was also aware that every man on the boat was one customer fewer for the bars in town, and if the impact was significant enough the owners would make trouble.

But Manolis had bragged that this was the very thing that gave him the idea; the laws of the land did not apply to them. He said he had got the idea from a boat that sat in the harbour and sold vegetables. Their 'shop' was on the water, at sea; they were outside the laws of the land, and they needed no licence. With some superficial investigation this appeared to be true, and Mitsos would have loved to believe it, but he knew that, in Greece, things could never be that simple.

The 'Love Bar' bobbed gently in the bay; the black water of the night danced with light from the windows, pink and red, laughter echoing off the liquid surface. The success of the first evening was not a one-off, and the next night, and the night after that, tourists and locals filled the boat to capacity. Mitsos was delighted and wondered whether he should have joined Manolis as a partner after all.

After ten days, Manolis' pockets were full and he handed out money to Mitsos with the air of a millionaire tipping the hired help. Mitsos, now almost sure he had been overly hasty in rejecting the offer of a partnership, wanted no free money, nor was he a hired help, and he kept his fists clenched shut. But Manolis stuffed the notes in his pockets at unexpected moments, laughing at Mitsos' sour expression.

Mitsos declared that he was being a friend, and he tried to give the money back, but Manolis said it was fair pay. Mitsos could no longer reach Manolis, whose mind was now occupied only by the pink boat's earnings. He would no longer look Mitsos squarely in the face; his eyes were like black glass, expressing no feelings, reflecting only money – and the girls that surrounded him. He seemed ugly.

After deliberating over the unwanted pay, and following an argument with Manolis about the girls in the bar in relation to his marriage vows, Mitsos began to justify taking the cash by sticking it in envelopes which he then, as regularly as money was given to him, slipped under Marina's door as he passed on his way home each night.

Manolis, by now, rarely went home. He was at the bar from dawn till dawn, sleeping in amongst the empty bottles, living on peanuts and beer.

Marina was no longer talking to either of them. Eight months pregnant, and alone, she walked with her head held high, trying to weather the storm. There was no mention of any envelopes when she passed Mitsos in the street: she just looked straight ahead. He presumed she did not know who they were from, and he was hopeful that she might even believe they were from Manolis – although he knew this was probably fantasy. At least she had money. He wondered what more he could do.

'Hey, Mitsos, stop your thinking.' Manolis slammed six shot glasses down on the bar and poured from one to the next, leaving a sticky residue between them on the bar top. The four Scandinavian girls laughed and each took a glass, but Mitsos hesitated. The girls giggled and cajoled him until he picked up his glass and they all drank, throwing their heads back. Some local boys joined them, always ready for a free shot.

Manolis lined up extra shot glasses, changed the bottle to something cheaper, and poured again. The crowd slammed their glasses back on the bar; the girls tossed their heads back, laughing, no longer caring what their hair looked like or if their lipstick was smudged. The local lads moved in and made contact, a hand on a shoulder, an arm casually swung around a neck in a brotherly fashion. One of them picked up one of the girl's hands to admire a ring. The local lads called for another shot. Manolis leaned in and whispered the price in Greek, and one of the boys nodded, his hand slipping more firmly around the blonde girl's waist. Another shot was poured.

'Skoll!' they shouted, and the arm around the waist became a claim of possession, the brotherly arm around the shoulder a right.

'Hey, boys, you should buy these girls a real drink! What'll it be, girls?'

Once they started, Mitsos knew the group would be ordering eight drinks at a time until the bar closed or the boys ran out of money, and he admired Manolis' tactics as much as he despised them.

At three in the morning, after two weeks of unimaginable success, Manolis was behind the bar looking pensive.

'What's up?' Mitsos was laughing at the tail end of a joke the town baker had been telling.

'It's this time every night.'

'What is?'

'People leave.'

'Maybe they want to leave with some money in their pockets, or they just need to get some sleep. It is three in the morning.'

But Manolis would not be pacified.

He was the same the next night.

Mitsos worried that trouble was brewing, and he took a walk along the pier to clear his head in the warm air. The stars seemed so bright and close that he felt he could touch them. There were various groups of people on the harbour's edge, drinking and laughing, and he wondered if, in some way, that was breaking the law. He sat on a bollard, shined by the seats of a thousand pairs of trousers before him, and wondered if Manolis had thought about Marina recently, dropped in to say hello, given her some house-keeping money even. How did he imagine she was surviving? As far as he knew, Manolis had no idea that he was dropping off envelopes of money.

He kicked a cork-edged net at his feet and looked about him. The harbour seemed a strange place to see people dressed up in their finery, instead of the be-vested fishermen mending their nets, stretching them between their toes and hands, weaving their shuttles across the broken lines. Now the toes were in platformed shoes or delicate sandals, and not even the local boys had bare feet. He finished his drink, and the world shifted slowly out of focus and he stopped thinking.

Two men in black trousers and white shirts marched towards him. Mitsos wondered if he was seeing double, and this feeling was accompanied by a strong feeling of déjà-vu.

'Who's the owner?' asked the shorter of the pair. Mitsos told them to wait, and ducking on board he whispered to Manolis. Manolis took all the money from the cash register and stuffed it into Mitsos' pockets before going ashore, a drink in either hand for the men in white shirts. They declined, and two delighted tourists received the free drinks as Manolis stuck his hands in his pockets.

'We have had many complaints about the noise.'

Mitsos, who had followed Manolis out, thought he recognised the tall speaker.

Manolis laughed, the relief on his face obvious. Mitsos wondered what law he thought he had broken if a noise complaint was a relief.

'I can't help the noise. The people are having a good time,' Manolis said.

'The noise must stop or we will close you down,' the shorter, white-shirted, man replied, and Mitsos remembered where he knew him from. It was the same man who had come to the beach bar all those years ago. Older, fatter, but the same.

'But all the bars are noisy?' Manolis swung his arm to indicate a string of bars along the harbour front.

'But not all night. They have licensing laws, they have to close at a certain time. This allows people to sleep. Your noise goes on all night and there is a law that says we can close you down unless you stop making noise.' The shorter one lingered on each word with his power.

'I remember you,' Mitsos interjected, but he was ignored.

'Presumably I can make noise until the bars close. You cannot stop that?' Manolis was still smiling, as if they were good friends of his.

The white shirts considered. One took out a pack of cigarettes and offered them around; only Manolis accepted.

'No, I suppose we cannot stop that.' The man in the white shirt blew out smoke as he reluctantly conceded. 'So you have one hour from now, but if there is any noise after that we will close you down … again,' he added, with a certain menace.

'Power-crazy nobodies,' Manolis spat after them, through clenched teeth. He sat on the bollard Mitsos had vacated, his head bowed to finish his cigarette, unreachable.

'Hey, who's serving down here? We're parched, and these girls really need a shot of ouzo,' a local lad, barely able to stand, shouted from the doorway of the boat.

Mitsos went in to serve and left Manolis on the pier, thinking. This worried Mitsos more than the men in white shirts. He watched through one of the boat's portholes, as he lined up the shots. Manolis' head jerked up quickly and he leapt to his feet.

'All aboard the Love Boat!' he shouted. Mitsos finished pouring the drinks, took the money and dashed up on deck.

'What are you doing?' he demanded.

Manolis ignored him. 'Tonight, a special event, only for the lucky few – a free moonlight cruise. All aboard the Love Boat bar.' With this, he started releasing the mooring lines.

'Tell me you are joking, you are not going to sail this thing?' Mitsos could hear the panic in his own voice.

'What's happening, man?' a local boy asked.

'A free cruise, my friend. Take your girl on board and you are assured of her company till dawn.' The boy grinned.

'Lads,' he called, 'I think we've scored here ...' The boys on the pier quickly manoeuvred their new tourist friends back inside.

'You can't sail her, Manolis, she is not seaworthy.'

'We will go out to the island.'

A little island sat in the bay, five hundred metres from the harbour, with a tiny whitewashed church like an iced topping, blue in the moonlight, at its summit. 'Go round it once and anchor till dawn. Then if the damn thing sinks at least there is the island.' Manolis was laughing. 'Those guys did me a favour. Move the noise out to sea and stop anyone leaving till dawn. Ha!'

'No, Manolis, it feels like a bad idea.' Mitsos was not even aware whether the engine worked and if it did who had carried out the work.

But Manolis had cast off all the ropes and was aboard. Mitsos hung back on shore and watched the departure with trepidation. The engine coughed a few times and then started, and the people on board cheered, raising their glasses to the skies. As the boat began to edge away from the pier, 'What the hell!' muttered Mitsos, and at the last moment he jumped across the widening gap and landed with a heavy thud on board. He grabbed at the cabin roof to steady himself before going inside. Manolis grinned at him; they were boys again with carrots in their pockets.

The heat of the evening sank into a heavy warmth of night, the sky expanded out in the bay and the stars grew sharp against the darker corners of the sky, dimming only around the orange moon. The pink cabin shone as the light caught it, from a distance looking like nothing more than a child's toy.

Inside three Germans had drunk themselves into a stupor and were hauled, a limb at a time, into a corner to sleep it off. Some English girls insisted on going on deck, and when they anchored by the tiny island they stripped to their underwear and jumped in the water. Some of the Greek boys followed, wearing nothing but a smile. One of the local lads insisted the music should be Greek and became self-appointed DJ.

As the traditional music filled the cabin the boys seemed to grow in stature in the familiar musical territory. One stood to dance and the others clapped in encouragement. In the tiny space, with his arms outstretched, his head thrown back, his chest full of pride, he kicked and strutted to the familiar tune. The music picked up speed and the boy increased his flamboyancy, slapping his ankle behind him, stomping the ground in front. He slid to his knees and slapped the board behind him, first one side, then the other. The girls cheered and he leapt to his feet. Someone put a full shot glass on the floor and he danced around it, then dropped flat to the floor, suspended above the rough wooden boards only by toes and finger tips. His head above the glass, his mouth encompassed the whole, leaving only the base showing, he bounded to his feet, his head back; the contents disappeared and he took the glass from his mouth, his arms outstretched in triumph. The boat's company cheered even more loudly, the girls' eyes shining, the boys emboldened. Manolis served drink after drink. Mitsos, intoxicated more by the music than the drink, forgot himself and clapped encouragement to the dancers who followed.

Dawn slipped over the horizon. The Germans awoke, the engine was started and they headed for the harbour. Boys and girls, arm in arm, happy, and still a bit drunk, headed for the bakery; the Germans staggered towards their hotel; the local men ambled to the kafenio for a much-needed coffee.

Manolis stretched and filled his pockets with the cash he had taken, handing a wad of notes, uncounted, to Mitsos. Mitsos' pockets were still full of the money Manolis had stashed on him when the men in white shirts appeared. Manolis waved it away as Mitsos offered it back. Mitsos wondered if Manolis knew he gave the money to Marina, and this was why he was so generous. He was too tired to talk about it so he ruffled his hair smooth and sucked on his furry tongue.

The girl who made the cushions was at the harbour. She smiled longingly at Manolis, who winked at her and told her he did not know what he would do without her. He pointed her towards the boat, indicating the bucket and mop by the pile of nets on the pier. She smiled at him but he offered no intimacy or money, instead kissing his own finger ends gathered around his thumb before opening them, throwing the kiss at her. She giggled, delighted, and turned to the boat with energy.

'Coffee?' Mitsos felt he should get some sleep and go home to deal with some of the dried brown weeds in his olive groves before the summer heat was really upon them, bringing with it the risk of fire. But coffee seemed like a good start to the day and he sat on the nearest chair in the nearest cafe.

They had been there five minutes when they were joined by two port policemen who smiled, ordered coffee and then said that they would have to inspect the boat and count the number of life jackets if Manolis and Mitsos intended to sail with tourists on board.

Manolis smiled broadly and offered breakfast as if they were long lost friends. Breakfast was declined but the coffee arrived and the men drank. They relaxed and asked Manolis how many life jackets he had already; it would save the effort of actually having to inspect the boat. Mitsos could see that Manolis was about to lie, and he caught his eye and shook his head, just a fraction. His tried to convey in his expression, 'Give them credit for some intelligence …'

'Actually, I haven't got around to that yet. Where do you suggest I get them from?' Mitsos was impressed with this cunning answer. This was Manolis thinking on his feet; it reminded him of school days. Wherever the port police decided to send Manolis to buy the life jackets they would be credited as a source of customers. As the order would be for many life jackets, and probably for distress flares, a medical kit, maybe a life-raft too, it would ensure discounts for the port police in the future, whiskys bought, dinners paid for, everyone happy. The port police were happy to discuss with Manolis what to buy, and where from.

When the port policemen stood to leave they shook hands with Manolis and patted him on the back.

They hoped he would make the purchases this week and Manolis assured them that he would. They reminded him that he already owed over two weeks' port fees and would he mind dropping in to pay sooner rather than later.

Mitsos, once again, was left with the impression that Manolis was running a business and working for a living just like everyone else. He decided that when Manolis became more used to his success he would guide him back to spending some time at home with Marina. And perhaps Manolis would appreciate some home cooking and a little peace and quiet after the hectic environment of the Love Boat.

He leaned back in his wicker chair and sipped his coffee and looked out over the bay, the sun shining, the sky so blue, the sea breeze pleasantly cooling the warmth. He could happily spend the day here. He turned to Manolis to suggest they order breakfast for themselves. Manolis sat with his legs crossed in front of him, dark sunglasses hiding his eyes, his shoulder-length hair spread over the back of the chair as he had slid down into a comfortable position. Mitsos could just hear him snoring quietly. He turned his attention back to the sea and watched the seagulls lazily floating in the thermals.

The next day they went to the same cafe for breakfast. Manolis slept again and Mitsos ate before returning to the village, slipping an envelope under Marina's door, tending his trees for an hour or two before sleeping until the evening. As far as he was concerned, life could continue like this for some time.

Marina was alone, but at least she was spared the dubious pleasure of Manolis' company and she had steady house-keeping money. Manolis was not in trouble and was enjoying some degree of success. In all, it seemed like they had hit a balance.

A week later the port policemen turned up as they drank their morning coffee. Mitsos smiled at them but Manolis groaned as they approached. He sat up, forced a smile and called the waiter to offer them coffee.

'No, thank you,' the policeman called to the beckoned waiter before turning back to Manolis. 'It seems you have not taken our advice about the life jackets. That, or we must presume you bought them elsewhere. So now there will be an inspection, tomorrow, to make sure you have the jackets. No life jackets, and you will be fined. Also your harbour fees are now three weeks behind and there will be more fines if you do not pay what is owed soon.' Mitsos' eyes widened. The port police left.

'Why on earth did you not buy the jackets? They offered you a chance to make things friendly and you have just succeeded in annoying them. Now they will be down on you every chance they get. Panayia!' Mitsos called on his god for strength.

'Yeah, first it's jackets, then it's something else. The moment you comply they feel their strength and start pushing you around. To hell with them.'

'But that's crazy! They have the law on their side. They will fine you. Just buy the jackets from where they suggested, make them feel good, pay your harbour fees and get on with your life.'

'Do you want breakfast?' Manolis had his hand up to get the waiter's attention. Mitsos stood up and went home.

The following evening there was a group of students on the boat. It was crowded earlier than usual and the music was already loud.

'How'd the inspection go?' Mitsos shouted over the noise.

'Fine.' Manolis gave him a whisky and smiled. Mitsos looked him in the eye, but a red-headed girl clinked glasses with him and he turned to wish her good health. When he turned back Manolis was talking to Theo from the village, who had come to see what all the fuss was about. It wasn't long before Theo was dancing, with his mop of frizzy hair bobbing to the music.

'So where are the jackets?' Mitsos asked.

Manolis sighed heavily and pointed to one of the seat-boxes. He had written in marker pen in both Greek and English 'Life Jackets'. Mitsos slapped him on the back and enjoyed the rest of the evening.

The following morning two men from the fire brigade sat with them for morning coffee.

After they left Manolis was ranting.

'First the port police threatening to fine me if I don't comply and now the fire brigade.'

'Well, fire is serious stuff, and she is all wood.'

'Yes, but fire alarms! Why? If you are one end you would see the fire at the other, and who needs extinguishers when you are surrounded by water?' He pulled at the beads he was wearing round his neck that some girl had given him. He pushed his long hair out of his eyes as he put on his sunglasses. Mitsos could not tell if he was looking at him or not behind the big dark glasses.

'Do you know what they said? They said, "I am afraid you have already incurred a fine for not having the fire regulation met from the beginning."' Manolis tried to imitate an Athenian accent. 'They say I have a week or they will close us down. Didn't I say if we start to comply they will just feel their strength and push all the more?'

The trickle of official visits threatened to become a tide. Representatives from the council came the following morning.

'Licences!' Manolis bleated. 'Not just one like the bars have, but two, for business and tourism, because we are at sea.'

A short man in glasses came next, from the tax office.

'Taxes!' spluttered Manolis in a rage. 'Well, death and taxes ...' countered Mitsos.

Mitsos tried to pour oil on Manolis' waters. He said that with the amount he was making he wouldn't even feel the cost of the fire hydrants, or the small amounts of money to apply for licences; it was all just business, and once it was done he could continue to reap the huge profits he was making now. 'And everyone must pay taxes.'

But Manolis was not to be pacified. With his tension came his temper. That night, before they cast off, he was far from polite to some customers who left fairly quickly. He told them to go to hell as they left. Mitsos felt embarrassed and told Manolis to cool it, but instead he swallowed back a whisky and maintained his frown. He was rude again later that night and even returned to harbour to let off some people who had annoyed him. When the boat docked they were not the only ones to leave; others went too because it was no longer fun with all the arguments on board. No money came to Mitsos that day or the next couple of days as Manolis' bad mood continued and fewer people came to the boat as a result. Mitsos wondered how Marina was coping.

He tried to ensure that Manolis complied with the firemen's requests. He took him to pick up the hydrants. Manolis grumbled that it was using all the money he had made and that takings had dropped over the last week.

Manolis went to the bar, and Mitsos went to run some errands for his farm before returning to the bar later that morning.

'You see?' Manolis began as soon as he saw Mitsos. 'Now they say the fire hydrants are not enough, we need a fire door at the far end of the boat. Like it is a cruise ship. Panayia! I mean, the boat is so small that by the time you get to the end you meet yourself coming back. Fire door my ... Just leave the windows open I say, they are easily big enough for a man to dive through, but "No" they say, it has to meet with fire door regulations, sealing shut, push-bar opening. "What do you think we are," I say, "the King's yacht?" You do everything they say and then they ask for more.'

'You have to be kidding me?' Even Mitsos could see how ridiculous this was.

'Do you know what the fireman said? He said, with his nose in the air "Well, my brother who owns the Sunset Bar over there, he had to put in a new door for fire regulations." So I said, "Oh I get it, this is all about your brother making a living, is it? Jealous, is he? Well, he should make his bar more fun if he wants more trade instead of trying to put other people put of business. Let me guess, the carpenter who makes these doors is your cousin, is he?"' Mitsos' mouth dropped open, fearing the worst of the exchange Manolis was describing. 'The fireman did not answer so I added "Cousin or best man, or brother-in-law? Which is he?" Do you know what he said?'

Mitsos shook his head sadly; he didn't want to hear.

'"He's my brother, actually," said the second fireman, and then had the cheek to say, "But that has nothing to do with it, it is just that he knows what is required." So I said, "To hell with you."' Manolis had rekindled his rage in the telling and stood up and started walking.

They walked back to the village, Manolis not saying a word, Mitsos trying to soothe him, suggesting that they should comply but not use the carpenter the firemen had suggested, that they just needed to keep the business going and this was one of the costs. Maybe they could put the door in themselves. At the village Manolis went on to his house and closed his door behind him, leaving Mitsos standing in the street. No sooner was the door shut than he could hear Manolis shouting inside, and he said a prayer for Marina and crossed himself three times.

The next day the bar opened as normal but Manolis was in a foul mood. The people who came left fairly quickly, and by the time they pushed off for the little island they were not even half full.

All that week, because of Manolis' attitude, the bar was becoming emptier and emptier, and as it did so Manolis sank further and further into his own blackness. On the Monday the firemen came again, along with the council man, and the port police, and the little man from the tax office. They were all waiting on the dock as the boat pulled in and the remaining people got off. Each of them demanded their fine money. The firemen also demanded to see the fire door and the port police wanted their harbour fees. The man from the council wanted to see the application for various licences that Manolis had been told he needed to file for. In short, until their requirements were met he could no longer open for business.

Manolis sighed, expelling all the air from his lungs, and shook his head.

'You were never going to be happy until you managed to close me, were you? None of you were. You all just wanted a piece on the way down. Well, you didn't get a piece, you nor your shop-owning cousins and brothers. To hell with you all!'

Mitsos could feel his mouth open and close like a fish. Manolis' thinking was beyond Mitsos' comprehension. He was failing Marina – again.

Manolis dismissed the speechless assembly, kicked the Love Boat sign flat, and went into the boat and closed the door behind him.

Mitsos felt inclined to apologise for Manolis' rudeness but on reflection he didn't care if they thought him rude. He shrugged and the group began to disperse.

'We will arrest anyone on board if you open tonight,' the taller of the port police said, loosening his collar as he walked away.

Mitsos looked out to sea, past the island where the breeze ruffling the surface.

Chapter 15

Mitsos was at a loss. Manolis came out of the boat and strode across to their usual kafenio for a Greek coffee.

'Why?' Mitsos asked, as they sat in the wickerwork chairs. Manolis said nothing. 'If you don't obey the rules the result is inevitable.' Manolis still didn't say anything. 'Now you have to pay the fines without even having an income. I presume you have no savings?' Manolis pushed his sunglasses back onto his head, stretched out his legs and looked across the harbour to the bay but did not reply.

Mitsos gave up. He too stretched out his legs and sipped his coffee. 'Marina is due any day now.' He hardly opened his lips to speak.

'You are like a nagging old woman. Shut up or go away.' Manolis broke his silence.

'I was just thinking about your baby, your son or daughter,' Manolis qualified.

'It'll give her something to do, something to think about other than me. Now be quiet, I am thinking.'

They sat as the town came to life, the fishing boats 'putt-putting' out into the bay, laden donkeys arriving with goods from nearby villages, men in white shirts walking briskly.

'Got it!' Manolis stood up. 'Come on.' Mitsos threw some drachmas on the table and followed in his wake back to the boat. Manolis unhooked the ropes from the bollards and started the engine. Mitsos stood on the harbour edge.

'Where are you going? What's the idea?' But the engine drowned his voice. 'Manolis! Hey! What's the idea?' Manolis cupped his hand round his ear and shook his head; the engine was too loud. He began to pull away from the dock. Mitsos shouted again, and again, and at the last second he surprised himself by jumping the gap to land beside Manolis. Manolis' grin made Mitsos wonder if his spontaneity had been wise.

'The solution's simple. We cannot work this town any more because they won't let us, so we will work another town,' Manolis said, and relaxed his stance, one hand on the helm.

'You can earn enough to pay all the fees and fines and be back in a couple of weeks. Could be a good idea!' Mitsos said, thinking of Marina, and her need for Manolis once the baby arrived. Manolis looked out to sea. He was chuckling to himself.

The next town was bigger than the one they had left. A wide palm-dotted walkway hugged the harbour edge, a child's playground with swings and see-saws and metal rocking animals fenced in at one end. There were people walking in their best clothes, children running, men in white shirts, sleeves rolled up, smoking and talking, young men with nothing to do sitting side-saddle on their stationary mopeds watching the tourists. In all, it felt like a lively, prosperous place. The first night reaped a good reward. Mitsos offered to keep the fine and fees money safe but Manolis said he could handle it.

But within two weeks they had officials harassing them again.

Mitsos had had enough. 'We have more fines now than when we left our home town,' he observed, watching Mitsos fold the latest official letter into four and then eight before he slipped it behind the handrail by the door.

'You look like a farmer,' Manolis scoffed. Mitsos, for the life of him could not figure out what that had to do with the situation and replied that of course he looked like farmer, because he was a farmer.

'How can I forget it?' replied Manolis, but he didn't smile.

Mitsos said he was going home, he would walk.

'Let us sail today!' Manolis replied.

'You'll go back and face the fines?' Mitsos asked.

'A big breakfast, clear up a bit, a quick sleep in the heat and we'll be off,' Manolis replied.

Mitsos no longer cared or wondered why the change of plan; he just wanted to go home. He ate his breakfast, he tidied up the boat and he fell asleep early, wishing the time before they were under way would pass.

When he woke Mitsos could hear the lapping of the waves: they had already set off. His heart felt lighter, he missed his routine, the quiet, the view from the hill. He was eager to be on deck and see the familiar coastline.

The sun hit him as he came out from the shade of the cabin and, for a moment, he could see nothing, just brightness. He heard Manolis cough. The brightness dimmed and the sea shone a dazzling blue.

Mitsos sat by the helm to get his bearings. He was fuzzy with sleep and nothing looked familiar. He studied more intensely the lie of the land and the curve of the rocks. Nothing was recognisable.

'Where are we?' he asked. A churning in the pit of his stomach knew the answer before Manolis spoke.

'Thought we would give it one last go.' His voice was flat without even the pretence of believing his own lie.

'Where are we?' Mitsos demanded, but the crumbling medieval tower halfway up a hill gave him a bearing. He had been this far down the coast one time with his father on a week's fishing trip. 'Let me off,' he demanded, but there was no place to stop. It was all rocks and cliffs and seagulls shouting.

Mitsos was furious and he shouted and bellowed at Manolis, who sat and smoked as he steered, calmly looking out across the water. By the time they reached the next town along the coast they were too far for Mitsos to walk home; it would take days. He wondered if there was a bus, but he would have to stay and work that night as with the paltry amounts Manolis was giving him these days he hadn't even enough money for a ticket. He swallowed his anger, mentally washed his hands of Manolis' reform and planned his return home.

They worked that evening, but there were not many tourists and takings were slim. The port police had asked for mooring fees before they had even finished tying up, and the council people had come to them with forms that needed filling out before they had opened that night.

'They know who we are. They have been warned,' Manolis spat. He was as much thinking out loud as telling Mitsos.

But Mitsos wasn't interested. The night gave him enough money to buy a bus ticket home. The next day he took his afternoon sleep earlier than usual, forgoing his morning coffee. The bus left early in the afternoon. The whole thing with the boat and Manolis felt like a mess and he just wanted to go home. More than anything, he felt a failure.

He awoke to the throbbing sound of the engine and roused himself as quickly as he could to dash on deck to see what was happening. Manolis was smoking and steering and looking out to sea. He looked content. Mitsos looked about him. The rhythmic thumping he could hear was his own pulse in his temples. He clenched his fists tight, his breathing rapid. He felt on the brink of exploding and didn't trust himself.

'If we get far enough away they will not have been warned so we will sail the whole day and find a fresh town that isn't wise to us.' Manolis grinned.

'No!' Mitsos felt tears prick his eyes. 'I want to go home.' He heard the words leave his lips, plaintive and childlike. He could not retract them. The view of the endless sea did not calm him. It brought visions of his chicken shed, his kitchen, where he wanted to be.

'For God's sake, Mitsos, are you ever going to grow up?' Manolis scoffed.

'Drop me off here, right here, right now. You do everything you can to be outside the law and I'll have no part of it. You have not given Marina a second thought – she may have well had your child by now, and she doesn't even know where you are!'

'I thought that part of it would please you, Marina not knowing where I am!' And he gave Mitsos a nasty smile.

'Sod you!' Mitsos exploded and wished Manolis no longer existed.

Manolis refused to take the boat in to shore and Mitsos sat seething as the hours passed. The sun was strong and they had no water with them. Manolis was drinking whisky and singing to himself and lighting cigarettes one after the other.

Mitsos' money had gone, his worthless unused bus ticket crushed in his pocket. The sun on the sea was too bright for his mood, the seagulls too raucous. He went below deck and poured himself an ouzo.

The next town turned into another and then another, as they went further and further from their village. In each town Manolis gave Mitsos a little money, but not enough for the bus fare home, adding promises of debts being paid and dreams for the next day. Mitsos was repeatedly sucked in to Manolis' reality and found his own reality and reason ebbing away.

The only reality he knew was that the money he had he needed for food; nothing was left over. One evening, feeling brave (and just a little bit desperate) when serving a drink, he took the payment and put it straight in his own back pocket.

But he was not a natural thief, there was no fluidity of movement, no grace in his action, and Manolis caught him, and then, if that was not enough, accused him of being part of the problem, the reason why they had not saved anything for the fines. They stopped talking. Manolis no longer let Mitsos serve drinks. He could clean, wash glasses.

On two occasions Mitsos drank so much he took a swing at Manolis, but Manolis was taller and stronger and a return slug was the end of both fights. On both occasions Mitsos had wished him dead and had shouted as much in front of an astonished clientele.

They stayed in each town until, with the level of the fines, the authorities threatened to imprison Manolis. The fines he owed just grew and grew with each stop they made. Authorities from previous towns showed up in the new towns and the web of debt closed in around them. In each town Mitsos made it clear to the authorities that he was hired help and if they could offer him a way home he would take it.

They had just left one particularly busy town and Manolis was humming at the tiller, heading towards a very picturesque village. Flat-topped white houses coursing down the hillside to a palm tree-lined water front; the sea clear and blue and calm in the shallow waters, children swimming and tourists sunbathing under umbrellas. Manolis said he had a good feeling about this town. Mitsos asked for a decent day's wage, seeing as the last town had been so profitable.

'You cannot pretend you are saving for fees and fines any more, Manolis, so just give me a decent day's pay.' They were the first words Mitsos had said to Manolis in a week.

'What, so you can abandon me? No chance. This would not be half so much fun on my own. Besides, you enjoy the chase, and you have all the ouzo you can drink, and you are surrounded by different girls each night. What more could you want?'

'That's what you want, Manolis, not me. I want my almond orchard. I want my own bed. I want to watch the cats laze in the sun by the flower pots at my back door.' Mitsos looked inland to the hills. He had no idea how far from home he was now since Manolis had, laughing, thrown their one chart overboard when Mitsos accused him of kidnapping.

'Oh, for pity's sake! Cats and flower pots – can you hear yourself?'

'Shut up, Manolis. Pay up or go to hell. I am getting off here either way. I will get a job on a farm, whatever it takes. I am not staying any longer.'

'You'd have to work a month on a farm to get enough saved to take a bus home from here.'

'I don't care.' Mitsos hated the way he sounded like a child when he got angry. He stuffed his hands as far in his trouser pockets as they would go.

Manolis paid him no more attention. He was pulling in alongside the harbour wall. He stood up, and taking a rope jumped the gap and tied them to a bollard.

'Manolis?' A deep voice said.

'Yes. Who wants to know?' He turned to see a policeman.

'I am arresting you for non-payment of fines, for not complying with licensing laws and for failure to ensure the safety of the people that go aboard your boat.'

Manolis hesitated for a second before turning to Mitsos.

'Can you get my prayer book out of the first box seat for me, please.' Mitsos looked at him to see if he had gone quite mad. Why would Manolis even own a prayer book?

'He can bring it to you when you are safely locked up.' The policeman did not even look at Mitsos as he handcuffed Manolis and took him away. Mitsos made as if to follow, and the policeman made it clear he would be wise to stay away unless he, too, wanted to be arrested. He was left standing opened-mouthed, the pink Love Boat's engine still throbbing.

Mitsos, a little bit dazed by the event, wandered back on board and closed down the engine.

'"Get my prayer book"! He has never said a prayer in his life, God damn him,' Mitsos announced to the empty boat. He pondered his own words and went to the first box seat and lifted the lid. Two life jackets and a box with a crude cross drawn on it. Mitsos lifted out the box and opened the lid. There was no prayer book. It was full of money.

His first thought was to take enough for the bus home and just leave. But then he wondered if he could do anything for Marina. Should he just take her the cash or should he try to bail out the mess Manolis was in? It was bad enough Manolis being in prison the first time, but if she knew it had happened again the shame would be too great for her and the shame would be passed on to the child. Better he try to sort out the mess.

He went to the police station and asked to speak to whoever was in charge. The police were very helpful. They had a full list of who was owed what. 'You had better get some legal advice, my friend,' suggested the policeman, almost kindly. 'I will introduce you to my brother. He is a lawyer and will help you.'

Mitsos went, box in hand, to the lawyer. Together they went over the list and divided up the money owed to each. After Mitsos took what he needed to pay for the bus journey home there was just enough left to pay the lawyer his stated fee, which seemed to Mitsos quite a coincidence. The lawyer smiled, a gold tooth twinkling somewhere near the back of his nicotine-stained mouth.

Mitsos unbuttons his shirt and pulls it out from his trousers. His vest comes out with it. He can remember that the bus journey seemed to take forever. The bus had dropped him in the town and he had gladly walked to the village, his limbs joyous with the movement after sitting for so long. He had swung his arms with such freedom, freedom from the bus and freedom from Manolis.

The joy of the memory of that freedom does not last long. He twitches his shoulders. He hasn't even got two arms to swing now. Mitsos puts the old newspaper clippings on the kitchen table and finishes his ouzo. He shakes his shirt off his shoulders and it falls down his back onto the chair, the sleeves picking up dust from the floor. His vest is baggy and old and accentuates his thin frame. A tiny jumping spider in a white and black suit runs in staccato bursts across the table. As it comes to a stop, motionless, Mitsos touches its rear and it jumps, a hand span, to his ouzo glass. He played for hours as a boy with these spiders; they are old friends. Mitsos picks up the glass and talks to the spider. 'She had had the baby by the time I got back.'

Manolis followed weeks later. His lawyer had paid all the fines on his behalf. Bloody Manolis got off with nothing more than a strong caution. Damn boat – at least it wasn't allowed to be sailed again.

He slams the glass down, and the spider retreats to the edge of the table. Mitsos is glad of the company of his eight-legged friend, and encourages him back with three tail-touching jumps. He is tipsy. He stands up, and looking at the motionless spider says, 'I heard one rumour that Manolis had insured the boat with what money he had left in his pockets and that the boat had sunk in the harbour.' He leans over to peer at the spider to make sure it is listening. 'But the insurance refused to pay up as they believed someone had scuppered the vessel on purpose.' He stands up straight, glass in hand. 'Ha! Served the scoundrel right!' His ouzo slops over the side of his glass.

'The talk in the village at the time was that we were in the whole thing together – as if! – and that I had got away and left Manolis to take the rap.' Mitsos slumps into a chair, and says through closed teeth and unmoving lips, 'That hurt.' He pours another drink and traces his finger around the top. The spider makes a few hops towards the bottle. 'Marina crossed the square when she saw me coming after that. I never got to meet the child, but she grew to be beautiful, like Marina.' Mitsos dips his finger in his ouzo and lets it drip just in front of the spider, which backs up a fraction. 'Even Manolis himself did not speak to me for some time, which only added weight to the village gossip.'

He swallows the aniseed liquid and pours another. He lifts the glass as if in a toast.

'When he finally did speak he asked why the hell I had handed over the money, saying that because of that the whole summer was for nothing. Damn the man.' He drinks his toast and pours himself another. Mitsos downs this drink in one, no toast needed. He surveys the table top, but the spider has gone.

He picks up one of the clippings and wonders who kept them all this time and why; his mother perhaps. It is a time he would rather forget. He searches his pockets for his lighter and lights the corner of one of the clippings. It burns more quickly than he expects and he leaps to his feet to put it in the fireplace before he burns his fingers. As the orange flame dies down he drops the other clippings on top. He watches the flames flicker, casting dancing shadows across the unlit room.

He knows that Marina only knew what she saw and what had been told her. In her eyes he was no better than Manolis, in fact he could see how she could easily think he had been egging him on. His pledge to help her had done nobody any good.

Now he has to make the biggest decision of his life. Will he be helping her this time or damning her and himself somehow?

With this thought in his head he lies down on the day-bed to sleep, not bothering to undress fully.

Chapter 16

The mellow morning light shines in, muted by the kitchen curtains, although the heat is already apparent and for a moment Mitsos does not know where he is. His dreams had taken him from the pink boat to chasing his broody hen, to the army and then up the hillside with his goats. He focuses on one thing. Slowly, it becomes a table, and after a minute or two it becomes his kitchen table. At this point he recalls his reminiscences of the previous night and the excess of ouzo that accompanied them. He sits up. His head spins; he hasn't drunk so much in years. It takes a while to stand, but once he is steady he shuffles across to the sink and puts his head under the tap, both drinking and refreshing himself. He can remember doing the very same thing as a young man, before he knew any better. 'You old fool,' he says to himself.

The kitchen curtains have not been drawn for a decade or more and they feel paper-brittle to the touch. He carefully pushes them back and opens the window, which is stiff. Thick cobwebs tear as he pushes it open. A moth makes its escape and the morning breeze blows in past Mitsos to refresh the room. He yawns at the day and then shuffles to the back door and opens it wide. The area at the back of the house has not been swept for … Mitsos tries to recall how long, but he cannot remember.

Pots line the edges of what used to be the brushed area of ground, some devoid of both flower and soil; Manolis had stolen them for his moped shop all those years ago and Mitsos has never bothered to replace them. Those with soil sprout weeds, which grow profusely.

Mitsos picks up the broom. He has not mastered using the broom with one arm, even after all these years. In truth, he has never really tried. When he was a lad and his mother made him sweep, how little he knew that just the action was a privilege, something to be grateful for. After a few pushes he finds it is not so hard, and he can manage with one hand. The dustpan and brush are a different matter but he pins the dustpan with his foot and finishes the job. He takes the pan to the end of the almond grove and pours the dust over the wall, where he is still keeping an eye out for the broody hen. The goat bells clonk and rattle in the hills above. He steps over the wall and climbs to the hut to feed the chickens, which cluck and fuss their gratitude. He turns and considers sitting for a while, but something prompts him to saunter back down the hill into the orchard.

The sound of a car stopping and the gate at the end of the track being opened, he checks the time. Surely his nephew is not due till later? He does not quicken his pace back to the yard.

Adonis is wearing a suit despite the heat. 'Hey? How ya running?' Mitsos finds the expression odd. Is his little brother becoming age-conscious and trying to be cool, using this phrase of the youth?

Mitsos sniggers. 'What? What's up?' Mitsos shakes his head and takes the baby-seat.

'Hey, little man, you're awake. Shall we go and look at the black branches against the sky?'

'Look, I have to go, here's the bag.' But Mitsos isn't listening and is halfway to the far wall, carrying the car seat. He sits down with his back against the stones, his charge beside him, and waves to Adonis, who has stopped in his car to look back. The wave makes Adonis smile. His face relaxes and he drives off, leaving the gate open.

'So, how have you been keeping?' The baby smiles and waves its arms at the fluttering blossom and flies and buzzy creatures that fill his vision. 'I made a bit of a night of it last night. You see, that is the other thing with age: not only do you not have a blank sheet in front of you but you have countless memories to haunt you, things you should have done but didn't, things you did do but shouldn't have. It can all get a bit much at times.' He pauses to watch a dragonfly. The baby squeals with delight. 'You are right, though, we should live in the moment. But you know what I realised going over these memories?' He pauses but there is no response. 'No? Well I will tell you. Your Uncle Mitsos may have been naive and easily taken in, maybe even a bit slow, but his heart was in the right place, at least up until the day he lost his arm. It's funny, that. All these years people have silently thinking that I am bad 'un, a trouble maker, a bit of a villain, but you know what? I wasn't. Sure, you begin to believe the looks after a time, and it hurts because it doesn't fit who you believe you are until you think, "Well, if they keep implying it, it must be true," and then you believe it and you behave accordingly, but it never felt like it fitted.' Mitsos settles onto his side, on his elbow, his head resting in his hand. He watches the innocence of his nephew's face.

'Because until the whole Love Boat thing I still knew I was a good 'un. It was after that I began to doubt. I had failed in my pledge to Marina. So I pulled as far away from Manolis as I could to show her, and myself, and the whole damn village that I was not the same.' Mitsos can feel the adrenaline coursing through his veins. He picks a grass and chews on it and is silent for a while, calming himself.

Five years after the beginning of the Love Boat episode Marina had another daughter. He does not want to even think how she was conceived. He pulls the grass from his mouth and throws it away. 'My hatred for Manolis only grew in his absence, and it was nearly eight years before our paths crossed again.' The baby's waving hands and happy gurgles indicate that he is not listening. Mitsos falls silent again, and he breathes deeply to steady himself and wipes away a tear. He sniffs loudly and clears his throat. 'But with what happened next I could never call myself good again. I deserved nothing. That's why I live up here alone, sit at the back of the kafenio.' He sighs through his nose. 'That's why I have such a problem with these envelopes that keep arriving and what to do about them. It would feel more right just to give them away.'

A butterfly lands on the baby's foot. He wiggles his toes and it flies in jerky movements up and away. Mitsos rolls back off his arm to lie in the grass, which is still surprisingly green for the time of year with its continuous heat. The almond trees thin out near the wall and Mitsos is dappled in sunlight, a light breeze keeping the pair of them cool.

'Shall I tell you? Shall I tell you how I lost my arm? You are young enough to have no prejudices. You tell me, am I guilty or am I not?' He picks another grass before he speaks

'Manolis came to the house one day …'

'What are you doing here?' Mitsos' back door had been wide open. He closed it a little when he saw who it was and leaned against the frame.

'Come on, Mitsos, it has been years since we have even seen each other. You've been farming, I've been farming, we are old men now and I thought perhaps we could just do a little fishing together.'

'We are not old men, we are forty-three and I have no desire to go fishing with you or anything else.' Mitsos stepped back from the door and began to close it.

'Marina has asked you to eat with us tonight. Will you come?'

'I seriously doubt she has asked me.' Mitsos paused.

'Well, don't come then. I'll tell her you didn't want to.' Manolis smiled his cheeky grin and turned to walk away. He clearly expected Mitsos to stop him but he didn't. He closed the door instead.

Mitsos debated whether to go or not. If he had been asked by Marina then it was an olive branch, a sign of peace. If he didn't go it would be a serious rebuff. He decided to go, and if she looked surprised he would leave saying he'd been misinformed.

Knocking on their door felt more than a little strange. A pretty dark-haired girl answered the door. This must be Eleni, with whom Marina was pregnant when Manolis had the Love Boat. She was tall for eight. She walked back inside, clearly expecting Mitsos to follow her into the kitchen.

The place had not changed. There were still Marina's parents, gilt-framed, on the wall, still only the bare essentials, a table and chairs, an oven, a fridge.

Marina sat in a chair with a blonde child of no more than three on her knee. The child was holding her knee and crying; Marina was kissing the little grazed area.

'Thank you for inviting me to eat with you.' Mitsos waited for confirmation but received none.

'Sit down, man.' Manolis seemed in a good humour. There were four wooden chairs around the table and a cheap rug that covered only part of the concrete floor, which had been painted white some time ago. The paint had worn off in paths to the sink and the door and to a lesser degree to the window, the dusty concrete eroding beneath.

'May I?' Mitsos asked Marina, who looked at an empty chair but said nothing. Mitsos sat in the hard chair and waited.

'Isn't it time those kids were in bed?' Manolis said, his words rushing out a little too quickly. He slowed his words at the end to make it sound more casual.

Marina put the little girl on her feet and the older girl took her by her hand and led her out of the room. Marina stood up to follow them.

'Stay, if you'd like,' Manolis said to her back. But it was not a question. She promised the girls she would be with them in a minute and came back into the room.

Mitsos crossed his legs and then uncrossed them. He folded his arms across his chest but let them slip into his lap.

'Are you hungry?' Marina's first words. There was no life in her voice.

Manolis pulled his chair to the table and indicated for Mitsos to do the same.

Marina took a cloth from a hook in the stone wall and used it to pull a deep dish out of the oven. The relatively modern oven looked out of context in such an old-fashioned room. She put the dish on the table and brought bread and feta and beetroot with a garlic sauce, which she placed next to the hot dish. Manolis helped himself and passed the serving spoon to Mitsos, who offered it to Marina, but she would not serve herself until his plate was full and he was eating.

Manolis offered a few pleasantries but Mitsos could not think what to reply. Marina said nothing. When they had finished eating Manolis pushed his chair back and pointed to the ouzo bottle on the mantelpiece, and Marina stood up to fetch it.

'Here's the thing,' Manolis said. Marina put two glasses on the table and he filled them. 'The oranges didn't do too well this year.' He re-corked the bottle. 'Well, actually it is not that they didn't do so well so much as the man we sold them to has not paid us and the oranges are gone.' Marina cast a look of grim disdain at him but said nothing.

'What about the olives?' Mitsos asked.

'I admit I was not on top of the olives this year and they have not done as well as I would have expected.' Marina cleared her throat. Manolis glanced at her fleetingly before continuing. 'So I thought I would try to do a little fishing until next year, just to tide us over.'

Mitsos looked at Marina but she refused to look back. 'What has this got to do with me?'

'Well, there's the thing. Since our little business venture with the boat bar I have no boat and there is no one else in the village who will lend me one.'

'What do you mean "our business venture"? It was yours, and yours alone.' Mitsos tried to keep himself calm but felt this emotions being hooked in.

'Will you not help us, Mitsos?' Marina's voice was like silk across a harp to Mitsos. He turned to look at her. Her eyes were liquid, her pupils dilated.

'Of course I will help you, Marina.'

'Right, so it's agreed then. We will meet tomorrow at dawn and go fishing.' Manolis clinked his glass against Mitsos', a boy again. The sunlight from the window behind the sink lit his face, bright one side against dark the other.

Mitsos takes a break from the story-telling. 'You see, my little friend, how keen I was to help, how eager to make Marina's life better, how easily I was led? You see that kindness was my downfall?' The baby begins to cry, and Mitsos realises time has passed and the poor little mite is probably hungry. He stands slowly, shakes his legs into action, brushes off some leaves and picks up the car seat. Adonis has left the bag by the back door. The car seat sits on the table as Mitsos warms the milk. Then he chuckles as he manoeuvres his nephew into the crook of his bent leg. He sits in the high-backed chair by the unlit fireplace facing the open kitchen window. The baby's little fingers come up and wrap around his own big rough hand as he offers the bottle. He bends over and kisses the child's hair with a tender lingering kiss.

The baby drinks deeply and his bright eyes look up at Mitsos.

'As I left that night Marina walked me to the door. I said goodnight and I assured her we would do well with the fishing. She said – and here is something that has haunted me ever since, and I could not swear it even happened – she said, very quietly, that the only good outcome would be if I drowned the bastard.' Mitsos sighs and looks out of the window, his hand holding the bottle steady. 'I say I could not swear to it as I had had two ouzos and I had never heard Marina use bad language before, so no sooner did I think I had heard it than I doubted myself. Maybe it was what I had wanted to hear, who knows? Time has made the memory more and more fuzzy; that, and I have replayed the scene until it is no longer real.'

Mitsos looks around the room and sees the appointment card for his meeting with his lawyer in town later that afternoon. He watches his nephew enjoying the milk, the baby's eyes reflecting rapture, not even trying to focus now.

'Anyway, we did go fishing, and we did ok, but Manolis wanted more, as always, so he came up with one of his ideas. Are you ready for this, my little man? He no longer wanted to trail a line, nor did he want to use a net. No, he came up with a revolutionary way of killing lots of fish in one go and all we had to do was scoop them up. I will tell you ...'

'It makes perfect sense. I don't know why the practice is not more widespread,' Manolis said hopefully as they walked back from the day's fishing with only two fish.

'It must be illegal for some reason. Anyway, it sounds dangerous to me. I will trail a line, I will use a net but I'll not do this, Manolis.'

'Marina will be disappointed.'

'That's your problem, not mine. She's your wife.' Mitsos tried to keep his tone level.

'Ah, but that's not how you want it to be, is it?' Manolis laughed.

'What's that meant to mean?'

'You think I don't know how you have been envying me my wife all these years, pretending to be my friend to get near her? I am not a fool, Mitsos, you are doing this to please her. Well, if you want to please her then …'

'Go to hell.' Mitsos could feel his temper rising, his muscles shivering in response.

'Yes, I probably will, and you'll be right by my side and you'll be no closer to her then either, unless a little infidelity drags her down with you.' Manolis laughed.

Mitsos lunged at him with all his strength, his fists flying, his eyes glassy with temper. Manolis landed on his back in the dust of the lane, Mitsos on top of him. Manolis brought his knee up sharply and Mitsos rolled off him doubled over, his hand to his groin. Manolis stood up chuckling.

'I am going to kill you one of these days you son of a ….' But it was not Mitsos' habit to swear and the sentence was left unfinished.

'Come on.' Manolis offered his hand to help Mitsos up but he refused it. 'If you were going to kill me you would have done it long ago.'

Somehow the knee to the groin and the obvious winning of the fight constituted a silent agreement that they were going to do it Manolis' way. Mitsos was hauled to his feet and the two of them went to Manolis' storage barn on the corner of the square.

Mitsos had been in there many times before. The place contained barrels of wine and crates of whisky, carpets and fishing tackle, and random items Manolis had won in card games: leather jackets, watches, a pair of cowboy boots, a pair of lamps. It was an Aladdin's cave.

Manolis opened a bottle of ouzo and sat down on one of the rickety chairs.

'Ha, we have had some times, Mitsos. Do you know what I heard the other day?' Mitsos was still standing so Manolis pushed a chair back for him and moved the glass of ouzo he had poured nearer his side of the table. 'You remember that trainee Papas we had some fun with? Well, he's done very well for himself, got a taller hat and coloured robes, I hear. But do you know how he came by his rise in the church? This is funny.' He stopped to laugh a little. 'He did not stop believing that the water into wine was a miracle of God and that the change back again was an equal miracle. It was this steadfast belief, when all around him were ridiculing him that made the archdeacon notice his solidity and commend him for it. Apparently the archdeacon said that if all the church could have such faith in the face of such adversity, the world would be a better place, and then he promoted him.'

Mitsos sat down; his legs felt shaky.

'So we did the guy a favour. We are heroes,' Manolis concluded.

'Not exactly heroes.' But this happy outcome for the priest relieved a little of Mitsos' guilt, and he smiled, and took a drink of ouzo.

'Also – and this one is even better – you know Katerina and Aris the tractor mender, who have just had their tenth kid, do you know how they met?'

Mitsos was still thinking about the positive effect of their teasing of the Papas. It made him feel lighter.

'Hey, I said do you know how that loving couple met? They met when they were eight. They met when they returned each other's donkeys the day after our all-night mischief. We played cupid without even knowing it. Heroes again!'

Mitsos' eyes widened and he looked Manolis square in the face.

'No word of a lie, I swear. You can ask them.'

'Manoli, they are the same age, they were at school together…' But Mitsos did not really mind Manolis' creativity with the truth. He expected nothing more. And maybe the day of the donkeys had made Aris and Katerina notice one another – who knows? Manolis swallowed the remains of his drink and poured more. He offered a cigarette and before long they were chatting like schoolboys, their common history bringing them together. But when Mitsos smiled it no longer quite reached his eyes, nor did it lighten his heart. When he laughed it was not from his belly, it was from a tight throat with an edge of nervousness.

Manolis showed him things in his barn and told of how they came to be his: a little card game here, in return for a job, or some information there. He had hats piled high from a tourist shop that went out of business; the loan of Manolis' truck to remove the remains of the stock had been paid for in goods. He had boxes of pans that he had taken from a gypsy in return for letting him off when he caught him stealing oranges from the neighbour's tree. The goods were varied and they were acquired by every possible means, but nothing, according to Manolis, was stolen, not in a straightforward way anyway.

'Ah, here we go.' Manolis was behind a ceiling-high pile of boxes, scratching about in the dark, the single bulb offering little light into the far corners, and the doors and windows blocked up with boxes, tools, goods and rubbish. He had unearthed some small boxes. He lifted the first one and passed it to Mitsos. It felt cool to the touch as it had been sitting on a compacted earth floor, and it was also heavy so he put it down on the table. Manolis passed two more and then straightened up.

The cardboard boxes were not closed and Mitsos flicked one open. There was a loose paper package inside. Manolis took one out and unwrapped some red sticks, the length of his hand: dynamite.

'Now, where would you be getting those from?' Mitsos asked. He folded his arms across his chest and exhaled.

'The guys up at the marble quarry were very partial to the three cup shuffle. They ran out of money so they bet dynamite.' Manolis laughed, nasally. 'Come on, there is no time like the present.' He took a wide rubber band off a hook in the wall and bundled together some of the dynamite. Mitsos was up and out of the door before him, trying to make some distance between him and the dynamite, wishing he had been more firm, said no more clearly. He did not like the idea, not one little bit.

The two of them strode out into the afternoon, the heat a slap in the face. The whitewashed village basked in the summer sun. The kafenio, usually full of old men and farmers taking a break from work and wives, was empty; the chemist and bakery that also flanked the town square, closed. The area in front of the church was devoid of shirtless boys playing barefoot ball. The school on the edge of town had finished for the day. The sun was past its highest and people were asleep during the afternoon's heavy heat. All was quiet. Not even a dog barked.

'Shall we do this when it is cooler?' Mitsos asked.

'Nah, come on, we will be selling to the tavernas as soon as they open if we go now. Imagine how pleased Marina will be.' He grinned and winked. Mitsos glared at him and strode ahead. Manolis made no attempt to catch up until he could see the sea and then he broke into a trot to draw level with Mitsos, the dynamite in his two hands clutched against his side.

'Hey!' Mitsos turned at Manolis' call. 'English rugby,' and Manolis threw the dynamite to Mitsos. In a mind-opening flash Mitsos saw his potential death and shock waves ran through his whole body. Legs sprang, arms extended, fingers spread, his whole being tensed to catch the bundle. With a huge sigh he hugged the dynamite bundle safely against his chest. He could not bring himself to believe that Manolis had just risked their lives over such a petty thrill. Mitsos felt his anger rising over Manolis' irresponsibility. This was the second time Manolis had nearly killed him.

'Come on, English rugby.' Manolis grinned and held out his hands for a return pass. Mitsos' muscles reverberated with his anger; his mind seethed with

Manolis' lack of responsibility, playing with peoples' lives, hurting people through lack of thought, or worse, from considered forethought. He felt dizzy with his emotions; there was no place for the weight of them to go, he felt like he might explode.

Manolis, still grinning, beckoned Mitsos to return the throw. 'Come on!' There was such derision in his voice, years of scathing, and in that blind moment Mitsos threw the dynamite at Manolis as if by doing so all the emotions would follow and he would be free of them. As the bundle left his hands time rolled and elongated. Mitsos saw where he had thrown the dynamite and where Manolis' hands were, and it was clear Manolis would not make the catch. Manolis took his eyes from the airborne bundle and for a fleeting second he looked to Mitsos, his eyes those of a ten year old boy with love for his friend. Mitsos pushed off his back foot and dived for the dynamite, but Manolis lunged forward with his whole body. The dynamite finished its arc and began its descent. Manolis had missed the catch; the dynamite was only feet from the floor and its inevitable impact. Mitsos reached down towards it with his left hand, his head only feet from Manolis', whose eyes were on him, and Manolis smiled, a kind smile, allowing his body to fall in unison with the dynamite, the two hitting the ground almost at the same moment, one on top of the other.

Mitsos was blown backwards, stunned into incomprehension. His ears rang with such intensity that it was all he could focus on. Awareness crept back on him and he looked for Manolis, but he was alone.

He wondered how far Manolis must have been blown. He looked about him but could not see Manolis anywhere. Mitsos felt angry. This was not a good time for a joke. Then he noticed the dog food all down his shirt, on the ground, hanging off the bushes. Time switched gear and reality was restored. Mitsos understood all he saw, and from deep within his gut a surge of love and anger and fear and repression swelled into his throat and he could hear the noise he made as something beyond himself, the cry of a hurt animal, loud, drawn wailing and inhuman.

Mitsos reaches for a baby wipe, his face wet with tears, his emotions catching in his chest causing it to spasm. The child on his knee is asleep, bottle hanging from his lips. He rolls the baby into his own chest and pins him there with his one arm so he can stand. He gently places the still sleeping baby in the portable car seat as quickly as he can before hurrying out into the yard. The air is no more breathable there. He runs through the almond trees to the wall, the wall where Manolis had hidden. He steps over the wall and strides up the hill till he is breathless, the need for oxygen dominating his chest full of emotions. On past the chickens and up into the pine copse. He throws himself face-first down into the stillness of the pine needles and grieves. His muffled howls release the plug in his throat, and sobs and tears follow. His shoulders shake with his suffering and he lies there engulfed in his own anguish until time is kind enough to release him from the torment by bringing the safety of the baby back to the forefront of his mind.

He rolls himself over and sits up, looking down at the village: his judge and jury who said nothing and in that silence implied everything. He stands up and walks back to his home, to find the baby is still asleep.

'Sleep on, my friend. All too soon life becomes a nightmare.' He rubs the stump of his arm, remembering his amazement that he didn't even notice it was missing until he woke up in the hospital. They had amputated the shreds of what was left, because really there was nothing to save, they had told him. He was so lucky to be alive. He would not be so if his friend had not fallen on the dynamite and in doing so contained the blast.

He was in the hospital for weeks, haunted by the image of Manolis falling and looking at him and smiling like a ten-year-old boy, with love in his eyes.

Chapter 17

Mitsos goes for lunch at Stella's after Adonis comes to pick up the baby. He feels he needs to get out, see people. Stavros is fussing with the grill, trying to get it going. Stella is standing, hand on hips, a look of resignation on her face.

'Hi, Mitsos. We've got one chicken cooked but the sausages will take longer. Stavros just spilt lemon sauce over the coals.'

'Stupid place to leave the bottle,' Stavros grunts.

Mitsos says nothing but slips through to the dining area. There are two of his peers there, Theo the kafenio owner and Cosmo the postman.

'Hey, Mitsos, we were just talking about you,' Cosmo says.

Mitsos' eyes widen and he feels his pulse quicken.

'Well, not you exactly,' Theo qualifies. 'We were talking about Manolis' funeral, what a carry on!'

What's that?' Stella comes in with her notebook and pencil.

'Manolis' funeral,' Cosmo smiles.

'No, please guys, not now,' Mitsos says.

'His funeral, what about his funeral?' Stella asks.

'No, of course, you were living in Stavros' village then,' Cosmo says.

'Come on, we don't need to hear that all over again.' Mitsos shuffles his feet.

‘Oh, go on.’ Stella sits down. ‘We have to wait for the grill now, anyway.’

Mitsos presses his lips together and shakes his head.

‘Come on, Mitsos, it is twenty-odd years ago and it is no disrespect to your friend,’ Cosmo says.

‘Some friend,’ Theo mutters under his breath, and Mitsos looks at him, his brow furrowing.

‘What?’ Mitsos asks.

‘Nothing.’ Theo offers him a cigarette, which he declines, it isn't his brand.

‘So, the funeral?’ Stella settles into her chair ready to be entertained.

‘The funeral.’ Cosmo titles his speech, and leans forward to set the scene. ‘Bear in mind that this was a while ago, when we were still using the old cemetery down in the gully between the two hills over there. I don't know if you have been there, Stella? It was the ideal spot to bury a man, maybe even a whole family. The sides are step and the flat area at the bottom narrows to a V at the back; it is very enclosed, quiet, peaceful. Yes, fine for a family, but a whole village!’ Cosmo takes out his cigarettes and offers one to Mitsos, who declines again, still not his own brand. Stella waves the offer away; she does not like smoke or smoking. ‘So bearing that in mind and bearing in mind that the old cemetery was packed to the gills with dead folk, I will tell you the tale of Manolis' funeral.’

He leans back in his chair and takes a big breath to begin.

'Well, as everyone knows, the poor sod blew himself up and very nearly took our friend Mitsos with him.' Mitsos looks up sharply from contemplating the grain of the wooden table. He has never heard anyone make a comment on what happened before, all through the interim twenty-two years, not a word. Mitsos had felt accused, but here is Cosmo saying that he was very nearly the victim. He focuses on Cosmo.

'Anyway, they gathered up what was left of him and put it in a coffin. So the coffin was in the church and the mourners did their duty and came to say their goodbyes. The villagers passed by the closed coffin, not sure what to do, as usually the coffin is open and everyone has a little something to say to the dead. But with the coffin all closed up people didn't say much, they just sat in the chairs, said a little prayer, and left. His family sitting either side of the coffin, Marina and her two girls, dry-eyed, his brothers looking morose. Who can blame them?' He pauses to take a drag on his cigarette.

'Not too many came as far as I can recall. People who had done business with his dad, farmers who had fields alongside his family's, neighbours, church-goers and cousins. Some gambling acquaintances of his turned up with their high-heeled girlfriends and sat at the back. You couldn't go,' He faces Mitsos, 'You were in a bad way, besides you wouldn't have wanted to go and no one would have expected you to go anyway.'

Mitsos screws up his eyes and frowns, trying to make sense of what he has heard. 'Why would no one expect me?'

'Well, after what he had done to you ... Anyway, those that were there, were there, and then the bells rang and the Papas led the procession out into the road.' Cosmo chuckles. 'You'll never guess which Papas it was. Do you remember that trainee Papas that came here when we were boys?' He turns to Theo, who nods vaguely. 'You know, who said he saw the water become wine that day when we were playing football? It was him, I tell you, no word of a lie. Someone said he had requested it, said he owed Manolis something. Funny bloke. Anyway …'

Mitsos looks at Stella, who shakes her head slightly as if to say 'What?' Mitsos points to his mouth with his thumb and mouths ouzo. Stella nips next door and returns with a handful of glasses and a bottle. Mitsos fortifies himself and pours one for each of his companions.

'Manolis, in his closed coffin, was put in the hearse and they started the steady drive to the cemetery and all the mourners walked behind. So there was Marina, who held hands with each of the girls, at the front, his brothers second; I think his mother was crying. Then there were the villagers and at the back the gamblers and their blonde girlfriends, all slowly following the hearse, the girls wobbling in their heels.' Cosmo takes a drink of ouzo.

'Stella, come and put the sausages on,' Stavros' voice shouts from by the grill. Stella stands and tells Cosmo to wait, and he draws on his cigarette and takes another sip of ouzo. Stella returns with a basket of bread and knives and forks.

'Not long now, boys.' She sits back down.

'Ok, so the hearse arrived at the cemetery and the brothers and the funeral arranger carried the coffin along the path to lead the way. The rest of us followed. We got to the end of the central path and there were no paths off from it. The graves were back to back and end to end, so we started to step over graves, following the Papas and the funeral organiser, who was pulling the coffin this way and that as he climbed over gravel beds and around the headstones, the brothers trying to follow his lead. They nearly dropped the thing on several occasions. The women in their high heels tottered and hung on to anyone available to stop themselves falling over. People chose different routes, and we all felt that soon we would have nowhere to go as we were heading up to the apex of the V, when the Papas suddenly stopped at the signal of the funeral guy. There, squeezed in between the wall and three graves, was the newly dug hole, the base of the wall and the bordering stones of the surrounding graves determining its size. People stopped, and those behind who had been watching where they put their feet walked into those in front of them and there was nowhere for anyone to stand.

Finally, we all gathered around, the women in heels pulling down their short skirts which had risen in the hike across the tombstones, neighbours saying what a disgrace the organisation was, and so on. Then the Papas said his little bit and the brothers and funeral organiser began to lower Manolis into the grave.'

Mitsos finishes his ouzo and pours another, and then fills everyone's glasses. He offers some to Stella, who shakes her head and points to the grill room where Stavros is. Mitsos nods his understanding.

Cosmo takes a breath. 'So they lowered the coffin, and the foot end, which was lower than the head end, began to go into the hole. Down it went, but as the head end, which was wider, was lowered it got stuck. So they lifted the foot end and levelled the coffin and lowered it again but now it wouldn't go down at all. All this while the Papas was trying to say holy things, but now everybody's attention was on the lowering of the coffin. So the funeral man told them to lower the foot in again, which they did, and then he told the brothers to push the head end down into the hole with their feet. The eldest brother lifted his knee and stamped on the head end with such force the lid could be heard cracking. "Careful", the organiser cried, "it's only plastic." Then all the men at the funeral had an opinion of how to get the coffin in the hole but everyone was talking so no one could be heard. In all this chaos the funeral organiser, who did not know the circumstances of the death, said, "It is the lid that is wider than the base. If we take the lid off we can put the coffin in and the lid on top."'

Cosmo pauses for dramatic effect and leans forwards to whisper. 'Everyone fell silent, horrified at the thought of the remains of Manolis being opened to the daylight, some, I swear, just a little curious, the girls in heels edging forward. At this point not a word was being said and everyone waited for someone to do something.

'That was when the eldest brother raised his foot again and stamped even harder on the lid. There was a crack and the coffin fell sideways into the hole, and before anyone could say or do anything the Papas said the words and the funeral man threw a handful of earth down into the hole where the coffin lay half on its side, with the lid ajar, closed to the day but open to the earth. The brothers quickly threw in handfuls of soil, and shovelled a bit over the edge with their feet before the mourners could look in to see what of Manolis remained in the coffin and what had fallen out. Each took their own handfuls of soil and leaned over for a good look.' Cosmo sits back and takes a good long sip of ouzo.

'Unbelievable!' Stella exhales.

'It's as true as I sit here, isn't it, Mitsos?' Cosmo raises his glass to him.

'Can we eat?' Mitsos asks Stella.

'Well, from what I have heard it seems a fitting end to a bit of a rogue. Who wants sausages with their chicken?' She scribbles the answers on her pad and goes through to the take-away grill room.

'Still, it was a bad day for you when he died, eh, Mitsos?'

Mitsos swallows and bites his lip.

'Yes, no one deserves what happened to you.' Theo nods.

'What?' Theo's words do not match Mitsos' feelings. It was a bad day for him because of the decision he made, not the consequences. His head feels airy, as if he might pass out. Spots of light dance in front of his eyes, the tears try to fall and he rubs his hand down his face and picks up a paper napkin to mop his brow and hide his eyes at the same time, wiping them surreptitiously before he scrunches the napkin and puts it neatly in the ashtray. Everything he thought he knew as being the truth feels as if it is melting. He focuses on the table top.

'Man, you put up with that guy for years, stood by him when everyone else thought you should walk away, supported his stupid schemes, took care of his wife, and for all that you lose an arm. It's not right,' Cosmo says.

This perception comes as such a revelation to Mitsos, he blinks new tears from his eyes. He is not sure he has heard correctly. In his confusion his mind wanders. He has visions of the chicken hut bar after Manolis had run it over, the sea breeze coming and one by one picking up some of the splintered pieces, carrying them away so the whole could no longer be the whole, it no longer existed. He wants to say, 'You don't blame me?' but he is still afraid he has misunderstood so instead he says, 'We were as bad as each other.' He meant it as a statement but it comes out as a question.

'No, my friend,' Theo answers. 'Marina told me about the envelopes of money you were putting under her door when the boat bar was doing well. Manolis wasn't giving her any. She survived that period because of you. In the end, the whole village knew.'

Mitsos opens his mouth and closes it again. He needs a moment. So many thoughts strive for precedence, clamouring for his attention, but the biggest sensation is the crumbling of a weight he didn't even know he had in his chest. Have the years of self-blame twisted his perceptions? No one spoke to him, surely that was condemnation.

'No one spoke to me.'

'What could we say? You had lost an arm from helping a friend, and you had lost the friend. We watched you struggle with him since we were boys but none of us helped. We just watched. We watched him take advantage and let you take the rap.' Theo offers a cigarette, but Mitsos does not trust his hand not to shake and tuts his refusal.

'Whose is the chicken, sausage, chips and lemon sauce?' No one answers Stella; they are all focused on Mitsos.

'Mitsos, you didn't think that we, that you, that …' But Theo cannot find the words.

'You are kidding me! Mitsos, man, you're the hero! Goodness knows where Marina and her kiddies would be without you. It is us that need to be ashamed. The whole village, we just stood by and you took the weight.'

Stella puts the plate in the middle of the table, wipes her hands on her apron and smiles at Mitsos. 'Idiot,' she says quietly, still smiling, and leaves the room to get the rest of the food.

Mitsos can feel with every beat of his heart his internal map of the world crumbling and in its place a non-condemning community that he can be part of, years of self-inflicted guilt melting away. All he can hear for a second is a large fly buzzing at the window.

'He did it on purpose, you know,' Mitsos says.

'What?' Cosmo asks with a mouthful of food. Stella comes back in with Mitsos' and Theo's food.

'We saw the explosive dropping, I reached for it, he reached for it, and in that split second we knew neither of us would catch it. He threw himself forward and had the time to smile at me when he realised his body was between me and the explosives.'

Mitsos allows his tears to fall. Cosmo stops eating. Theo puts his hand on Mitsos' shoulder. Stella, who has just entered the room with two plates, hears this last sentence and stops and stands in the middle of the room, tears welling in her eyes. The fly at the window stops buzzing to clean itself. The weather vane on the roof creaks round as the wind changes.

Mitsos' silent tears run.

'Stella, these sausages are burning,' Stavros shouts from the next room. Stella puts the plates in front of Mitsos and Theo, wipes her eyes on her apron, and hurries out of the room.

Mitsos stands up and goes to the toilet in the corner to wash his hand. He washes his face whilst he is there. He bears in mind how many years ago they are talking about and dries his eyes. He returns to find a whisky by his lunch. Theo and Cosmo are busy eating and Stella is not in the room.

'Cosmo, my friend.' Mitsos smiles and begins to eat. 'Now about my mail ...'

Chapter 18

Mitsos watches the rain streaming down the kitchen window It is warm but the rain is falling with some strength. He has seen it coming with the season, building slowing, promising, retreating. Today, all day, black storm clouds have been gathering and the water is drumming on the roof, a month's rain in half an hour. He gets up from the day-bed where he has slept again and opens the back door. The rain is pouring from the roof like a mountain stream in the winter. The wind blows the rain away from the door so Mitsos sits by the table and watches the ground soaking up the raindrops as quickly as they fall. It rained at the same time last year, just for an hour or so but not quite as hard or as strongly as this.

The appointment with his lawyer yesterday went well and things are progressing quickly. He needs to make up his mind what to do about Marina. Things have changed a bit. She spoke to him that day in the square and now he knows that she was aware who the envelopes were from. How many other things are not as he thought they were? He has a strange feeling of hope.

Thunder echoes over the hills and the rain increases its intensity; the noise is almost deafening. One of the empty flower pots is filling quickly. A couple of beetles swim in panic on the surface, finding twigs and leaves to hang on to. He watches the smooth packed-earth yard grow darker in colour, puddles forming as the ground becomes saturated. The almond branches are a deep black against a grey-blue flat sky at the horizon. There is a cat up one of the trees, curled in a hollow of two branches, the leaves making a roof protecting it from the rain. Another cat makes a dash for the barn. Mitsos still thinks of it as the donkey barn, although it is now inhabited by a solitary tractor, and has been for years.

Mitsos is about to get up and make coffee when he hears a 'ping'. The copper kettle hanging from a metal spike in the fireplace pings again as another rain drop hits it, the chimney open to the elements. Then Mitsos feels a drop on his face. He looks up; the open rafters are showing no pinpricks of light and yet a drop of rain has come in, not from the chimney. Another. And another. Mitsos stands up and takes a pan and waits for the next drop to show him where to position it. No sooner has he placed the pan to catch the drops than another leak becomes evident. He watches and finds the spot where the rain is coming in. He looks up again; there is no sign of light through the tiles. He takes a bowl this time and places it to catch the rain.

Outside the wind is picking up. He cannot hear it howling, the rain is too loud to hear the wind, but it is blowing the rain to a very steep angle. It rarely rains when the wind is blowing from this quarter, and when it does it is never this strong. Mitsos recalls gossip of global warming and melting icecaps, but it feels too far-fetched that this has anything to do with that. Besides, the problem of the leaks is too pressing to leave room for speculation on such a scale.

He reasons that the wind must be blowing the rain under the tiles. The pitch of the roof in the kitchen is such that the wind must be blowing diagonally across and down them, but the pitch in the front room goes the other way; the wind there will be blowing diagonally across and up under them. Mitsos goes through the narrow hallway and opens the door to the little-used front room. He stops in his tracks. Water is coming in from the rafters in several places, running along the beams before dripping onto the floor in many places. A cascade is flowing from under the trim round the window, the windows themselves a timpani of sound as the wind blows a hard rain against them.

Mitsos darts into action. He tries to carry two bowls at once and nearly drops them. He puts cups and bowls and saucepans and even his grandmother's soup tureen around the front room. He pushes the chairs into areas where there is no water, arranges a towel under the window and then considers the bedrooms. These are in the oldest part of the house which has evolved, over the centuries, to accommodate his ancestors. The newest part, with the kitchen and front room, is mostly plastered breeze-block, the bedroom nearest the kitchen, where he and he brothers slept when they were young is made of *plithra,* a baked mud brick as dense as concrete, and the end room, his parents' room, is built of stone. From the outside it all looks the same, all plastered over, painted white. On the inside, the bedrooms, although they too are plastered now, have holes in the base of the walls where insects, over time, have gnawed and scraped away the mud brick and the soft grouting between the stones, creating tiny channels from the outside to escape the heat and, no doubt, in the night scuttle to the kitchen and clean the floor of breadcrumbs. Tonight the holes will be refuge from the rain for a multitude of tiny beasties. Mitsos likes this thought.

In the heat of the summer his parents' bedroom keeps coolest and in the winter warmest. With the rain, the wind and the condition of the roof, in this, the oldest part of the house, his concern is that it might now also be the wettest. He passes his old bedroom and opens the door at right angles to it, into the cool stone-built room. He had moved from his childhood room into here one particularly hot summer, a few years after both his parents were dead. He had stayed right up until he got too lazy to even move from the kitchen at night. His day-bed became his night-bed when his limbs flopped into apathy with the introduction of regular nightcaps to blank his mind.

The stone room is cool and neat, the bed is made and smooth, the shutters closed, the rain drums on the roof. Normally the room is so quiet he can hear the death-watch beetle quietly scratching away at the timbers that hold up the roof. He looks about the dusty floor for dark patches, the sign of rain pooling, but there are none. He runs his hand across the bed on both sides but, amazingly, it is dry. The wardrobe door hangs open, his vests neatly folded and stacked from a time before he stopped caring.

He pictures Theo's clean shirt at lunch time. He strips off his undershirt and puts on a fresh one and takes down a shirt from one of the hangers. He used to silently ridicule his dad for wearing a vest and shirt in summer, but now he does the same, it stops his shirt sticking. The rain is getting even louder. He changes his trousers whilst he is there; he cannot remember when he last did so. Then he recalls what he was doing and decides to check the second bedroom.

In years not much has changed in there. Two beds are pushed up against the walls and one in the centre, with not even leg-room around it. White sheets cover the mattresses; the floor is dry except for a spot by the door. He puts his dirty vest there to soak up the moisture and returns to the kitchen and flings his dirty trousers over the back of a chair.

It is a while since he has shaved. He heats water on the camping stove by the sink, leaving his lighter next to it. The razor feels harsh and his bristles are tough; it takes a while. As he shaves, he listens to the sound of the rain hitting the assembled pots inside his house and wills it to stop. He puts the blade down to feel the smoothness of his jaw. He looks younger without the grey stubble, but he needs a haircut too. He smooths off the remaining shaving foam from around his ears with a tea towel which he then puts down, on top of his lighter.

Two of the pans in the front room are full so Mitsos pokes his head out of the back door for the bucket. It is by the donkey shed. The rain is so fierce that he will not make it there and back without being soaked. He takes his rubber fishing coat and hat from the wall, kicks off his slip-on plastic sandals, slips his feet into his rubber fishing boots, and with his sou'wester on his head and his long rubber coat around his shoulders he makes a dash for it. He grabs the bucket by the handle but it immediately comes away in his hand. He throws the handle into the barn. He lifts out the mop, but the head remains behind, an indentation in the stringy mess suggesting that something has been nesting in it at some point. He discards the mop handle and picks up the handle-less bucket, and as he runs back to the house he upturns it to discard the mop head.

He exhales as he steps back into the dry, puts the bucket down, and pulls off his hat and hangs up the coat, creating a pool of rain water on the floor. He takes the bucket through to the front room, but as he carries it he sees that the sun and time have cracked the plastic and it is useless.

'For goodness' sake.' He puts the bucket by the door and thinks for a minute before he takes a baking tray out of the range and puts it to catch the drips in the front room. There is nothing more he can do.

He sits back down on the kitchen chair, looking out at the rain, and crosses his legs; his foot jiggles. He knows he will need a mop and bucket as soon as the rain stops. The roads into town will be flooded. He will have to go to Marina's corner shop to buy one. He decides he needs a coffee first and returns to his little camping stove by the sink. He searches his pocket for his lighter but cannot find it. He looks on the mantelpiece but it is not there. He reaches across to the shelf behind the sink by the window for a box of matches; the soggy box disintegrates in his hand.

'Oh, Panayia!' he exclaims to his god and looks out at the rain, wondering if he should make a dash down to the square and get coffee either at Stella's or at the kafenio. The rain is easing. He hopes it will stop as quickly as it started. He gives it another five minutes.

It eases but does not stop. He puts on his fishing gear and closes the door behind him. He is aware that he has not fed the chickens, but they will survive. His neighbour takes care of his goats for a cut of the profits and the trees don't need much work at this time of year. He has organised his life well for a one-armed farmer. He smiles to himself as he hurries down the track to the road. He quite likes the rain.

The downpour has all but stopped as he reaches the square. He decides coffee comes before mops and buckets and he climbs the few steps into the kafenio. He begins to walk towards his table in the back corner when Theo approaches him with a coffee.

'Coffee?' he asks, and walks past him to a table in the front window-corner. 'There's a leak over your old table.'

There are a few other men sitting drinking coffee, and they acknowledge Mitsos with a nod of a head, or a raising of a finger. One says 'Yeia', a casual hello. Mitsos turns to the table in the window. This is where his Baba would sit. Theo walks past him again with a second coffee.

'You don't mind if I join you, do you?' he asks.

'Er, no.' Mitsos pulls off his sou'wester and his old-fashioned, thick yellow rubber-coated jacket. He hangs them on the coat rack at the back and notices one of the other old men is barefoot with his trousers rolled up, another is wet up to his ankles, sporting socks but no shoes.

'Everyone's been caught short, it seems.' Theo nods his mop of hair at the wet shoes lining the window's edge. 'Should have seen the rush to Marina's to buy buckets and mops the first time it eased. It was almost comical.'

'Oh, I am on my way there myself,' Mitsos says.

Theo looks at him but says nothing.

'I know it's early, but could I have a whisky with this coffee? A bit of courage is what I need.'

'No you don't.' Theo stands and retrieves a bottle of whisky and a glass from behind the counter. 'You want this in a separate glass or in your coffee?'

'Theo, can I ask you a question?' Mitsos looks over to Marina's shop through the rain.

'Sure.' Theo is smiling, looking out at the world, leaving the whisky bottle on the table for Mitsos to decide what to do with it himself.

'No, it's ok, never mind.' And he gulps down some coffee and stands to leave, dropping some coins on the table.

'Here anytime,' Theo reminds him.

'Actually, I might come back in a minute.' He looks at his coffee cup, still half full. 'I'll just go and get a bucket and mop from Marina's.'

'Ok, then get me a bucket whilst you're there, will you?'

Mitsos doesn't bother with his sou'wester or rubber coat. He makes a dash in the light rain across to the shop. The bell rings as he enters. Marina is sitting behind the counter, her feet up on a beer crate. The English woman, Juliet, from the old farmhouse, is talking to her. She turns and smiles, her hair no less gold in the artificial lighting.

'Hi, how are you?' she asks with a smile, picking up a new bucket she presumably has just bought.

'Fine, thank you,' Mitsos says politely.

'I imagine you are.' She smiles even more widely and leaves the shop.

Mitsos watches her leave and then turns to Marina, who stands.

The stare at each other before they both look away.

The rain starts again.

It intensifies suddenly.

'Bad weather,' Mitsos says.

'Sold all my buckets,' Marina replies.

'Oh, that's what I came for,' Mitsos says, and turns to leave, clearing his throat.

The skies open and the downpour over the square startles them both with its ferocity, and with it comes a sudden gust.

'The wind's changed direction,' Mitsos observes. The shop door, that the English lady left open, bangs shut. The leaves of the palm tree in the square are swept over to one side and, to Mitsos, the view through the half-glass door looks like pictures of hurricanes he has seen on TV; but as dramatic as the scene is, he knows the wind is nowhere near as strong. The man in the kiosk has boarded up his two side windows; he is now pulling in all the boxes of chewing gum. He is screwing up his face, so Mitsos knows the wind is blowing the rain even in there. His kitchen is going to be flooded, with the wind in this direction. The tiles might not even hold. He wonders how much of the ugly furniture will be salvageable.

The sky visibly darkens before everything is lit for a fraction of a second with lightning that bleaches the clouds. There is a crack of thunder. Marina jumps. The rain pouring off the roof is beginning to seep under the door. Marina pulls a beach towel from one of the shelves, releases it from its cellophane and hurries to pack it into the crack under the door.

'Can I help?' Mitsos asks as Marina rights herself. She has stopped the flow. They are standing very close.

Another flash of lightning, and they wait for the crack of thunder which follows sooner than either of them expects. The lights in the kafenio blink as the electricity is interrupted. The rain is too intense to make out anything clearly outside.

'Marina, whilst I am here I have something I need to talk to you about.' He can smell her shampoo.

Marina looks up to him, her mouth a hard line, the whites around her eyes so clear.

There is a tearing noise and water starts gushing in from the ceiling directly over a shelf of toilet rolls. In the moment that it takes to register, Mitsos recalls this was the area where Manolis had kept his whisky when it was his store room all those years ago, whisky and water. The situation is far from funny but the thought makes him chuckle.

'Panayia!' Marina squeaks and runs as fast as her legs will take her to the far corner where she grabs at the toilet rolls and throws them, one after the other, behind the counter, away from the leak. Mitsos leaps after her and he stacks the toilet rolls neatly. When the space below the hole has been cleared they peer up at the grey daylight beyond. At least one tile has slipped. The next lightning flash is accompanied almost immediately by a drawn-out rumble of thunder. The wind is howling now, and tiles can be heard lifting and falling back into place in several other parts of the roof.

'I've just sold my last bucket,' Marina wails as the rain, which is now pooling in the corner, begins its route across the floor to a dip in the centre. There is another noise, a smashing sound, and this time they both look up expectantly, as rain begins to course in down the corner by the flour, where Manolis had kept the dynamite. Mitsos blinks rapidly for a second to rid himself of the memories.

'Not the dried goods!' Marina shouts above the noise, and both of them hurry to the corner to empty the shelves, placing the flour with the magazines, the bird seed on the counter. Marina pulls a pack of dustbin liners off a shelf and opens them, and taking one out she begins to fill it with newspapers and magazines. Mitsos helps as much as he can to put all the paper goods into the bag she is holding. Once it is full, Marina opens a second bag. Mitsos struggles to open a bag by himself between his hand and his teeth, cursing quietly into the plastic. Finally it opens and he hangs it on a shelf corner and begins to transfer the sugar and the cake mixes, adding a few packets of flour that have made it to the same shelf into the sack until the hanging corner tears and the contents spill back on the floor. Marina is bagging the knitting-wool and the bread.

Mitsos tries again, the flimsy plastic stuck to itself so the bag will not open. Turning his back on Marina he chews it and pulls at the ragged edges with his teeth. Again he is letting Marina down. The plastic gapes, this time he holds one edge in his mouth as he salvages all that has fallen onto the wet floor. The flour is ruined. The sugar on top is ok.

The lightning flashes and they hear a crack so loud that Marina puts her hands to her ears. The thunder rolls louder and the two of them duck at the sound. Mitsos looks out of the window in the door but all he can see is rain. Marina has gone to the stockings and tights section when Mitsos looks up to see the central roof beam bending. He stares transfixed. It snaps with an awful splintering sound. The whole roof caves in and a tree branch follows through the rip straight towards him. He dives in front of the counter and all he can hear is ripping, tearing and splitting of wood and glass smashing, until there is no sound except the pounding of the rain.

'Marina!' he shouts but there is no answer. He stands and tries to orientate himself but the shop is a mass of rubble and he cannot tell where Marina was. The elements are suddenly in the room, the rain lashing from all directions. He feels dizzy and the air is filled with new smells from all the broken packets of food mixing with the rain. He starts toward the household products and gets as far as the crisps, which are still all lined up on the shelves. He rubs water from his eyes, his shirt is stuck to him, the empty sleeve flopping heavily. The branch is across the roof beam; both are a metre or so above the floor, held up by shelves and tins. The lightning flares again and the accompanying roar of thunder is immediate. Mitsos climbs over the beam, beyond which is a mess of foodstuffs, toiletries, cleaning products and rubble.

'Marina?' he shouts. He can hear his heart beat in his ears. The dark, cloud-filled sky is casting shadows. Nothing is clear, the lights have all gone out and the corners of the shop are in semi-darkness. He sees a movement and moves towards it only to jump back. It is a rat. He swallows and wipes more rain from his face. He is stepping on things that break and crush. He steps on something hard and round; he fears it is Marina's arm. His throat constricts, but reaching down he is relieved to find it is a torch. He flicks it on but there are no batteries in it and so he drops it. He feels along the floor and pulls up a packet. Ten-denier tights. He throws them behind him and waves his hand across the floor, feeling for what his eyes cannot see. He touches something soft and warm.

'Marina!' She makes a sound, and he laughs out loud with joy. He reaches under the beam along her arm to her shoulder; he lies on the floor and wriggles under the beam to see her face.

'Are you ok?'

'What do you think?' Marina smiles.

'I'll soon have you out.' Mitsos smiles in return.

The grating of stone upon stone silences them. The beam above them is sliding sideways. Mitsos begins to back out; there is a screech of wood, ripping, tearing, splintering. Mitsos scrabbles, the beam drops. Mitsos is hit full force across his back and he sinks to the floor, head to head with Marina.

'Mitsos!'

He coughs and wheezes; the wind has been knocked out of him. He blinks, looking into Marina's eyes. He gasps for air. His legs feels as though it is submerged in warm water and he isn't sure if he has fallen in a puddle, wet himself or if it is blood; flashes of Manolis pulling him into the sea.

'Mitsos, are you hurt?'

'I don't know. Are you?'

'I don't think so.'

Mitsos tries to move. He can scrabble about with his legs but the weight across his back is too heavy to move. He labours for breath.

'Can you move, Marina?' He hears some noises from down by her hips.

'No, my legs are stuck.'

'Hey! Mitsos, Marina.' It is Theo's voice. A light sweeps across the debris.

Mitsos tries to shout but he is gasping for air and cannot make a sound.

'Theo, we are here. The roof beam is on Mitsos, he cannot breathe.'

'Marina, when we were kids ...' Mitsos whispers and reaches for her hand.

'No you don't! Don't go soft on me now, Mitsos. I have seen it in the films, they go all soft and then they die, so pack it in, do you hear?'

'You silly woman.' Mitsos laughs and passes out.

Chapter 19

There is a smell of gunpowder and dog meat and Mitsos kicks and scrabbles, willing himself awake. The room is too bright. The gunpowder lingers and then distorts and becomes flowers, jasmine. He raises his arm to shield his eyes. The bright light dims as something is drawn across his field of vision. The shade brings focus and there is a man pulling a curtain. Mitsos looks down. He is in bed, with white sheets, a thin blue cover.

'How are we feeling?' the man asks.

'Where am I?'

'Have you a temperature?' He does not so much ask as command and Mitsos feels a hand on his forehead.

His senses begin to return. He recognises the signs of a village house, a rough wood floor, a door made from floorboards. He tries to recall why he is there. The last time he was in a strange bed it was after the dynamite. His arm! He feels his shoulder, but the wound is not fresh, the shape of the nub familiar.

'Rain's stopped,' the man comments.

An image of a tree flashes though his mind, the crushing pain across his back, and …

'Marina!' he shouts, pushing the hand away from his forehead.

'Steady on, she's fine, she's next door.' The man leaves the room.

Mitsos looks around the room. There is a chest of drawers and the narrow iron bed he is on. The walls are stone, unplastered, the mortar in between is crumbly, the floor bare, a village house that has not been modernised. There is one window, with so many layers of paint the corners are rounded. The cotton curtain is drawn, the sun strong behind it. Mitsos tries to move and a pain darts across his back on the left and down the front on the right. He puts his hand to his ribs; he can feel that he is trussed up. He moves a leg at a time to check them. His left one feels bruised but they both work.

He pushes himself up slowly and sits for a while, replaying what happened in the shop, gaining consciousness, orienting himself. Then he stares at the curtain across the window and becomes impatient. He does not feel unwell, but bruised to the point gasping for breath. Swinging his legs over the side of the bed, he tries to stand. The world feels like a rocking boat and he bends his knees to compensate for the motion, his hand holding the edge of the bed. The swells subside and he takes a tentative step. There is air round his legs. He looks down; he has no trousers on. He feels his legs to see where they hurt. He has a bandage round his right knee and he can see blood soaking through. He looks about and sees a dressing gown at the end of the bed. It is a thick navy-blue velour. He inspects it and finds in the pocket a receipt. Mitsos stares at it and realise it must be Theo's. Who else would order 20 kg of coffee grounds and 30 bottles of ouzo? He wonders if Theo does his book keeping in bed.

'Bless him,' Mitsos mutters, and puts it on,

The landing is plastered white but the floorboards are bare. The ceiling light flickers, neither on nor off. Mitsos keeps his hand in contact with the wall, just in case, and looks in the next room, a single brass bed with someone in it facing away from the door. Mitsos enters the room and looks over the blanket lump. It is Marina; she is sleeping.

'Yeia sou, Marina.' He greets her softly, even though her eyes are closed. He looks around the room. There is a stool by the wall and he drags it next to Marina's bed.

'It seems every time I come near you I cause you pain,' he states as Marina sleeps on.

A man enters the room. 'Ah, you're up. How do you feel? You broke a few ribs, I'm afraid, not much we can do about that but they will heal.' He takes a stethoscope from round his neck and puts it in the bag he is holding.

'Is she ok?' Mitsos asks. His face tries to disintegrate into tears but he will not let it.

'Well, she has a concussion and a broken leg from the accident but she is mostly just shaken. I was wondering if she has had a heart attack.'

'But she's not even fifty!'

'Coming up to fifty, a bit overweight, unfit and in a bad accident.' The man smiles as if he is imparting good news.

'Well, has she?'

'I don't think so, but I have taken a blood sample and I will check for high levels of enzymes to be sure.' He smiles even more broadly and leaves the room, his steps echoing down the wooden stairs.

Mitsos looks back at the sleeping Marina. Her face is still turned away from him. He senses a tear welling on his lower lid again and wipes it away with the back of his hand, biting his bottom lip to bring him to his senses.

'Marina, I have so much to say to you.' He sniffs and falters; he should say it to her face, not when she is sleeping. But there is a deep comfort in her deafly being there. A confession without consequences.

'In some ways we have changed, you and I. Life does that.' He draws himself up and rubs his stump. He should have said all this years ago. He dubs himself a coward, both then and now. 'I was gutless. I had the chance to marry you, give you a good life, I turned it down.' He struggles to keep his voice from quivering. He rubs his face in the crook of his dressing gown sleeve. 'I have never been able to say to you how sorry I was for that, or for the day Manolis died.' Mitsos blinks a few times and swallows, but his chest spasms as he fails to control his emotion. He holds out his hand to stroke Marina's hair, but when his fingers make contact with the first strands he watches them just pick bits of debris from the hair instead. He pulls the big pieces out and he puts them in the dressing gown pocket, not knowing what else to do with them.

He must tell her. This is the safest time he will ever get. 'But what I really need you to know is I think

I was angry when he urged me to throw it to him.' He waits for a response he hopes won't come. Marina makes no movement. He continues. 'You know how he was, he always pushed me, pushed and pushed until I was no longer sure which were his thoughts and which were my own.' Mitsos shakes his head gently as if that will clear his mind now. 'I feel that on that day maybe I lost it, maybe I wanted to harm him, maybe I wanted the dynamite to explode, maybe I wanted to shock him, or at least stop him bullying me.' He screws up his eyes and drops his head. 'There is no sorry big enough for that, Marina. But I am truly sorry.'

'And I am not sleeping,' Marina says.

Mitsos sits up straight with a start and the pain shoots through his ribs. He groans and Marina turns her head. 'Are you ok?'

'Hurts,' he gasps, bending over to ease the pain. 'I broke some ribs.' Doubled up, he looks across at her, looking for condemnation in her eyes but finds none. 'How do you feel?' he asks politely, slowly straightening, as if his monologue never happened.

'Sore, my leg aches. They have given me pain killers so it isn't too bad.'

'Are we in Theo's house?'

'No, this is upstairs at my house.' Mitsos is relieved to know that the tree has not hit the house as well as the shop, the two being only separated by a courtyard.

'Oh!' He can think of nothing else to reply.

'So, you were saying?'

Mitsos quickly looks down at his dressing gown. His head swims from the sudden movement and he puts his hand up to steady it but moving his arm feels impossible, his ribs sear with pain and his lungs are restricted in their movement. Marina waits until his breathing is steady.

'Mitsos, I don't blame you, and I wasn't sad.' Mitsos looks up in stages. He is not sure he can meet her eyes. 'It was shocking but it was not the worst day of my life. In fact, after the initial horror, it was a relief.' Mitsos' jaw drops open a little. 'Yes, can you imagine the guilt I felt, this was my children's father?'

They both pause silent in their own thoughts.

Mitsos can hear the quiet, steady, scratching, munching sound of a death-watch beetle in Marina's ceiling, in more than one place. He wonders if the whole village is infested. He can hear people downstairs, or maybe they are out on the street. Everything feels a little confusing. He sits without thought for a while.

'Marina, can I ask you something?' Marina nods, but her features become immobile as if she is bracing herself. 'That day, when we first went fishing, did you say that the best outcome would be if …'

'Shhh!' Marina hisses, and closes her mouth firmly. She is silent for a long time. Mitsos shifts his weight, almost constantly, to try and take some pressure off his ribs. 'You think that I didn't wonder, didn't worry, that you might have taken me literally?' She closes her eyes tightly. Mitsos can see a tear squeezed from the corner of each. He looks around for a handkerchief. Marina pulls from under her pillow one with black butterflies embroidered on it and she wipes her eyes. 'Hearing that it might have happened because you were cross, although it burdens you, gives me such relief. To hear your confession without my name being in there!'

'You do think I killed him, then?'

'God, no! I am quite aware of how Manolis pushed and pushed until your mind was no longer your own. If he wanted you to throw the damn thing at him he would have talked on until you did, using his twisted logic, igniting your emotions. He had had years of practice on you, he knew exactly what to do. God no, Mitsos, you are not to blame.'

'But I did throw it.' Mitsos' chest feels heavy; he wants to let it sink, his shoulders to roll forward, but pain keeps him as he is, sitting stiffly upright.

'Let it go, Mitsos.' She puts her hand out to pat his arm, but withdraws it as his arm is on the other side; touching his ribs would be too personal. She blushes.

'But if you don't blame me, why did you not speak to me all those years?'

Marina starts to laugh. It has a bitter, sad edge, but her bruises resist the movement and she sucks in through pursed lips and holds her side. As she relaxes, she says, 'How could I talk to you when I thought that, well, that you had, that I …' She pauses to reflect. 'You reminded me of what I had said. I feared that was what had killed him.'

'So you did think I had killed him!'

'No, I thought I had killed him.' Marina's pupils are wide as her truth is revealed; she looks into Mitsos' eyes to face her fear. Their gazes lock, each in their own guilt, each searching for reassurance.

'That's enough of that!' They both turn to Theo in the doorway. 'It was an accident!'

Theo looks from one to the other and shakes his head. 'That man was so good at making other people responsible for his life that you even believe you were responsible for his death! He's dead, in all honesty it seems like no one cares, so forget about him! By the way, the colour suits you,' he says, looking at Mitsos.

'What?' Mitsos asks.

'The colour, the navy blue suits you.' He pulls at the lapel of the dressing gown. 'So, do either of you want coffee?'

They both nod and Theo leaves the room.

Marina slowly manoeuvres herself into a sitting position. Mitsos tries to help but it causes him too much pain.

'Can you draw the curtain, Mitsos, let some light in?' Mitsos stands slowly and shuffles to the window. His knee hurts and it is hard to take in air without his ribs complaining.

'We are in a bit of a mess, aren't we?' he says by way of conversation.

'Well, we are alive.' Marina sighs as he shuffles back and sits down again.

Mitsos tries to think of something to say. For years he has been dreaming of a scenario, perhaps not exactly like this, but similar, time alone with Marina, time to talk, to explain, but now it is reality he cannot think of anything to say to her.

'Although I am actually in one heck of a mess now, what with the oranges not being paid for this year …' Marina says suddenly

'What?' Mitsos asks.

'Yes, with all this struggle in the economy, everybody's broke. I sold to that new man, from Athens this year, you know, that scoundrel Mr Froutokleftis. I am not the only one. Others sold to him too, because he gave a good rate, and none have been paid. No one can afford to take him to court so it's a thief's market.' Marina laughs at her own turn of phrase but it is a sad, tired laugh. Mitsos remembers a time it had happened before, when they had both blamed Manolis.

'Have you considered telling the authorities?'

'How can I prove it? Anyway, it's done.' She looks far out of the window. 'And now with the shop gone what am I to do?' But she says this quietly, as if Mitsos is not in the room. He shuffles in his seat and wonders if he should leave. Theo returns with some well-timed coffee and asks if they are hungry. The both shake their heads.

'Widow Katerina, in her usual organising manner,' Theo chuckles gently, 'has arranged a rota in the village.' Marina groans slightly as she smiles. 'So someone will bring food twice a day until you are up and about.'

'Oh no, there's no need,' Mitsos says.

'Mitsos, you barely look after yourself when you are well, let people take care of you a little for a change.' Marina says. Mitsos' eyebrows rise with the implication that Marina has noticed something about the way he lives his life. He can feel the colour in his cheeks and picks at some fluff on the sleeve of his dressing gown, shifting his weight again to ease the pressure on his ribs. No position is comfortable

'And I'll pop over and bring coffee,' Theo offers.

They hear him leaving, trotting down the stairs along the hall, and a slam as the door is closed behind him, a patter of leather on tarmac as he disappears across the square.

The hours turn into days and Mitsos can feel his ribs healing, but slowly. Marina's daughters have visited and he has finally been introduced. His conversations with Marina become easier and easier, and they talk for hours, sometimes discussing their mutual history, or current affairs, sometimes observations about nature. They find they have a lot in common. Mitsos cannot believe that life has finally thrown him together with Marina. He is experiencing being happy, they get on so well. But something is missing.

'So what exactly do you do all day if you have arranged for your goats to be taken care of? Your oranges only need a little work until harvest and that's down to the orange pickers, same with your olives. Your days must be pretty empty?'

'They don't feel it. I go up and see the chickens and then ...' Mitsos thinks for a moment and wonders what he does do all day. 'I go to the kafenio for coffee and then on to Stella's for lunch.'

'She got a rum husband. I feel for her.'

'Nice lady, though. I often sit and talk to her.'

'I've never really spoken to Stella. What does she like to talk about?'

'Oh, everything and anything. She is very understanding, cuts up my food for me.' His voice tapers to a whisper. He wonders what Stella is doing now and how she is coping with her husband and the foreign girl. It is hard to remember how attractive Stavros was before he got such a huge round stomach. The bigger it got, the more pushy and unpleasant his flirting seemed, his blue eyes bloodshot and bulging from his ruddy complexion. Funny that, when he was slim and good looking he didn't seem so lecherous, or maybe that was just Mitsos' perspective.

'What are you thinking about?'

But Mitsos does not hear. His mind is on Stella and her position. Poor Stella, he wonders what he can do to help. Surely he must be able to do something. Does Stavros give her enough house-keeping money? At least they do not have children that she has to provide for like Marina did. Mitsos reels at the comparison and then pushes it aside.

No, he will find a way to make Stella's life more pleasant. He will find the times when Stavros goes to town and spend more time with her, talk to her, show that someone cares. Maybe he can find a way to take her to a taverna in town without upsetting Stavros, or having to take him too. If she is still having lessons with that English lady, Juliet, he could take them both out together, a thank-you to Juliet for her translation and a chance to spoil Stella.

'Hey, what are you thinking?' Marina breaks into his daydream.

'Oh, I was just thinking about Stella.' Mitsos looks at his fingernails, not sure if he wants to talk about what he was thinking. 'It seems she needs a friend,' he says vaguely. 'I don't think Stavros appreciates her as much as she deserves.' He can feel his heartbeat. He is talking to Marina, whom he has loved from a distance for over thirty years, about a woman with whom he spends most of his time with when he is not alone. He cannot deny he misses Stella.

'Well, you are good at being a good friend.' Mitsos hears this but he can feel some anger stirring inside him. He has tried to be a good friend to Marina and it has brought him nothing but pain. He is sick of being a good friend. Damn it, he wants someone to be a good friend back, someone who will listen to him, share his woes, help him with his life. Like Stella does. He looks up and out of the window. He has a swelling feeling in his chest and a need to see her. He feels as if he is suddenly going a little bit mad, his thoughts becoming irrational. He can just see the edge of her shop through Marina's window. His heart is now loud enough to hear inside his ears. His mouth has gone dry so he looks down at his coffee, which will be difficult to drink as he is holding the saucer. It hurts to lift his arm but he does so in stages and sips the coffee off the top with the little cup still sitting on its plate. Once the coffee level drops he can probably balance it on his knee and lift the cup off. That is one thing Stella would immediately think of, to help him with that, but Marina is oblivious.

He looks at Marina, who is staring at the bedspread as she drinks her coffee. His pledge comes to mind; he is haunted by the promise, he cannot leave it unfulfilled. If he is not true to his word then what is he? A man without integrity, a rogue, a Manolis? His foot starts jiggling. He looks up to the ceiling, he lets his head roll backward and rest against the wall with a bump. He feels unsettled, his mind is spinning and nothing is making any sense. His thoughts juggle, he can almost understand his own dilemma and at the same time almost touch the answer, but actually there is nothing but confusion going on in his mind and his heart. He bangs his head gently against the wall. On the last knock, with surprising ease, quite without effort, everything slots into place. If Manolis is gone and Marina is provided for, then he has fulfilled his pledge, but also there is a way – and here he congratulates himself and begins to breathe easily and then even deeply, as far as his bruised ribs will allow, because he can bring her pride, allow her to walk with her head held high – he can bring Manolis back from the dead and make him provide for her himself, give her the feeling she is a wife worth providing for, that she had a husband that took care of her, a husband who assured her future.

And it won't be a lie, well not completely.

And once his pledge is fulfilled maybe he can be some help to Stella, poor Stella, someone needs to make a pledge to her. He thinks of all the smiles he has received from her, the care she takes when she cuts his food, the hours they have spent talking. The disinterest she has in Stavros, the hurt he has seen in her eyes when Stavros flirts in public. The joy he has seen there when he comes for his lunch. The eye contact. He is not wrong, slow maybe, but not wrong.

Mitsos smiles to himself. He suddenly feels a great deal better. He balances the saucer on his knee and lifts off the cup and sips it until it is drained. Theo does make the best coffee. He replaces the cup, takes hold of the saucer and stands, slowly.

'Are you going?'

'I was just thinking I felt quite a bit better. I thought I might try to get dressed today.'

'Well, you are grinning like a gypsy. Something must be feeling right.' Marina smiles back at him. He delights in her face, so familiar and yet so unknown after all these years. She isn't the same person he remembers at all. He wonders if she changed in all the years they never spoke or if he never really did know her. But his mind is made up, and he knows what he must do to right all the wrongs in his and her world, and then he can start with a fresh sheet, like his little nephew.

It must be nearly time for his baptism by now.

Chapter 20

'I am not going to stop you, but I have had broken ribs too, and the longer you rest them the quicker they heal. How's your knee?' Theo asks.

'It's sore, but I have had worse.' Mitsos tries to hold his trousers up by trapping them between his hip and the wall so he can zip them. He has lost weight since he has been laid up and putting the baggy old things on one-handed is a struggle.

Theo steps forward to help but steps back again as he hears the zip.

'What? You're going to do my flies up for me now?' Mitsos laughs. His eyes glint a little.

'Good to see you fighting back for a change, Mitsos.' He takes a cigarette out of his pocket and offers one.

'No thanks, I don't think I smoke any more. It's been so long now,' Mitsos says as he smooths his empty sleeve flat and tucks it in his waist band.

He pops in to say farewell to Marina but this time she really is sleeping. He strokes her hair but it is with the touch of a friend, not the stroke of a lover.

The effort of going downstairs hurts his ribs and he leans on the wall and does his best to slide down, his feet catching up.

The outside air feels fresh even though the sun is shining and the heat is already building. He can hear the birds in the bushes and children laughing and the sound of kicking as they play football by the church.

Mitsos smiles and wishes he could skip or jump or just run, but his ribs won't allow it and so he whistles instead. Turning towards the square he catches his first glimpse of the corner shop, or what little remains of it. The tree has been removed; judging by the sawdust, cut up for firewood. The roof tiles litter the area and it now looks like any one of a thousand decaying forgotten buildings in Greece. There is no sign that it was a shop; all the goods have been removed without a trace, leaving just rubble and dust and one or two broken beer bottles. But Mitsos does not feel sad; he is in a position to fulfil his pledge to improve Marina's life. He crosses the square.

Cosmo, who has been feeding the chickens whilst he recovered, has left the gate to the track open and a rather forlorn dog runs out to bark at him.

'Sorry, dog, but this is my patch. Shoo!' He waves his arm at the dog, which runs away up towards the pine trees on top of the hill.

The roof of the house does not look too bad from this side but he knows the front will have taken the force of the storm. He begins to pick his way up the front path but the roses have grown over it and the bougainvillea, sharp with thorns, is in full blossom. He will have it cleared. The view of the village from there is just lovely, laid out like a map, the world at his feet. The bench by the front door, covered in bindweed, is still there offering a place to sit and ponder. He returns to the back yard and pushes the door to the house open. The pans and bowls are where he left them, looking strangely out of context; the water gone, evaporated by the heat. He goes through to the front room and is greeted by, but not surprised at, the mess. Several tiles have blown off and some of the supporting laths split; there is a small hole in the roof and his furniture has water stains and jagged tide marks where the rain found a path.

He raises his eyebrows and decides he will just throw it all out; it was ugly and old-fashioned anyway, and it reminds him of his mother's hopes for visitors competing with his Baba's temper, which assured that there would be none, at least none that would warrant opening up the 'best' room. Neighbours who dropped in for a chat and a coffee when his father was out in the fields did not fit into this category.

He opens the drawer with all the bits and pieces where he had found the newspaper clippings. His bank book is still there; he had thought that was where he had seen it, and is happy that his memory had not been deceiving him. He had opened a bank account when he was in his twenties but had found little use for it. Everyday transactions were conducted using cash. Cheques were used by businesses, post-dated and passed from one to another, like promissory notes. A useless system that impeded everyone's cash-flow. He has not used the account since the first month or two after he opened it. He rubs the cover against his shirt and looks at it. He opens the stiff-backed book with a little difficulty to find he has five hundred drachmas still in the account, worth about a euro now. It amuses him that it hasn't been used since the drachma. He pockets the book and takes some money from the sugar jar on his way out. He would like to go up and see the chickens but he is excited about his newly formulated plan; the birds can wait. He sets off at as brisk a pace as he can manage to the bus stop in the village.

'Another five minutes,' Vasso calls from the kiosk.

Mitsos looks up and down the street to be sure; there is no sign of any bus. 'Oh!' he replies. 'Thanks.'

The bus pulls round the corner early and one person gets off. Mitsos climbs the steps and pays the driver,

'Hey hey, if it isn't the hero! Glad to see you up and about,' the bus driver greets him. Mitsos scans his face but cannot place him. He pulls at his shirt collar, nods in acknowledgement and looks for a seat. Travelling by bus gives Mitsos an elevated view. He sees Stella's shop is open but he does not see Stella. On the outskirts of the village he can see down into people's yards, all concreted over, swept with flowers in pots. As they move into the open country between the village and the town he looks across the tops of the orange trees which line so much of the road; he feels like a god, all-seeing.

Concrete apartment blocks mark the outskirts of the small metropolis, three and sometimes four storeys high. He remembers them being built in the seventies. The balconies are covered with shrubs and flowers and trees in pots, but for all these efforts they are still ugly to Mitsos' eyes and he looks down into his lap until they pass into the older part of town where tiled roofs top grand stone buildings.

The bus stops and Mitsos gets out last so he can take his time and avoid any jarring.

The bank is close to the bus stop. It has had an electric door put in since his last visit. He tries to push the door open but it is locked. He steps back and sees a green button; he pushes this and can hear the door click open. There is a second inner door and negotiating the two proves to be a matter of waiting and pushing another button at the right moment. A line of people queuing to be served watch him. Emotionless faces, bored and expressionless. They look away as he finally gains entrance. Mitsos can feel his cheeks glowing, embarrassed at his inability to negotiate the door. Mitsos wonders how Adonis can live in the cold environment of town, where people don't know each other, where faces are blank.

'Mr Mitsos, how nice to see you.' A man in a suit shuffling papers behind a desk stands up and comes round, his hand stretched in front of him ready to shake a warm greeting. 'So nice of you to call in person. Would you like to see the manager?' He ushers Mitsos to a lift recessed in the wall. The people in the queue are staring at him again, one with an open mouth, two whispering to each other as they watch his every move. The man in the suit presses the button to call the lift and opens the door for Mitsos.

The lift is slow. Mitsos has time to see himself reflected in every mirrored side of the interior, his hair shaggy round his collar, his oversized trousers done up with a leather belt that is twisted and worn with ragged edges. He looks very much the farmer. He is about to say to himself that a farmer is what he is when the lift stops.

The door opens into a light open room with a big desk at one end. Low square ceiling tiles, with the occasional one missing to house a reflective lighting unit. Bank logos framed on the walls, blue padded chairs, industrial carpet.

'Ah! Mr Mitsos, how nice of you to call.' Mitsos is not used to being treated with such regard; he finds it all a little fake. He puts his hand in his pocket and remains standing when the manager sweeps his hand to offer him a seat.

'Coffee?' A girl appears from nowhere and asks.

'No thanks.' The girl draws out the chair for him and smiles, inviting him to sit down. Mitsos does not smile back but he sits. He feels like a rabbit edging nearer and nearer to the trap, wary and untrusting, until … snap!

Mitsos offers his bank book but it is waved away as if he is beyond all that.

'So, your account looks healthy. The final balance has come in.' The bank manager stares into the computer screen; his cufflinks glint as he taps his keyboard. Writing out the amount on a Post-it note, he slides the paper across the desk to Mitsos, letting go of it as it levels beside his name plate, Mr Pseftico. Mitsos absorbs the name slowly. The manager beams, one hand on the other, rubbing his own knuckles. Mitsos notices there is a line of biro on one of his shirt cuffs.

He picks up the paper and reads, consciously keeping his face passive. He pushes his chair a little away from his desk and crosses his legs.

'Can you make me a cheque out? To Marina …'

'Marina?' Mr Pseftico sounds delighted. 'From the corner shop in the village? Marina who came from this town?' Mitsos nods; the bank manager smiles, relaxing. 'Her parents lived next door to us back then, did you know?' He grins broadly, as if glad to have found some common ground.

'For this amount.' Mitsos ignores Mr Psefticos' social interaction and takes a pen from the pen holder on his desk and writes in the corner of his jotter before scribbling it out and looking around him to assure himself that he is not overlooked. The bank manager, having read the amount, looks at him in horror and then a sly grin spreads across his face and he nods in a knowing way.

'It is hers by right,' Mitsos clips. He is surprised by how authoritative his voice sounds. The manager stops smiling and makes out the cheque. Mitsos examines it, folds it and puts it in his shirt pocket, noting that the stitching has come away a little down one side. He smooths it flat against his chest.

'Something else. Would you happen to know how much a good suit costs?' he asks, looking Mr Pseftico up and down.

The manager's eyebrows rise. He seems to sum up the situation and leans back in the chair, his hands folded on his belly. 'A really nice suit from "Panomiti" can cost anything up to six hundred euros; a pair of trousers is less, obviously. He also sells some nice shirts, they cost round about a hundred and fifty. But of course ...'

Mitsos sniffs and shakes his head. 'Can you give me a thousand in cash then?'

The manager counts out the cash and begins to tell Mitsos how delighted he is to have him as a costumer and he must be sure to give his regards to Marina, who, if she doesn't have a bank account, must be sure to pop in and he will help her out, and any other friends Mitsos would like to point his way. It is so nice to have a good calibre of clientele.

Mitsos is glad of the quiet safety of the lift, but looks himself over again in the mirrored box and is a little shocked for the second time at his unruly appearance.

He steps out at the bottom and an entirely new set of blank faces waiting for the teller stare at him. He struggles with the timing of the buttons on the door going out, and releases a huge sigh as he finally escapes.

He is not at all sure if he wants to go to 'Panomiti' but decides the walk will be pleasant, through the narrow streets, bougainvillea dripping from stems as thick as his arm, growing up the sides of the buildings, reaching as high as second-floor balconies, some of them spanning the street, bougainvillea arches.

Through the town square lined with a dozen cafes, the tables and chairs creep toward the central point where, for now, children play ball and gypsies sell balloons to Greeks with children and hand-held battery fans to the tourists.

Out of the other end of the square, back into narrow roads, he comes to a halt. He stands outside 'Panomiti' looking at the shiny shoes with labels from England. The pinstriped shirts look crisp and clean, and he wonders how long they would stay that way living as he does. The trousers don't look like they would last more than a week and the shoes are completely impractical for the track to his house. There is a rather nice tweed jacket, but it will be a while before it is cool again. He walks on and goes into a shop he knows, which is used by farmers.

The stock is in wooden drawers and boxed in the back. In the front are three chairs and a table with old magazines. If you didn't know it you would have no idea what the shop sold.

He is greeted perfunctorily. His size is estimated and he struggles to try things on, the man offering no help. Mitsos buys a good solid pair of shoes, two pairs of decent trousers, and five shirts of the best quality they stock. Once he has tried on one of the shirts and the trousers he does not change back again. His ribs are aching and he wishes he had some painkillers with him.

In the changing cubicle there is a free-standing full-length mirror. He does not recognise himself with the new clothes on but he does notice, again, his shaggy hair, and he heads straight to the barber's. The barber's shop offers a continuous stream of commentary on matters as important and diverse as football, politics and local gossip for no charge, and a serviceable short back and sides for eight euros.

He feels he has done all he should for a man in his position. Suited and booted with short hair, he sets off for the bus stop. He stops as he catches someone walking beside him and is startled to find it is his own reflection in a cafe window. Again, he does not recognise himself, his baggy trousers replaced by a pair that fit, his threadbare shirt for a crisp one with sharp creases. He feels distinctly uncomfortable. Men like this are noticed, they have a voice, rights even. He suddenly feels too visible. With this thought, he watches his shoulders hunch over. An edge of defiance brings a smile: the boy he once was loves the new image. He is as much alive as the next man. He stands tall. For so long he has felt he deserved no voice, no place in the community. He smooths his hand over his hair. It was not all as it seemed; people do not condemn him. He turns from the glass and walks on, his gait a little more upright, his balance a little more sure.

He feels in his pocket where there is still a ridiculous amount of money. He wonders now why he asked for so much cash, and considers that he must get a better grip if he doesn't want to make a fool of himself.

He looks out over the bay. The tiny church atop the little island looks idyllic, the sea beckoning, the view hot and seductive. He feels lucky to have been born here. He walks on and his attention is drawn to a picture in a shop window of the pyramids in Egypt. It occurs to him how much of the world there is to see, and he wonders whether if he saw it all he would still think he was lucky to be born in his village in Greece.

There is a girl smoking in the doorway of the shop.

'Amazing, aren't they?' she says.

'Yes, indeed.'

'We have a group going next month if you fancy seeing them?'

Mitsos is about to pat his trouser pocket to indicate the problem is not the offer or the girl but that he has no money, a habit of sixty-five years, when he stops himself. His pockets are bulging.

He allows the girl, who introduces herself as Anna, to draw him deeper into the conversation and they spend the rest of the morning talking. Although she is Greek, she was born in Birmingham, England, and she has a very strange Greek accent.

'I wonder if I am very ungrateful, wanting to go off and enjoy new horizons, not to be content with what I have?' Mitsos shifts his gaze back inside, to a poster of the Great Wall of China.

'Oh no!' Anna seems almost offended. 'No, a desire to see more of the world only goes to prove that you still have a spark of life.' Anna neatens some papers on the counter. She looks up as Mitsos. 'I mean if you read one book and enjoy it and then read a second book it doesn't make you ungrateful for the first, does it? The enjoyment of the first is what makes you want more. It shows you are alive!'

In a rash moment he allows her to arrange two tickets to Rhodes, where he will board a cruise ship for Egypt. There are no direct cruises to Egypt, she tells him.

'But on the bright side, it will allow you to see Santorini and Rhodos, both beautiful islands,' Anna enthuses.

She arranges a week in Egypt followed by a flight to Morocco, with another week's stay. Mitsos feels thrilled and just a little scared, having never flown before, or for that matter been any further than down the coast from his village. He hasn't even been to Athens, so none of these plans feel very real.

'You'll be home within a month, with memories that will last a lifetime,' Anna says, and then reminds him to pass by with his passport.

'You do have a passport?' she asks. Mitsos frowns. 'Not to worry, it will take about a week, go to the police station ...' She reaches for a pen and paper. 'I'll make a list of the documents you will need.' She scribbles and hands it to him.

'When it arrives I will need the details and those of your travel partner so I can finalise the arrangements.' She wishes him good day.

Mitsos feels dizzy with emotion as he continues the walk towards the bus stop for the village. Excitement and fear mingle in his stomach. He cannot believe what he has done. Not having the nerve to even take Stella out for dinner, he doesn't know why he feels sure that Stella will come, but he does. Will she have a passport? Instinctively, he knows this is going to work out. Maybe just as a friend but, he decides, that is ok. In fact more than ok; he would no longer be alone.

She has intimated that it is only through lack of choice that she has stayed with Stavros. He gently chastises himself for being so slow on the uptake; he feels wonderfully happy and free. The tickets go in his new shirt pocket next to the cheque and he indulges himself, forgoing the bus, and takes a taxi home. Besides, he is sure he has missed the last bus and he cannot face the walk with his bags of shopping and aching ribs, even though he feels so light.

The taxi driver provides his own opinions on football and politics, contradicting the barber, and wishes Mitsos well at the village square. He has the greatest urge to run straight to the take-away and tell Stella everything, but he also likes the feeling of savouring what he is going to do. He waves at her from a distance and she waves back and smiles. She looks happy to see him, he is not wrong. He taps his pocket to confirm everything is in place and makes his way up to his land.

He is surprised to see his house looks the same. In his mind, the mess of weeds and tangle of thorns has gone from the front of the house and it has been repainted a clean sparkling white. He makes do with the back door and goes to his camp stove to make coffee. He lifts the tea towel from the side to fold it.

'Ah, that's where you are,' he says as he picks up his lighter. He puts two teaspoons of coffee and sugar in his ‘briki’ pan and fills it with water from a bottle. The tap water comes from his well and isn't good to drink. He watches the mix move, the granules floating around, then dancing and bubbling. He picks the pan off swiftly and lets the writhing brown liquid settle for a moment before pouring it into a tiny cup.

‘Perfect.’ He takes it through to the spoilt front room and balances it on the arm of a rain-stained chair so he can open the front door. The door is fast but the bolt slides open more easily than he expects. It opens with cracks and groans, insects darting from the uncovering of the hinges.

The village is spread before him. He pulls some of the bind-weed from the bench but it is a big job. He takes a cushion from indoors and puts it down on the seat outside. He can see the sea sparkling both towards the town and along beyond the village, a church-crowned hill interrupting the continuum of the view. The orange groves seem to want to march inland forever, only coming to a halt where they surrender control to distant mountains. Everyday sounds drift up from the village below. A cockerel crowing, dogs barking, a tractor amongst the oranges, a car engine idling, its door wide open by the kiosk where the driver stands to be served. A child laughing, a baby crying. Life as always, just carrying on.

The sun on his face would be uncomfortably hot were it not for a gentle breeze that tempers the heat to a warmth that is pleasant. When it is this hot the sky turns a deep dark blue and the rising air softens the edges of everything in the valley, the haze of the warmth seems to make everything glow. He remains, soaking in this view of his homeland for a long time, only taking a break to make more coffee before drifting into staring once again. The sun begins to sink and the sky near the horizon contrasts yellow to the blue. The hills in the distance become two-dimensional paper cut-outs in all shades of blue, deep to light as they recede into the sky.

The noises of the village quieten, the sound of shutters being closed takes over from the sound of voices, the sun sinks a little further, the divide between ground and sky takes on an orange glow and the hills turn softly purple, warm hues and a haze as dusk becomes night. The air cools rapidly although it is still light enough to see.

Mitsos sits and sips his coffee. A gentle movement startles him, a delicate snapping and crunching under small feet. Perhaps a cat? He sits still so as not to scare it. In amongst the roses and the weeds and the bougainvillea something is edging towards him. He stays very still, until all of a sudden his broody hen struts onto the path, and then disappears into a cluster of weeds and settles.

'So that's where you're laying,' he says, but takes no action, sitting longer to finish his coffee.

Sleepy, Mitsos decides it is time for bed. The sooner he sleeps the sooner he can go and see Marina – and Stella.

Chapter 21

He awakes to sunshine squeezing between the louvres in the shutters. He made the effort to go to bed in the stone room last night. It feels good to be in a big bed, with crisp sheets. He loves the early morning cool, a slight sharp edge to the air, almost enough to warrant putting on a vest but, really, just too delicious on the skin. He kicks off the sheet and allows the air to cool him all over. He still feels sleepy and considers turning over and going back to sleep when his plans for the day come flowing back.

He is up and out of bed in a heartbeat and he opens the shutters that face in the direction of the village. These too have not been opened for years and the rusted fixtures resist at first. He thumps the handle with his fist; it gives a little each time until they swing open freely.

The village basks in the early morning light below him. He takes a deep breath and stretches, his nub also lifting to the ceiling. At moments like these it still feels as if he has two arms; either way, it makes no difference. He smiles and puts on a new set of clothes from yesterday's shopping spree. He feels a little indulgent now for all he spent yesterday, nearly two hundred euros just on clothes. The last time he spent that much was on a new engine for the tractor. But, he reflects, it was just a drop in the ocean of all he can spend, if he wants to. He immediately recognises this thinking as the trap that it is. Reckless spending is a route back to poverty, and he makes a mental note to only spend after a great deal of thought.

Mitsos makes his way to the kitchen sink and washes his face and then goes out to the toilet which is in a lean-to in the yard. There is a hole in the wooden door and he looks up through the branches of the almond trees toward the chickens and the pines. He must feed the hens.

After the chickens are all pecking away he stretches again and makes his way back to his house for a coffee, but then decides he be kind to himself, just a little, and indulge his first coffee of the day in the kafenio. His father always took his first coffee at the kafenio, and Mitsos had always considered it a needless expense and an insult to his mother, but as he has no wife, he reasons, it is disrespectful to no one and he can now afford it.

He pats his shirt pocket to make sure the tickets and the cheque are safely in place and sets off with good balance and a spring in his step, but cautious of his aches and pains.

Theo shows no signs of shock with this change in his day's routine and is unmoved by his taking the table in the window again. He bobs to the table with his mop of hair flopping in his eyes, a halo of frizz, two cups, one in either hand.

'Mind if I join you?'

'Morning, Theo.' Mitsos has one of his feet resting on the front rung of the chair at right angles to him round the square table. He removes his foot so Theo can sit.

'Don't know about you, but I get a little lonely even though I am surrounded by people all day. I need someone with the same history to ground me, know what I mean?'

'Not really,' Mitsos replies.

They both take a sip of coffee.

'You don't get lonely up there, then?'

'No. But how can you get lonely when you are surrounded by the men of the village all day?' Mitsos' brows draw together as he thinks.

'Funny, isn't it? Because I bring them coffees they often, not all the time, but sometimes, enough to make the difference, talk at me rather than with me, know what I mean?'

Mitsos nods and takes another sip.

'And I overhear everything. You can't help it, and I forget who has said what to whom, who knows things and who doesn't, what's been said in confidence, what hasn't, so in the end I dare not say anything to anybody for fear of blowing something. I would have gone out of business years ago if I couldn't keep secrets.' He laughs at his reality.

Mitsos chuckles, and wonders what Theo would make of his secret. He considers telling him, but can find no reason to apart from to brag and he has no need for that, so he just smiles.

'Cigarette?' Theo offers. Mitsos shakes his head. 'What's with the new clothes?'

'Had a little windfall and decided it was time. Do you know what time Marina is waking up these days?'

'Oh, she's on her feet and downstairs today. She keeps talking about family that she has and how she has nothing to offer them now the shop is gone. I didn't even know she had family, apart from the girls, of course. She's having a bit of a panic about her future, I think. It's all she talks about at the moment. Can't blame her. Are you going to go and see her?'

'Yes, there's something I need to settle with her.'

'Do you want a whisky in your coffee?' Theo chuckles.

Mitsos snorts through his nose. 'No, I'm past that now.'

They sit for a while watching the village go about its morning's business. There are still a couple of immigrant workers waiting, hopefully, sitting round the palm tree. A truck pulls up and takes the taller of the two and the other one sits back down, resigned. The man in the truck talks to his co-driver and they nod and the driver opens his window and motions for the second immigrant to climb aboard as well. The truck drives off with the two illegals sitting on the open back, at the opposite corner from the goat that is tied there, bleating pitifully.

The place where Marina's shop was looks very bare now. The roof tiles that survived the storm have been removed, by gypsies probably. Well, Marina has no need to worry about that.

'So, Mitsos, my old chum, how long have we known each other now? Sixty years?' Theo begins. 'I probably knew you before you knew me, you and Manolis being the boys to look up to at school and you being a year older. Amazing how a year makes such a difference at that age. You wouldn't have noticed me then.'

'I noticed you. I noticed you because Manolis picked on you and I was glad it wasn't me. But enough, these are not happy thoughts.'

'All I was going to say was in all this time we have never eaten together. I am not a good cook but I wondered if you would like to go into town one night and we can try one of the restaurants on the front. I'll treat you to lobster,' he adds with a sly grin.

Mitsos smiles in return; he appreciates the teasing.

'Sounds like a great idea. Can we do it in about a month?'

'In a month? Why so long?'

Mitsos is tempted again to tell Theo everything but resists, he is not a show-off.

'Just because ...' Mitsos smiles so warmly that Theo shrugs in acceptance.

'Right, I am off to see Marina.' He drops a note onto the table. Theo protests that it is too much and Mitsos says, vaguely, that it is for next time as well, and strides out and across the road to Marina's back door. Just before he knocks he looks down the street to Stella's take-away. It looks like it isn't open yet.

The courtyard has escaped the storm unscathed and he sits with Marina under the lemon tree. Despite the high wall, it feels exposed on the side where the protruding shop roof used to shield the early morning sun. Mitsos is glad for Marina that at least the wall is still intact and nothing has changed in her home.

Marina brings out two coffees, which Mitsos cannot face so soon after his first one at the kafenio. He wants a glass of water and goes to get it himself as Marina is using a crutch with her broken leg. When he returns she is looking at the floor, her features pulled down by gravity. She looks so sad.

'Mitsos, what am I going to do?' she begins.

'Well, I …'

'I have no shop, no oranges, the olives are worth only enough for a few months' living.'

'I can …'

'You don't know this, but I have some family I haven't seen for a while and I have asked them to come here to be with me. But how can they come now when I have nothing to offer?' She sniffs and sips her coffee. Mitsos tries to form what he wants to say in his head but the words are becoming scrambled.

'I said they could work the shop and live in the house and I would start to take things easy, no more five a.m. wake-ups seven days a week. I cannot begin to tell you how much I was looking forward to that.' A tear runs down her face and hangs on the end of her chin. 'But now?' She sighs. 'Panayia, why does everything always turn to …'

'Marina,' Mitsos says, loud enough and strongly enough to stop her in her train of thought. 'I have something I need to tell you.'

She looks at him with disinterest, distracted by her own woes.

'Manolis ...'

'Please let's not talk about Manolis now, in fact let's not talk about him ever.' She puts her coffee on the table and picks at a long thread from her old skirt.

'Would you feel different if he had provided for you? If one of his schemes had worked?'

'That was never going to happen, and talking about it is just raking over old ground.'

'But would you feel different?'

Marina looks up; her gaze wanders to the pots at the far end of the courtyard. 'The wisteria needs watering.'

'I have a good reason for asking.'

'OK, yes, if one had worked maybe things would have been different, he might have been different. But he would never have allowed one to be successful, he would have pushed in some direction until it went badly wrong – that is just how he was. If one scheme had left me provided for after his death, well then yes, maybe things would be different, maybe I would have romanticised him and his death by now and feel like someone once cared.'

'That's what Stella said.'

'What's Stella got to do with this?'

'Nothing, just that ... No, never mind Stella. I have something to tell you.'

'So you said, but it's not being told, is it?'

'One of Manolis' schemes did pay off. He has left you provided for.'

'What are you talking about, Mitsos? Did that beam land on your head?' She has filled the watering can from an outside tap but cannot lift it for her broken leg.

Mitsos takes the cheque out of his pocket and hands it to Marina. She is smiling at her own joke and glances at the paper, her face transfixed when she deciphers it. She hands the cheque back.

'Come on Mitsos, are you teasing me? You are not with Manolis playing a prank. You know my position now, this is hurtful rather than funny.'

Mitsos thrusts the paper back at her. 'It's real.' His eyebrows lift, the pitch of his voice is high. He starts to giggle. Marina sits down again.

She begins to smile but it doesn't quite form. 'Mitsos, I appreciate you wanting to make me feel better but this is not helping, really, believe me.' She doesn't take the cheque.

'Ok, let me explain, then.' Mitsos looks down at the cheque and back at Marina. 'Do you remember the beach bar?' Marina shakes her head, not to say that she doesn't remember the beach bar, but sadly, as if she is disappointed.

'Don't tell me you are resurrecting the bar and going to make enough to cover the cheque?' Her tone is light and she smiles, but it does not reach her eyes.

'What if I sold it? What if I sold the beet field?'

Marina giggles, the giggle grows into a belly laugh and her eyes become moist. She wipes away a tear and looks at Mitsos only to hoot again. 'Mitsos, it is a beet field, you'll get very little per *stremma*. It was ten *stremmas* max,' she says, using the local land measurement term. 'And who would want it anyway?

The soil's saturated with brine, it's useless.' She composes herself. 'But if you have sold it then that's great, best to be rid of it then you don't have to think about it.'

'Would you agree that I would not have the land if it wasn't for Manolis?' Mitsos asks.

'What, are you turning American on me, are you going to sue me now?' Marina laughs and sits down again, the wisteria remaining thirsty.

'No, I want to know that you agree with me, that he is responsible for me having the land, and if so, would you say, if he was still living, I would be fair in holding him to be responsible if the price was way short of the fertile land I swapped it for?'

'You can't really hold him responsible, as ultimately it was your choice to swap the land, but I do know how he'd twist logic and make you feel like you didn't know your own mind until you agreed with him. So in some ways I would say he was responsible in the way a conman is responsible for the tricks he pulls. But for that he'd go to jail, not pay the difference.'

'So we are agreed he was responsible. In one word, yes or no.'

'In that case I would have to say yes, sorry Mitsos, but you were had.' There is pity in her eyes.

'Good, then you must take this.' He hands the cheque back to Marina. She takes the paper again and puts it on the cracked wooden table under her coffee cup and then reaches out and pats Mitsos' hand, a slightly pitying but compassionate gesture.

Mitsos can feel his breath shortening as he looks at Marina. 'Look, I sold the beet field and did not make a loss, I made a profit.' Marina looks once more at the cheque and seems to find something funny.

'Mitsos, what you are saying and this piece of paper you are showing me do not relate. I cannot tell where joking ends and reality begins. Something has happened but you are not doing a very good job of explaining. Perhaps you'd better tell me in a bit more detail what has happened, and forget this cheque joke.'

Mitsos up at the blue cloudless sky and tries to calm his racing pulse. 'The man at the bank wrote the cheque because I said I …'

'No, Mitsos, from the beginning.'

Mitsos takes a deep breath and tries to think where the beginning is. He takes a sip of his coffee which is now only tepid.

'A man from an estate agent's in town came to see me. Well, he said he had been contacted by an estate agent from Athens who had a client from Germany who wanted some land.' Marina nods her understanding. 'He remembered me from the beach bar; he had been there that night. So he came and found me all these years later and asked if I still had the land. He told me he had a client who wanted remote land by the sea.'

'So you have sold the land, then?'

'Yes, I said so.'

'But some person wanting to buy a bit of land in a remote location to build a house does not write cheques like that.' She points to the cheque and smiles at Mitsos' joke.

'But it wasn't some person.'

'Who was it, then?' Marina picks up the cheque and looks at it again.

'Well, I didn't know at the beginning. One of their men came and looked at the land and he said it was perfect so the estate agent man from the town winked at me and told me not to say a word. I kept my mouth shut and we all left. But I didn't hear anything. I just thought nothing was happening so I stopped thinking about it. Then a letter came from their lawyers in Germany with an offer and the agent made a counter-offer and asked for more money and back and forth it went. Anyway, now it is settled and they put the money in my bank.'

'So who was it that bought it?'

'They are called Geld-drukken Hotel Group. They are going to build a hotel complex with pools, restaurants, cinema, somewhere that the tourist doesn't have to leave and even if they did where would they go, all the way out there?'

Marina straightens the cheque out, now a little creased by her dismissive handling, and looks at it again. 'So this is really real then?'

'Yes, it is real.' Mitsos feels a lifting in his chest, the beginnings of a sense of freedom.

Marina begins to smile and then pulls her face straight. 'Then this is yours, not mine. I cannot accept it,' and she places the cheque on the table again as if it were too hot. Mitsos' chest sinks.

'I thought you would say that,' Mitsos says. 'But tell me, did you not inherit his house and his orange and olive groves, and did you not agree that he was responsible if I was to make a loss from swapping my prime land for the beet field?' He pauses. 'Loss profit, same difference.'

Marina's face drains of colour. She picks up the cheque again, and then holding it carefully by the corners she looks at Mitsos, her mouth gaping until she shuts it to swallow before asking, 'But what about you?'

'I didn't split it exactly fifty-fifty, it was a bit in my favour, but I figured you wouldn't mind.'

'Mind! What the heck am I going to do with a million euros?'

'What am I going to do with one and a half?' Mitsos laughs. Marina's round belly begins to wobble before the noise comes from her throat, a warble that rapidly loses control. Tears rolling down her face, she stands, forgetting her broken leg and nearly falls. Mitsos jumps up to catch her, wincing with the pain in his ribs and she falls against him, laughing. Their faces so close, eyes shining in their mutual joy. Marina looks up to him, Mitsos bends towards her and kisses her tenderly, on her forehead, recovering from his hysteria.

'You are safe now, Marina.' He holds her to him and smiles. Years of tension leave his face. He has fulfilled his promise, he has righted his wrongs, he has set them both free. He releases her slowly and she pulls away gently. They look into each other's eyes and know of their shared history but also see the possibilities of their individual futures reflected there.

'Will you rebuild the shop?' Mitsos asks.

'I have no idea. First, you must tell me how I change this bit of paper into solid money I can feel.'

'You are such a village girl, Marina.' And they both laugh as they recognise their mutual lack of sophistication.

Mitsos leaves Marina with joy in his heart. Her future comfort is assured, his pledge concluded. He walks with light feet to Stella's. She is not sitting outside so Mitsos pops his head in. Stavros is poking at the grill trying to get it going, using a lighter and pulling his hand away quickly so as not to burn himself, but too quickly for it to ignite. It is clearly a tricky process, and one that he has still not mastered after years in the shop. Stella is not with him.

'Not open yet,' Stavros puffs. Mitsos could have the grill lit with one match but does not feel inclined to help. He would like to ask where Stella is but feels this may not be in her best interest.

'Oh, ok, what time are you opening?'

'When they get back.'

'Who?' Mitsos is confused by the plural.

'Stella and the English girl, gone off somewhere.'

This surprises Mitsos. He cannot imagine Stella wanting to spend any time with the English girl whom Stavros is clearly hunting, if not bedding.

Mitsos feeds his chickens and wanders under the pine tree. By midday he is hungry so he saunters back down to Stella's. The tickets are burning a hole in his shirt pocket.

He does not see her on his way in; the shop is particularly busy. Stavros himself takes the order. He waits a long time for his food to come. It is Stavros who brings it. Mitsos squirms on his seat a little, feeling guilty for his thoughts but reasoning with himself that Stavros cannot see inside his shirt pocket or his head, or his heart. He must just be cross with the grill and have her working in there or washing up behind. He finishes his lunch more quickly than usual and looks for Stella on the way out but as there is such a jostle of people he decides not to add to it. Wherever she is in the throng, she is clearly busy.

He stops to recruit an immigrant on the way through the square and a grinning Pakistani man accompanies him up to his land, where Mitsos sets him about clearing the path to the front door, showing him the difference between a weed and a flower after the grinning fool pulls up a rose bush.

Mitsos drinks coffee and watches the world, motorbikes racing through the village in pairs as young boys get their first taste of freedom, women in garish housecoats chatting on corners and the blue sky above going on forever, over the mountains in the distance to faraway places.

When the immigrant has finished the weeding he gets him to clear the front room of the rain-spoilt furniture. Not sure what to do with it, Mitsos asks the man if he would like any of it. The Pakistani says he would like it all and he piles it neatly by the gate. He pulls a mobile phome from his pocket, talks swiftly in his native tongue and grins all the more. A friend will come for it later, he says.

Mitsos is about to pay him ten euros for half a day's work, when he recalls the man without shoes that the English woman had bought a sandwich for. He never did give that man his gloves, so he compensates his past omission by paying this worker for a whole day, despite his irritating grin and the truck full of furniture he will, in all probability, sell.

The front room is a lovely bright space with all the heavy furniture gone. Mitsos paces around in it to enjoy the change but he can't quite settle as he is hungry again.

It is dinner time and he taps his shirt pocket and heads down to see Stella. He is excited with what he can offer her but worries about Stavros.

It occurs to Mitsos that he has chosen an unavailable girl again. He combs his short hair in the small mirror by his back door.

'But this time, Mitsos, you are grabbing the opportunity, whereas with poor Marina you clearly left it too late,' he tells his reflection before walking, as eagerly as the warmth will allow down to the village square and along to the fast-food restaurant.

Stavros is sitting outside. Mitsos walks in with a smile. Stella will know from the look on his face that something good has happened. Stavros follows him into the empty take-away.

Before Mitsos has sat down or gathered his thoughts the words come out. 'Where's Stella?'

'She's not here. What can I get you?' Stavros grunts. Mitsos feels confused and then disguises his perplexity by searching his pockets. He pretends he has forgotten his money and leaves. He has a curious feeling in his stomach but it is not like any hunger he has experienced, similar but definitely not the same. It slowly grows into his chest cavity and images of Stella fill his mind. He crosses to the kafenio and sits in his old seat by the counter. Theo is making a coffee and looks up at Mitsos and nods.

'Are you ready for tomorrow?' Theo asks. Mitsos looks at him.

'Ah, there you are,' Adonis calls as he trips up the few steps into the cafe. He ambles over to Mitsos' table and sits down, patting him on the back. 'Coffee,' he commands Theo, who nods and picks up another cup.

Mitsos is still looking at Theo, who smiles benignly and commences his task.

'So, tomorrow, did you remember?' But Mitsos' face is blank. 'Tomorrow is his christening. You hadn't forgotten, had you?'

'Oh!' Mitsos squeezes thoughts of Stella to the back of his mind and scrabbles for some memory of the christening date, but finds none. He lies, 'No, of course, tomorrow. Here in the village.'

Theo is sniggering at the counter.

'Yes, everyone says they will be going. We are having food here afterwards. Theo will put tables in the square and we will have a party. The whole village will come. It will be great.' He smiles widely and looks out to the square over the tops of the old men's heads.

'The whole village … you have invited everyone?'

'Yup, everyone.'

Mitsos smiles very slightly. He likes the idea of giving Stella the tickets in the church.

Chapter 22

Mitsos is at the church early. The brass chandelier is lit, the glass in front of the icons with their gold leaf halos is polished, all is shining and shimmering in the cool, partially lit interior, the dark corners a relief from the ornate holy items.

To Mitsos' amusement the trainee Papas, who is now an old man and highly respected in the church, has come to the village to perform the baptism. He says he offered to do it because he has fond memories of the village. He does not recognise Mitsos when he shakes his hand.

Mitsos slinks away from the Papas' verbosity and stands against the wall by the wooden side door. He doesn't really want to get caught up in all the social graces. His brother says he has invited many of his friends from the town and he watches their arrival in their town clothes, jeans made to look faded, thin shirts, expensive rags. They are full of vigour and life's energy, happy to see each other. One of the women smiles and Mitsos imagines the smile that will be on Stella's face within half an hour. He transfers his weight from foot to foot at the thought. He wonders if she will let him buy her clothes, ones without designer patches.

A petite woman in a floral dress comes in. Mitsos catches a glimpse and stands on tiptoe to see, above the growing crowd, if it is Stella, but it turns out to be a teenager with a rather old-looking face. Mitsos can guess exactly what she will look when she is middle-aged.

Cosmo arrives, supporting his mother. He nods at Mitsos, who nods back. All the chairs have been moved from the centre of the church to line the edges to give more room around the font. Cosmo takes his mother to one of these chairs. Adonis arrives with his wife Leni and the baby, who is crying; Leni is trying to soothe him. Adonis ignores the baby, doesn't see Mitsos, but greets his friends from town. Theo hurries in and speaks into Adonis' ear, receives a reply, and hurries out again. The psaltis begins to sing the prayers. The church is filling now; Mitsos sees his neighbours arrive. Vasso has emerged from the kiosk in a new dress, her hair done. The two ladies from the chemist's have exchanged their white coats for flowing dresses. He keeps looking for Stella but she has not arrived yet. He wonders if she has travelled any distance by boat before.

Juliet enters, quietly, alone, and finds a corner to stand in. She has a pale green dress on, which suits her. He taps his shirt pocket to make sure the tickets are still there. Stella will be so excited. Or maybe just relieved to be able to leave Stavros. He imagines the shop will shut without Stella, and Stavros will return to his own village. There won't be a fuss.

The light from the open main doors is blocked and Mitsos turns to find a clique of people entering all at once. The women in the group go and light candles, as do some of the men; the rest of the men shake hands with those they know, smiling at the joy of the gathering and the prospect of the party and feast in the square afterwards. Mitsos recognises them as village people who work in the town. Some of their wives have ridiculously high heels on and not a hair out of place. Mitsos feels they are trying too hard, overdressed for the village. They are too gaudy to be easy on his eyes. He looks away and thinks of Egypt.

To his surprise he sees Stavros come in, wearing a crisp white shirt that stretches over his belly and is too tight to do up at the collar. He is sweating profusely and the shirt already has stains under the arms although he looks as if he has dressed specially for the occasion. Mitsos checks that Stella is not with him and watches as he moves between the people, lights a candle and kisses the feet of an icon before crossing himself three times and finding a chair to sit on. Mitsos loses sight of him as he sits. Mitsos reasons that he and Stella may have to leave separately; they don't need a scene.

The incense is blowing about the church and it is particularly strong where Mitsos is standing. He likes the aroma but the smoke itself bothers him. He coughs. Leni notices him and smiles and lifts the baby's hand to make him wave at Mitsos. Mitsos smiles to be polite but thinks what a ridiculous thing it is to do, to make a baby wave as if it is a puppet. He chastises himself for thinking such unkind thoughts and then realises that he is still shifting his weight from foot to foot with his growing impatience.

'Where is she?' But there is no one near him to hear. He stands as tall as he can to look over the heads towards the door.

Several young farmers turn up with their wives. The wives have made an effort, but look distinctly uncomfortable in their brightly coloured clothes. Their husbands are wearing clean versions of what they wear every day and, with a relaxed manner, chat amongst themselves.

Still there is no sign of Stella. The church is almost full now and the Papas stands and people settle down and stop talking. Mitsos searches through the crowd that is already there to check that he has not missed her coming in, but there are too many people to see clearly who is there and who is not. The brass chandelier hangs low overhead; the gold of the icons shimmers in the artificial light and the illumination from the dozens of prayer candles that have now been lit and stood up in the sand trays near the entrance.

There is a small parting of people around the door and he sees Marina's dark head as she shuffles in on her crutches. Mitsos stops leaning against the wall and goes to assist her to find a comfortable place. She insists on being near the font and Mitsos takes a chair from the edge of the room and pushes his way through the crowd to provide this comfort for her.

The psaltis nears the end of his singing and the Papas begins his prayers over the child. The crowd is hushed as the ceremony has begun.

The child is taken away and undressed. The Papas blesses the oil and the baby is brought to the font wrapped in a towel so he can blow on the child's face three times. Mitsos stays by Marina but looks over his shoulder constantly for Stella. The baby struggles as his godmother wipes the blessed oil all over him with her hands before pouring the rest in the font with three tips of the bottle.

'Who are you looking for?' Marina whispers to Mitsos.

'No one, why?' Mitsos was not aware it was so obvious.

'Just wondering.' She becomes absorbed in the Papas' words. The baby spreads his legs to brace himself against the font, to avoid being dipped in the cold water. Marina then whispers, 'Talking about looking for people, did you hear?'

'Hear what?' Mitsos whispers.

'Stella. She walked out on Stavros and he has not seen her since. She took the English girl with her, yesterday morning.'

A shiver runs down Mitsos' back. The hairs on his arm stand on end and he feels slightly sick. He tries to swallow but he has forgotten to breathe and feels as if he is choking. He coughs until his airways clear and someone pats him on the back. He doesn't trust himself to say anything but, without his consent, he hears himself ask in a high pitched whisper, 'Where's she gone?'

The baby is now in the font and the Papas is trying to pour the water over him but the baby is wriggling and slippery with the oil. The Papas stops his prayers as he tries for a better hold.

'She just left a note saying she has gone a long way away and that she is not coming back. Stavros has been out looking for her since last night. He has not slept a wink. Good for her, I say. It's what I should have done instead of spending those years with Manolis.'

Mitsos can feel his chest caving in. His knees tremble and he thinks he might fall over. He grabs the back of Marina's chair and grips until his knuckles are white. He concentrates on his breathing, getting a steady pace, filling his lungs, slowing his heartbeat. The moment passes and he dares to let go. His breathing becomes normal but his sight is out of focus for a minute.

'You ok?' Marina asks, frowning. Mitsos dares not answer and just puts his hand on her shoulder. He has done it again. He has found someone, not recognised his feelings and left it too late to take action. His face is like stone but a tear runs down the edge of his nose and into his lip. He wipes his hand across his mouth and stares intently at the priest. He knows now she is not coming today. She has gone. The Papas is getting to the main part and the crowd move towards the font so they can hear the name.

'Cheer up, Mitsos,' Marina whispers, looking him in the eyes. 'We each have the world at our feet now,' she says, patting her skirt pocket as if it were full.

But Mitsos remains looking sad. The Papas is still struggling with the slippery baby.

'Oh come on, Mitsos, whatever you are thinking, nothing can be as bad as you have already been through.' She smiles. 'Hey, at least we need never mention you-know-who again.' She takes his hand and squeezes it.

'Who?' Mitsos is in his own world. The baby's cries are becoming deafening.

'Manolis.'

'What about Manolis?'

'I was just saying, at least we need never mention his name again.' Marina turns back to hear the priest in his final prayer before he announces, 'In the name of the father, the son, and the holy ghost I baptise this baby Manolis.'

'Panayia mou!' sighs Marina. Mitsos looks up sharply and all life drains from his face. A mask of resignation blanks all emotion. He takes one last look around the church before leaning forward and tapping Adonis, who is standing in front of him, on the shoulder. Adonis turns and smiles. 'I have a present for you and Leni,' Mitsos whispers. He takes the two tickets out of his shirt pocket and gives them to Adonis. Adonis is still grinning and thanks Mitsos without looking at them, and puts them in his top pocket before turning away.

'See something of life before it is too late,' Mitsos whispers to the back of his head before he slips out into the empty street, remembering that he has forgotten to feed the chickens.

The Explosive Nature of Friendship

Sara Alexi is the author of the Greek Village Series. She divides her time between England and a small village in Greece.

http://facebook.com/authorsaraalexi

24647988R00177

Made in the USA
Lexington, KY
01 August 2013